Angel Song in Shawl by Steve Willis.
Mixed media on paper, 16" x 22". 2012.

Moon City Review
2015

Moon City Review is a publication of Moon City Press at Missouri State University and is distributed by the University of Arkansas Press. Exchange subscriptions with literary magazines are encouraged. The editors of *Moon City Review* contract First North American Serial Rights, all rights reverting to the writers upon publication. The views expressed by authors in *Moon City Review* do not necessarily reflect the opinions of its editors, Moon City Press, or Missouri State University.

All other correspondence should be sent to the appropriate editor, using the following information:

Moon City Review
Department of English
Missouri State University
901 South National Avenue
Springfield, MO 65897

Submissions are considered at http://mooncitypress.com/mcr/. For more information, please consult www.mooncitypress.com.

ISBN: 978-0-913785-61-4

moon city press
springfield missouri

Staff

Table of Contents

Poetry

Fiction

Nonfiction

Translations

The Missouri State University Literary Competitions

The 2016

Moon City

Short Fiction Award

• The Moon City Short Fiction Award is for an original collection of short fiction, written originally in English by a single or collaborative author. Anthologies will not be considered.

• Individual pieces in the collection may be published in periodicals, but not yet collected and published in full-length manuscript form.

• Entries may include short shorts, short fiction, and/or up to one novella. Please include a table of contents and acknowledgements page.

• Open to all writers not associated with Moon City Press or its judges, past or present. Students, employees, and alumni of Missouri State University are ineligible.

• Manuscripts should fall between 30,000 and 65,000 words.

• Manuscripts should be submitted via Submittable, https://mooncitypress.submittable.com

• A $25 entry fee is due via Submittable at the time of submission; entry fees are nonrefundable.

• Simultaneous submissions are permitted, though manuscripts should be withdrawn immediately if accepted elsewhere.

• Deadline: October 1, 2015. Winners will be notified by Spring 2016 and the winner will be published in Spring 2017.

• First prize: $1000, publication by Moon City Press (including international distribution through the University of Arkansas Press), and a standard royalty contract. Ten additional finalists will be named and considered for publication.

• For questions, please visit http://mooncitypress.com/ or contact Moon City Editor Michael Czyzniejewski at mczyzniejewski@missouristate.edu.

Marjorie Stelmach

Complaint of the Dark Matter

On learning that the expansion of the
universe is speeding up

Too long I've slogged this cluttered universe,
        stumbled on meteors, skidded on that spill
    of milk it's useless to cry over now; I feel
in my bones the bruises of the bang; creation's dust
        obstructs my throat: I'm old. And worse,
    it's Light, that bitch, gets all the glory. Riddle
me this: whose holdings are more vast? Until
        the first eye opened and the cosmos burst
    into tears and bloom and sex and sappy verse,
what *good* was Light? But now I sense it, dullard
        though I am: Her pace is picking up, until,
    in time, she'll have surpassed herself. My curse:
that first *Let be*. No matter, though. She'll see.
The worm will turn. Then: payback time … *eternity*.

Charles Harper Webb

Half in Love With Easeful Death

He had sexy hair—black as Tiffany's cat Sin (for Singularity)—accentuated by tomato lips and cream-cheese skin.

"He looks like Dracula," her best friend Pammi said.

"His name's Kevin D. Smith," admitted Tiff.

"Well, I wouldn't cut my finger near him," Pammi said. "Or let him give you a hickey."

Riding in his hearse creeped Tiffy out. But her mom loved the white lilies he brought to every meal, and his thank-you notes in Gothic script. "The man has manners," she said. "And a distinguished hand!"

"Two of them," Tiff said, then blushed so hard that she felt slapped. After *le petit mort*, she'd lie in his arms and sleep like the … whatever ….

"He's my own Jones," she thought: *Angel Lust* or *Sexstasy*. In all her nineteen years, she'd never felt so free.

Still, she panicked at, "Will you marry me?"

"It's so soon … I'm really young … I need to think …."

"Is it my job?" he said. "The scythe's a pain; you don't have to tell me. Try getting on an elevator. Or catching a cab. Airports are hell. And the hours—worse than OB/GYNs'. I'm looking into other work. The military, maybe. Or the FDA."

"Lawyers make good money," she said.

"*Kevin D. Smith, Esquire*. Does have a nice ring," he said, and slipped a big one on her wilting hand.

Charles Harper Webb

Hungry

When, after hard and bloody labor, he emerges, doctors are amazed to find no afterbirth.

"Did he eat it?" a nurse asks. "Look at those teeth."

"Don't stereotype the boy," one doctor warns.

The baby leaps at Momma's breast. She needs stitches where the lactation coach pries him away. "Some babies do just fine on formula," she sighs.

This baby thrives on formula—all he can swill. When he runs out, he eats the rubber nipple, then the glass bottle.

"A go-getter!" gloats Dad.

Baby eats Aunt Gayle's knitted b'anky, with his birthdate and eight embroidered sheep. He eats his mattress, guaranteed for fifteen years. He eats the crib his grandma air-freighted from France.

"He's not fat; he's husky," Mom insists.

"A take-no-prisoners guy," Dad boasts. "He'll be a CEO before he's 35."

Next day, Baby eats them both. He eats his room, and then his house. He's starting on his yard when Social Services arrive.

He eats the social worker's forms, then her car, with her, shrieking, inside.

He eats the house next door—ornamental brick sidewalk and all. He eats the whole block, including the street. He eats the city, then the state, then the country, then the continent.

He drinks the oceans, and chomps the earth like a cheese ball.

He eats the stars, the galaxies, the space between. He eats until there's nothing left.

"Waaa!" he cries, "Waaa!"—and eats the tangy nothingness.

He eats until only one speck is left, smaller than the tip of a quark-sized pin. He gapes his mouth for that. A Big Bang begins.

Jeannine Hall Gailey

Interpreting Signs in Appalachia

In this story a girl grows up in a field of nuclear
reactors, surrounded by abnormal blooms, pea shoots
and peonies. She learns to ride ponies, goes barefoot
in the treacherous grass. Sickly, she dreams in the arms
of apple trees, spits out their green piths. It's likely
her thyroid grew to the size of a poisoned apple,
that her blood ran hot, that her hair grew long
with trace metals. It's likely you won't find her
happy ending here, sewn into the silent concrete.
Look to the swallows—they carry their mythic toxins
in the walls of their nests, tucked into nooks, hidden
between stones. Search for clues to the mystery, follow
the green light of foxfire into the sides of mountains,
beneath silos. Listen for the crackle underground.

Jessica Forcier

Climbers

It started with just one child, as these things do.

Bianca Fabrizio ran laps around the tiny piece of grass in front of her mom's unit in Marina Village. She beat a track around the edge, pounded her sneakers into the ground over and over. Her mother had said she had "ants in the pants" and sent her outside, but only where she could see. She didn't want her at the basketball court with the boys, who hassled her and caused trouble.

Bianca was small for her age, nervous. She ran and ran, brown puffs of dust blossoming under her feet, but it was no use. She couldn't get the feeling out of her bones: She had to keep moving, keep going up. She started jumping, bending her knees, launching herself from the hard ground. She tried to touch the top of the living room window. She surprised herself when she met her goal. She jumped, again and again, slapping the side of the building. She imagined herself Michael Jordan, LeBron James, going in for the dunk. She wanted to be higher, even higher than she could jump.

She noticed that the brick on her corner unit crumbled in spots. She reached up for a hole just big enough for her hand. Finding a place to rest her foot, she lifted herself against the wall. She was off the ground, and the brick dug into her fingers. She looked up again and saw another piece missing. She extended her left hand and grabbed. Before she knew it, she was standing on top of the brick overhang of the front door. From there, it was an easy climb to the top of the two-story unit. Hauling herself up the sloping roof, she stood and looked at the project, which sprawled over the South End. She was walking over her bedroom, and she jumped up and down, satisfied to hear the light fixtures bang in response. She screamed, "Yo, yo, look at me!"

Other kids peered up from their double Dutch, their Matchbox cars. They shielded their eyes from the sun and saw Bianca, arms waving high in the air in victory.

"What you doing, Bianca?" a girl yelled. "You wanna get yourself killed?"

"I did it! I climbed up here!" She danced a minute, with fist pumps and hooting, careful not to slip.

The other kids stopped what they were doing, frozen for a minute by the sight of her. Bianca called out to them, "Come on, chickens! You try."

They dropped everything and ran to her unit. Bianca moved closer to the top of the roof and smirked. "I bet you can't do it," she said, backing up even farther, sitting on the peak.

But they did, even Janet Rodriguez, who was wearing her Sunday best, a floral sundress and black Mary Janes. Each child followed the other, and they formed a chain to help each other up. Soon, ten children were walking around on the roof, waving to Marina Village, to the Sikorsky plant on South Avenue, to I-95 and the Metro-North trains passing on the tracks, to Long Island Sound and the horizon beyond. For all they knew, they were on top of the world.

Bianca's stunt sparked something in them, something wild.

It spread by word of mouth, one child talking to another. The kids from the Village were the celebrities of the moment, and every time the story was told, the number grew: ten, twenty, sixty-five kids on the roof. Soon, others wanted in on the action.

They started small: They climbed eight-foot-high chain-link fences, fire escapes on the sides of apartment buildings. When everybody in the hood mastered one challenge, they'd move on to the next. They did it freestyle, hand over hand, no spikes, no ropes, no knowledge that those things even existed. Each height they mastered was a victory and made them want more. They saw the city with new eyes. Everything looked smaller, scalable.

They scoped out the Remington Arms factory on Barnum Avenue. Access was easy under a corner of the fence that curled up at the edge, and this let them avoid the barbed wire on top. Remington had finally moved out after a hundred years in operation, and the buildings stood vast and empty. They raced across the yard, the wind scented with something vaguely metallic. Uninterested in the other factory buildings, they headed for the shot tower, once Bridgeport's tallest structure. It stood like a soda bottle, the bottom squat, the top skinny. The crumbling brick was again the children's best friend. They kicked out panes of already-broken windows to find better footing. Progress was slow, but once one child achieved the roof, he or she reached down and helped the others up. Children slowly snaked up the side of the building like ants, colorful T-shirts and jean shorts a bright contrast to the faded red brick.

At the Remington climb, a photographer from *The Bridgeport Post* drove by and couldn't believe his eyes. He pulled over and took shots of the climbers, and the next day a headline announced, "City Kids Love Dangerous New Sport."

Parents were horrified. "Don't you know what you're doing?" they asked. It was true, the children didn't think about consequences. As more and more had joined in on the climbing, statistically, someone should have gotten hurt. There should have been some kind of accident. But providence or dumb luck prevailed, and nothing had happened yet.

The public outcry forced the children to make new plans. The police took notice. There were complaints of trespassing, of being public nuisances. After the crackdown, kids were afraid to climb. For a few weeks, no children even attempted it, and the adults were satisfied that the trend was squashed.

But they couldn't forget what it felt like, to be that far up, to keep reaching higher and higher. They stared up at the tall buildings when they traveled downtown, their fingers itching to grab onto brick, concrete, chain-link.

Then one day, Bianca rode along when her mother picked up her aunt at the ferry terminal. When they pulled into the parking lot, she didn't look at the Sound. Instead, she stared at the power plant in front of her. It rose on the horizon, a mass of steel girders and coal chutes, power lines, and three smokestacks, a red-and-white-striped one highest of all. She couldn't tear her eyes away from it.

The next day, at school, she told everyone her plan. She pushed away her sandwich. They all ate free or reduced-price lunch, and the wilted lettuce and globs of mayonnaise never made the salty ham any more edible. Leaning across the table, she kept her voice low. Her tablemates scooted closer, glad to be in on a secret.

"We go at night," she said. "No chance anybody will see us." She hunched her shoulders down even farther. "Let's have one last big climb if we have to give it up for good."

The other kids nodded gravely. Bianca was eleven, a sage bound for middle school the next school year.

A third-grade boy timidly raised his hand, his glasses glinting from the fluorescent lights above.

Bianca nodded to him, acknowledging his presence.

"Um, isn't the power plant really hard to get into? And dangerous? I mean, it makes—power."

Bianca shook her head. "I got it covered. We go on magic night."

The third grade boy bit his lip. "What's magic night?"

The other kids laughed. "How do you not know?"

Bianca pulled the little boy close. "Let me tell you a story," she said.

This was what they knew, playground legend spread through years of whispers, then boasts. On a night in June back in the late seventies, a kid from the Pequonnock Apartments flew away.

He'd lived heaped with abuse, frayed by poverty and fear. He was stretched like a guitar string, skinny and taut. Quick to run around corners, light enough to jump incredible heights, he knew he was special, and he knew he needed a way out. He dreamed up the plan after nights at his bedroom window, up on the eighth floor, when he watched the planes buzz low overhead on their way to Sikorsky Airport. He decided he was going to catch one.

His friends heard of his plan, ripped on him, called him *loco*, *dumb ass*, any other slur they could think of. "You gonna throw a rope around a plane and pull it out of the sky?"

He wouldn't listen to them. He started sitting up nights, breaking the lock to the roof access door and climbing up. He stared at the sky. Each plane had its own distinctive signal lights, white and red starbursts. He guessed at angles, too young for geometry, but with a sharp eye for distances. The number of planes was different every night, and he kept a log of when they passed.

He prepared himself physically. He counted the number of push-ups he could do in one minute. He practiced and practiced, even though the gravel on the roof cut his hands. He kept pumping, sweat rolling down his skinny arms, dripping from his curly hair into his mouth.

A small playground at school also served as a training ground. He swung from the monkey bars, used the farthest one for pull-ups, his chin inching just above the bar, his fingers white with effort.

His friends didn't connect his training to his plan. They asked him questions: "Why you doing this? Somebody gonna fight you? When's the fight?"

He didn't say anything because he knew that they wouldn't believe him.

A night in late June, just after school let out, brought a heat wave. There were ninety-degree temperatures, unusual for that time of year. People poured out of the apartments, sat on plastic lawn chairs in the courtyard for the hope of a breeze.

And on the roof, he waited. He knew it was coming, knew the timing exactly.

The small yellow plane descended slowly, the engine humming, drawing everyone's eyes up. Then they saw the boy. He ran, jumped, and launched himself from the roof's edge. He reached his arms out to the small X near the landing gear, bungee cord struts that were just big enough for his hands.

To the people down below, he hung in mid-air, supported by invisible currents. They held their breath, doubting what their eyes were seeing.

The boy kept reaching for those struts, his arms pulling, straining. It shouldn't have worked. It should have been impossible.

But he caught them. He trailed behind the plane, his red T-shirt visible, a little boy banner flying across the night sky.

The people below cheered like hell.

From that day on, the story spread. The boy was never seen again, which seemed to give it credence. No one knew who started calling it "magic night," but it stuck. Ever since then, children believed that the rules of the universe were suspended once a year. No one could ever prove that anything else magical had ever happened, but the climbers were convinced. They knew magic night would give them protection for their last big ascent.

They waited for nightfall. They put on pajamas and kissed their parents good night. They pretended to go to sleep, but put their clothes back on and waited under the covers. Some kids didn't need to worry; their parents were passed out on the couch, or out somewhere they didn't know. They just waited for the appointed time.

Nine-thirty arrived. Some of the kids had to sneak out their windows, and they relished the chance to climb slowly again, even if it was down, hands and feet maneuvering the wood, the concrete. Some kids slipped out the front door, practically jumped down the flights of stairs to get to the ground.

Children rode their bikes from all over the city, covered miles and miles, avoided police cars or the shady corners. They pumped their legs, every block one closer to the climb.

At about ten-fifteen, a mass of children met in a dark corner of the parking lot, abandoning their bikes in a pile. Bianca stood on the curb, overlooking the crowd. Janet was there, the third-grade boy, and a mass of other young faces, upturned and excited. Some kids stretched, some cracked their knuckles. Some couldn't stand still, and they walked in tight circles, over and over, wringing their hands. But no one spoke; they all knew their silence was paramount.

Bianca held up her hands to her flock. Everyone stopped in place to look at her. "We're here," she said. "No one is going to keep us from climbing!"

A small cheer went up, followed by, "Shh, shh, shh."

Bianca raised her eyes to the power plant. "This is it. We go in under the fence, then we spread out." She pointed to two shovels lying on the ground. "First, we dig."

A few kids grabbed for the shovels, and there was some shoving over the privilege. The stronger ones prevailed, and started moving the earth.

They dug and dug until they had two child-sized holes. Bianca slipped under first and waited for the kids to come through, two by two. She held a few of the most enthusiastic back from the plant. "Hold up," she said, over and over.

When they all entered, they stared up at the structure. It was bigger than they could have imagined, as big as a dream. It had to be at least forty stories high, much larger than any of the office buildings downtown, the decks of blue-and-white steel stacked up on top of each other, layer upon layer like birthday cake. Yellow lights blazed from each level, better than anything they ever saw at Christmas. The three smokestacks had signals that flashed every other second. The rings of white lights on the surrounding structures that held the coal sparkled like crowns.

The children itched to climb, wanted to go right away. They rushed the building, but the plant's foundation was smooth concrete, no chinks, no places to grab on to. They scrabbled against it, jumped up, but couldn't reach. It was several stories high, and nobody could see any stairs or ladders to the upper levels.

When the impossibility of their situation settled on them, some children started to cry. Others held back, but the sniffles started. Hundreds of sets of eyes turned to Bianca's.

She looked up at the plant, and the tears in her eyes made the lights seem like distant stars. "This is magic night," she said. "The magic will come."

The children repeated her words in their minds like a mantra, like a Tinkerbell wish. *The magic will come.* Some of them held hands, the words pulsing through their blood, their eyes fixed on the plant.

No one wanted to believe it would end like this. They'd come so close. They couldn't have this taken away from them, not like every other good thing. The climbing was theirs. The power plant was theirs. They looked up at it, and the coal dust floated gently, coating their bodies like snow.

They stood pressed against the side of the foundation to avoid detection from the crew above. Some kids shoved their disappointment deep down, underneath the rest, shook from the effort. Some of them turned on Bianca, walked right up, got in her face.

"You promised. What are you going to do?"

She couldn't bear the betrayal in their eyes. Her mouth was dry. She opened it, but couldn't find the answer they wanted.

A deafening electrical buzz assaulted their ears, and they looked to the city. The lights of the high-rises downtown flashed and were gone. They turned back to the plant, and the layers of lights on the decks flickered and disappeared. Loud emergency horns filled the air, and the children turned to each other, amazed.

Bianca shook off the defeat that was sitting on her chest. This was their moment, the magic she believed in. Now she needed to get them to the plant. She looked up at the power lines that connected to the decks. The electrical tower was to their left, smooth metal, an easy climb. She turned and pointed. "We have a couple minutes, maybe. We'll climb the wires."

She started climbing the tower, hand over hand up the side. She looked down to the rest of the kids. "It's the only way! We gotta go now!"

But they waited. She reached the power lines. She held out a hand, hesitated.

The third grader called to her. "Bianca, don't do it!"

Bianca looked down at him, the concern on his face. But she was too close, she thought. She couldn't quit now. Her hand trembled as she reached for the line. The children gasped as she reached out and grabbed it.

She started swinging her way across, perfectly alive. "Come on guys, now, now, now!"

The children silently cheered and scrambled up the tower. They crossed the power lines, aided by their strong arms, all the way to the platform. They saw no adults, all probably inside the interior plant, dealing with the outage. They spread out fast, grabbing onto the steel girders.

Children climbed, some like squirrels, some like caterpillars. They went fast, all pent-up energy, excitement and nerves. They moved with confidence, eager to scale their biggest challenge.

Shimmying up steel girders, they reached and grabbed the next beam, and the next, imagined that they were climbing a giant Erector Set. One or two of them would freeze for a minute when they realized the height, but another kid would offer a hand, which they'd gratefully take, glad for a friend. They stared inside at the giant machines the girders protected, and wondered just what they did.

Some of the kids went to the smoke stacks, which had easy ladders on the sides. The tallest one was red-and-white striped, a giant peppermint stick. There was no higher place in the whole plant. Bianca was with them, wanted to see it, be there, when the culmination of what she'd started that day back in the project reached its peak. She climbed rung after rung, the heat coming off of the stack growing more intense with each foot they ascended.

They reached the top in a few minutes and stood on a small, circular deck just below the smokestack's opening. The stack released enormous billows of white smoke, which made them cough, but still, none of them would move. They were five hundred feet up, forty stories, and the wind rushing past made them hold onto the railing very tightly. They stared out at the skyline again, and the only lights were from I-95, a steady stream of cars and trucks on the highway, going somewhere else. The city was so quiet, so dark. They knew they'd never see anything like this again.

Bianca looked around her at her friends, kids she didn't even know, her fellow climbers. She'd started something big: bigger than anything she could ever dream for herself, for them. She wanted to say something, call out.

But then the lights popped on, neighborhood by neighborhood. The smokestack tower signal flashed again, and the children were flooded in white. They froze for a second, knowing that the moment was over, but not wanting to leave. Then they scrambled down the ladder, knocking feet against heads, hands slipping on the metal.

Back on the highest deck of the main plant, the kids huddled together, looking down at the lines below. They knew they couldn't go back the way they came. Even Bianca didn't know what to do. She'd never thought the trip out that far.

Then a little voice cried out: "Look! Slides!"

The children turned to their right and saw the sloping coal chutes, three in all. Inside, they contained conveyor belts to bring the coal up, but their smooth surfaces could bring the children down.

The climbers rejoiced. They laughed and screamed as they slid down the chute, wind blowing back their hair. They stomped off to the next level, the following chute just as fast and thrilling.

When they reached the last, the entire group of children stood still. It hung directly over the Sound.

"What do we do?" the third-grader asked. He pushed his glasses higher on his nose.

The children searched, but there was no safety ladder, no shortcut to the ground.

"We could find an adult," a little girl said, but she turned and realized that there was no way to climb up the previous chute.

Bianca peered over the side. What else could they do? It was the last one, not that big a drop, and nothing was in the way. Finally, she sat down and looked back to the other kids.

"Let's be brave," she said. She pushed off and slid down, and the children watched her disappear.

One by one, they followed her, sat down and let the chute take them. The cool metal whizzed by beneath their legs. The wind blew in their eyes, made them teary, and the lights reflecting off the Sound looked like shiny coins on the surface. They reached the edge and flew off. Their stomachs dropped when they hung for a split second in the air, and they braced themselves to be accepted by the cold, dark water below.

Mary Quade

The Middle-School Cheerleader

She vacillates between losing
and an unpredicted win. In the living
room, in front of the picture window at night,
its murky mirror,
she runs through the choreography
of cheer, the path of satellite
around some sun.
                        From outside,
she seems to mime the workings
of a particularly impenetrable
machine—the circulation of arms,
knee cranks, hands stamping the air
into discreet, clattering parts.
                        She mouths
Go, Go, Go—a plea.
                        Afternoons, she
launches across the lawn
in flaccid roundoffs, legs
never quite gathering
the elastic snap.
                        She's here
because she couldn't possibly
catch the ball herself, feed it
to the carnivorous goal. It stays
too much alive in her clutch,
flees.

So she lifts one girl
to another girl's shoulders. Her sweater
hugs nothing, her skirt
flirts chastely
with her thighs.
                In high school,
she won't make the squad—with their tease
of flips, their victory of firm
towers, their incommunicable
congenital pep, their splitting
themselves in two.

Mary Quade

Amish Boy Gesturing at the Road

Where is the boy who looks after the sheep?

He's pumping
his fist
vigorously, elbow working it
up and down
in front of his body,
tight with clothes—

an obscene gesture!
How? I gasp. Behind him
turquoise and pink dresses shimmy
on the line. They look cotton,
but they're polyester. They feel
like motel sheets, I think,
never wearing out. Some have no
buttons to fall off,
only pins
biting the placket.
These people seem very practical
and impractical—
with their linoleum-floored bedrooms
and oil lamps burning
near white curtains always perfectly
open or perfectly closed.
Shouldn't the boy be using
this energy
to milk a cow or something?

Amish Boy Gesturing at the Road

His straw hat begins to slip.
A horse takes a step;
the blade slices through earth.

The boy's elbow
never wears out.
Oh. I see
what he wants. He wants
a passing semi-truck
to blow,
blow the horn.

Mary Quade

Measuring Exposure

—*after Nina Berman's* Wounded U.S.
Marine Returns Home From Iraq to Marry

Your light meter believes
that the shadows
                    and highlights
and tones in between
average out to 18 percent gray, a shade like
the hide of something tough.

                              So, the young bride's
white sleeveless gown
cancels out the groom's midnight blue dress uniform.
But how much light do we find
in her red bouquet of roses
with its one white flower?
                              Or the portrait studio's
all-purpose backdrop?
                              Or the reflection off his
bald head, his facial features lost to scars, ear fused
into jaw, nose into mouth? Inside, a plastic dome
has replaced his shattered skull. His left hand,
a prosthetic, deflated of gesture.
His expression, entombed;
                              and hers,
a blank neutrality
we ache to shape into something—

                              shock,
sadness, the bravery of vows.
                    Yet moments earlier
she was smiling,
            or maybe moments later.

One flash defined
the suicide bomber,
blacked out everything before.

                    The couple
in the photo become famous, their story
detached from them, given its own
lasting future, an icon
to adopt.

            But it's a wedding photo,
a posed instant before a life,
                    in which
he takes pills to smooth out
several shapes of pain,
to make possible a day's routine. In a year,
they divorce.
                Still, always doubt a little
that bright and dark add up to gray.

Gabriel Houck

Homecoming

Etienne wouldn't see the sharks so much as feel them. A quick hard tug, then slack again. He would look back at the polymer-coated wire that ran from a loop around his waist through the quaking necks of drum and speckled trout he'd caught, trailing outward behind his body in the water like an S-curved tail, its tip a white foam buoy glazed brown with salt and sparkling in the afternoon sun. The tide was leading the stringer behind him, and the backs of the fish he'd caught swished and boiled against the surface. There would be a tug, sometimes two, but rarely a splash. The buoy would sink to its fat midriff, tremble, and then bob up again, jaunty and slick.

When his father had lifted him out of the boat, he'd been terrified. He slid down to a standing position in the water, his feet lost in the deep green beneath him. He could only feel the sand through his shoes, the caress of the current, the cool-to-warm settling of the water on his skin. The waves came to his chest and slapped against the hull of the boat. He was eye level with the rail, the metal gunnels flecked with fish blood, the white resin surface stained along the waterline. His father was haloed by the sun, an angular shadow rocking above him, hair radiating like fire in the wind.

Remember to shuffle your feet when you walk, his father said.

I will, Etienne said.

If you don't, you'll step on a stingray. They'll get out of the way if you shuffle.

I will remember, Etienne said.

Then his father nodded at Gil Delacambre, who started the outboard. A cloud of diesel spun in the wind, and the boat motored off to the east, smaller and smaller, until the boy could only hear the soft *put put put* and the water licking against the fabric of his T-shirt.

In every direction, Etienne saw color. Coal-blue waves rippling in the summer wind, a white dome of sky patterned with cotton, mirage-haze at the horizon and oil rainbows that coiled and slid past him on the water's surface. He was simply a boy standing in the sea, impossibly here, on two feet, and now alone. Here there was the Gulf of Mexico and the sky and nothing else. For five minutes, he panicked. He peed, felt the warmth on his thighs and then the cold creeping back. There was no land in sight. He couldn't see the island they'd set up camp on, a spit of crushed shells and sand in the barrier group by Breton Sound, its white dunes peppered with oyster grass that nudged only six inches above the waterline. He closed his eyes. He felt the salt wind, the gooseflesh, then a gradual evening out of his heartbeat. He thought of how his body would adjust like this in cold swimming pools on boiling afternoons back in New Orleans. *Okay,* he said to the wind. Then he checked the gill string, unhooked his lure from the tip of his spinner rod, and tossed it out into the waves.

The park ranger is telling the sheriff's man and a couple of local reporters that Etienne's father may have had a death wish. This strikes Etienne as wrong, but nonetheless he considers it. He has come to understand the term in a detached, third-person kind of way, precise in how it describes people who are only characters to him. BASE jumpers and daredevils on TV. Soldiers who sign up for repeat tours overseas. Adventurers in airport novels. He calls upon these images to make a subtle demarcation between the idea of people who provoke death, poking its den with a stick to see when it will come hissing after them, and people like his father. It seems an unfair term here, yet maybe they are right. His father is now seventy-four years old, two bad shoulder sockets, a back that seizes daily and forces him to lie down and stretch. He is active for seventy-four, but this is the kind of mixed blessing that has already fueled speculation about his state of mind. Had his father been arrogant, paddling out into the swamp with a backpack, a sandwich, a pair of water bottles? No phone or emergency kit. No life jacket, even. He'd been doing this for decades, since his children were old enough to kneel in the canoes with him, to play with GI Joes and watch the morning steam lift off the water under the unrelenting southern sun. The man was a veteran. Military survival training, trips to the Arctic Circle, the Wind River Mountains, the steep basalt canyons of the Pacific Northwest. Etienne's mother had said once that he was born in the wrong century, and as a boy, Etienne had latched onto that idea with some sense of pride. A caveman father. A frontiersman in a wetland that sinks further and further into history. Arrogant, maybe. But for Etienne, arrogance doesn't fully square with a man who had a death wish. What is arrogant about a suicide? Moreover, what is a suicide without a body?

Etienne stands at the boat ramp and watches the assembled group of volunteers drink cold coffee from a thermos, talking and swatting mosquitoes. It's day two of the search, and everyone's face has the same flat composure. It looks a lot like boredom, but Etienne knows better, has seen that look from cops in the city. The only exception is the ranger, a woman in her mid-forties with hair the deep tea color of creek water, graying in stripes that almost flash in the sun. She is clouded with gnats, but there's a liveliness in her gestures when she talks to the reporters. Her hands are on her hips now, eyes looking back towards the darkening shapes of cypress that border the edge of the Atchafalaya Wildlife Refuge. Etienne follows their gaze to the trees, to the deep spaces between them that echo with crickets and cicadas and tree frogs. A white noise hums steadily until breaks in the conversation, swelling up through the pauses all at once, holding everyone momentarily in the sound of a freefall.

Like most childhood memories, the memory of the fishing trip in Breton Sound is so imprecise that Etienne discovers that he's changed details each time he recalls it. Sometimes he can still see the boat while he's wading in the Gulf, sometimes he's abandoned all on his own. Sometimes he sees a shark hit his stringer, sometimes he just feels the tug on the line and pees himself, too scared to look back, counting the seconds until the line around his waist goes slack again. He can't recall if Gil Delacambre stays overnight with them on the island, or if he simply drops them in the evening and returns the next day. It is thirty miles back to the marshes along Louisiana's crumbling edge, so it seems unlikely that Gil would've left and returned, but Etienne can't picture the boat in the surf, the man's tent, anything about his presence that night on the island. He can picture the thunderheads at sunset, white cliffs descending into a reddish haze below, grinding inexorably closer from the south. He remembers the halo of sun in his father's hair from the boat when he drops him off in the water. He remembers a flash of teeth, like a smile, before the motor revs to life.

His father had brought the dog with him. Five days ago now, in the morning, he'd strapped the old fiberglass canoe to the roof of the Jeep, singing a little song as he helped the dog climb into the passenger seat. The dog was fourteen and more visibly hobbled by age than his father had ever shown himself to be. She was a mutt of the swamp. He'd found her on a canoe trip with his students, pulled her tiny form from a spit of land at the edge of Bayou Sauvage, wrapped her in his T-shirt, and left her on his lap the whole drive home. First he was just going to clean her up before putting her up for adoption. Then he was just going to make sure she was inoculated and healthy. Then it had to be the right owner, someone whom his father could trust with the dog, not just some asshole who would tie her up in the yard and leave her there. Eventually, she just became their dog, without anyone saying so out loud. The situation just settled, like sediment in the water, until everyone saw it clearly and nobody felt it could be any other way.

Etienne is having coffee with the park ranger, whose hair is pulled into a ponytail and whose hat rests on the table next to her walkie-talkie. The café is a few miles up from the boat launch where the search is being organized. There, a thinner group of volunteers, quieter each day, are eating brown-bag lunches in the shade. There, he'd caught whispers of things he'd rather not hear. Strangely, this hadn't angered him so much as made him pity the men and women who were searching for his father. He'd feel their eyes on him when he moved through the sphere of their conversations, felt them bite their tongues and clip the sharper edges of their doubts until he moved out of earshot again. He wanted to hold their hands and tell them not to hold back, but in his head this had sounded disrespectful, like he was picking a fight. Maybe the park ranger had sensed something, asked him to lunch to get away. Maybe she just pitied him. Maybe she has brought him here to give him the "realistic expectations" speech.

"It's not a suicide," Etienne says, breaking the silence filled by the trailing end of a song from the kitchen radio. The ranger looks out the window and then back over at him. Her face is taut and tired-looking. Her eyes are a deeper brown, almost black, wet and gilded with half-moons of refracted neon from the overhead.

"I suspect you don't want it to be," she said evenly, "but if we don't find him soon this is going to move to recovery. And honestly, it might be easier to view it that way."

Etienne thinks about this, about what choice was easiest for framing the loss of his father.

"It's not a suicide because he brought the dog," he says.

She straightens her back and sighs. "The dog does give him a much better chance of being found." She looks back out the window again, her eyes still caught with that look he'd seen three days ago with the reporters. Active. Thinking. She is the last holdout.

"I mean, he wouldn't kill the dog," Etienne says. "Intentionally, at least, he wouldn't put her in harm's way. If he'd meant to die, he'd have gone alone."

"You said the dog was old too," the ranger says. Etienne finds himself annoyed by the pragmatism in the ranger's suggestion.

"He found her in the swamp," Etienne says. "Rescued her from an island, probably a day or two from starving. Nursed her back. There's no way he'd do that."

"Was the dog sick?"

"Yes, but find a fourteen-year-old dog that isn't."

A long pause, punctuated by the start-up of brass music from the kitchen and the clanging of silverware to the beat.

"Maybe he was taking her home," she says.

"I don't believe that," he says. "And I bet you don't, either."

She holds his eyes with hers. They both have a hand on the table, fingertips separated by a narrow strip of lacquered wood like a channel. After an extended silence, the radio next to her warbles and then comes to life.

That night on Breton Island, the storm had broken with such fury that they could hear alarms going off on the oil rig whose lights danced in the distance to the east. Etienne imagined all the roughnecks evacuating, sliding down firepoles and cargo nets into waiting Coast Guard ships. They were leaving him, he thought. He'd wished that they could call the rig, tell them a man and his boy were on the island.

Just so they would know, so it wouldn't be a mystery when the Gulf rose up and swallowed them without a trace.

Out of the south, from a blackness strobed with lightning, a wind came up across the island with the force of a steam engine. He could hear the sand blasting the fabric of the tent, and he huddled close to his father, who lay with his back to the windward side, headlamp and reading glasses on, narrating *Huckleberry Finn* with a deep Southern twang.

Golly, Huck, his father said, *If he a man, then why don't he talk like a man?*

At that moment, the tent came down around them, pressing them into the sand and dragging them along the dune. The light went out. They both gripped the ground through the fabric, searching for the rootstalks of oyster grass. He was screaming, deafly in the rush, and he held his father's shoulders, still bone and cartilage, still solid, still anchored to the Earth.

The dog is at the boat launch. Surrounded by volunteer searchers who offer her bites of peanut butter sandwich, she is turning in circles in the hot sun. She drinks from a bowl set down by someone, and then turns back to the treeline and whines, licking her muddy chops. Her fur is thickly woven with brambles and thorns. The volunteer who found her is an elderly, long-boned woman named Nelta, who owns a gas station in Picayune. Nelta used to help Etienne's father run the shuttle back when his family canoed the creeks of southern Mississippi. She knows the dog by name, sits by her and runs her fingers through the matted fur, whispers, *Good Bear, what a good girl, what a good good girl.*

Etienne is standing just outside the passenger door of the ranger's Jeep, shifting his weight from leg to leg, his pulse racing. Beneath his feet, the crushed oyster shells that pave the drive down to the boat ramp crackle and pop. Around him, several volunteers hover in a semicircle. All of them are upbeat. Several conversations are going at once. A middle-aged guy in hunting camo and a blaze orange penny stands next to Etienne, smoking a menthol in long drags and nodding. "Had one like that when I was a boy," he says, to no one in particular, the words uncoiling in white puffs from his sunburned lips.

"It's an excellent sign," the ranger is saying, handing a laminated map to Nelta for her to examine. Etienne watches the sunlight on the ranger's hair, imagines some change in color that is seeping in now, turning tea to amber and amber to gold. Nelta has one hand anchored firmly on the dog, who has now lain down at the edge of the launch, panting and running her tongue along her nose. Etienne watches Nelta's hand work the dog's fur. He pictures his mother, thinks of that same casual movement of the fingers, of the lazy and loving claim her hands would lay. This came during silent afternoons on the back porch, a hand on the dog, the sunbaked smells of autumn drifting lazily over the town. It came during lowlight nights in the living room, during mornings in the kitchen with breakfast-crumbed fingers dragging low for curious noses to find. He knows, quite suddenly, that his father is dead. As clearly as he now tastes the diesel on the air, he knows it in a way that feels almost transcendental. He can see his father. It is yesterday, and he is many miles to the northeast, in a clearing between cypress knees, lying in the shade. The canoe is missing. He has his leg bound with the torn sleeves of his sweatshirt, the short spare paddle for a brace. He has made a fire. He always makes fires, but this one is a small one, and he is out of matches, and he is watching the light through the trees with the knowledge that another night out in the swamp will likely be his last. His father is talking to the dog, pointing it southward across the wide inlet which they've paddled, towards the distant high ground that eventually links up to Route 105. He is whispering in his singsong voice, cajoling her. He keeps pointing and clapping, *Go go go*, he says, but she won't go. She won't go until later, when it's dark and the ground comes alive with fire ants and stick bugs and the wild night chorus of the sinking world. When he is no longer clapping and his skin has turned the coolness of the water. When enough time has passed for her to know that he won't whisper anymore, she will sniff the ground around him, turn in circles, lick his eyelids, and then turn uncertainly to where the inlet meets the land.

He'd awoken to the sound of gulls. The wet fabric of the tent lay pressed to their backs, filtering the light of morning into a pale red glow patterned with shadow droplets that slid and shimmered on their skin. Etienne had been asleep, although he didn't know how or when it had happened. Next to him, his father lay pressed into a depression in the sand, the folds of their collapsed tent obscuring his brow and part of his torso. Etienne could smell his breath, the unbrushed teeth and nighttime dose of whiskey, and watched the air from his father's lips move the loose pages of *Huckleberry Finn*. Outside, the oystergrass tickled the tent walls in the wind. The air hummed. The gulls cackled. Etienne kept still, long past when his body began to ache with the need to stretch, to go pee, to unfurl the wet plastic from their backs and step out to see what the storm had done to the island. One of his hands still clutched the sand through the groundcloth, and as the sounds of the world crept in around him, he stayed still, strangely certain above all things that he would stay this way, unmoving, until his father stirred

Jeff Pearson

Honda CR-X Fastback

*"Significantly worse than average" protection
for its occupants in the event of side impact*

I watched our first CR-X's wheel roll down the street,
all by itself, axle split with rust. A plea

from inside the blood-
red coat of paint, glove box stuffed with fast-
food, drive-
thru napkins for spills, a two-door

hatch-back with significantly better-
than-average gas mileage,
high like my dad's blood pressure.

The second CR-X collapsed
in on him, as a white pickup blew
right into his body, head and neck
followed dead Newton's number two law.

At night, the turn signal would stick
and turn off the headlights.

He bought the car
for me, for enrolling in wrestling,
where I would learn the firemen's
carry, the chicken wing, granby,
and to never use a full nelson

because it was a penalty,
and you will break a neck.

Brian Clifton

I've Become, He Said, Wary of Quick Things

In his flulike six-month wane,
my father nailed his Hepatitis C

treatments: the shots, the pills.

Over laundry, my mother assures
me my blood is safe, repeats.
I watched him lose weight, shovel

cottage cheese through the hole
in his beard. I remember splitting

a bottle of brandy with him—
it was his roommate who had lost
her mind all those years ago

and burrowed into the walls
until she found a passage
in the basement that led
her under their neighbor's

lawn; it was never my father.
In California, he traded dates
with the mayor's queer daughter

for rent. No one could know that

now he is too weak to lift a ream
of shingles. It's embarrassing

to hear my cousins whisper
each holiday about my father's
appetite: how it came and went

with my mother over the years.

They speculate if my mother needs
treatment. Next autumn, my father
will sit on his deck with an air rifle

and pop the overstuffed jaws
of each squirrel on his property.

Katherine Frain

A Southern Cold

In December, the luxury of flowers.
Of frogs like the speckled bodies of fallen
leaves, migrations of change congregating
in the ragged bite of moon. December,
South Carolina will sweet-talk the June
harvest's eye, mewl milk to lazy cats

lounging in rail-thin shotgun shacks, crow
rot to termites infesting splintered
spines of sandy breach. The North's palest
reach: the shame of anonymity

in our summer. Their claim to timelessness
the sliding name all icicles bestow
on covered trees, on roofs bowed under
blankets of dissipating white. As if
the china patterns clutched
tight under the frost would bloom

the same gilded lilies. South Carolina, clutch
your deer, the bright split of August and December;
what changes is not the crispness of the air
or red, but whose velvet brain bloods the fender.

Michael Robins

Paris of the Plains

Missouri runs late where language stands
beside the station at the end of a tunnel.

Missouri is starving for a story & starting
out in the world. Suitcase in either hand

shrills with crickets for the tired sermon,
shuts the narrow transom she'd opened.

Language in this poem need not speculate
like strangers along the rim of Missouri.

Rhetoric takes turns, gathers like wolves
about the brilliance of such encampments.

Language is useless as Missouri: She mates
sensibly, saying the names of cities once

& flowers, the sheer numbers of cardinals
breathless, naked atop the Missouri trees.

Cate McGowan

Let Go

It was 3 a.m. at the Krispy Kreme. I noticed her skin first. Lustrous and dark, like the coffee I was waiting to order. Before I started my hormone therapy, it had taken me at least two shaves and three layers of pancake to get skin that looked that smooth! So, that night, I stood there in line, and I checked the lady out, up and down, the way a good queen sums up the competition. Nothing else had fared as well as her glossy cheeks; her arms were rough and dry. When I looked closer, as I edged up to the counter, I saw her arms close. Track marks pocked the length of them. The poor thing had no fashion sense, either—she was stuffed into a tight magenta jumpsuit and was all portly like an uncooked sausage. It was when she moved that she had real problems. The woman jerked around like a puppet dragged through water. And she stood there, legs splayed, arms waving, and spoke in alternating tones, gibberish, mainly, bellowed questions and whispered cursing. Goddammit, all I wanted was some coffee.

So I stood close behind her, and magenta lady reordered and recounted her cash for the fifth time, ordering, then retracting, then ordering again. The clerk stood with one hand on her hip, the other on the cash register, staring into space, impatient, irritated. I needed my goddamn cup of coffee.

Some cute straight guy, who'd been pacing the fluorescent-bright restaurant, who was as keen as I was to get a move on with the ordering, started yelling. Into his cell phone.

"If you're *serious* about your recovery," he was saying, "you'll turn this over to your higher power. You know what I'm saying?" He walked back and forth, listened, shaking his head. "Screw that shit, man! Let go and let God. That bitch girlfriend can take care a herself. She ain't worth two sticks rubbed together."

He slammed his cell phone shut and stood, arms crossed, scowling at magenta jumpsuit lady, who was still trying to count her money.

"It's sixteen forty-five," the clerk said.

"'K, then, um, that's too much, too much. I need two dollars. Take off one a them Boston Cremes is all you need do." She shuffled through the words.

"Oh Lord," the clerk said. She rolled her eyes. "You know I already rang it up. Now you making me go and write up an overring? Again?"

"I just don't have enough," the lady said.

I peered over magenta lady's shoulder, counted her money myself. The cashier wasn't helping.

"You have eighteen dollars," I snapped. "Do I need to count it for you?"

The guy on the cell phone looked at me, eyes big as breakfast plates. It was as if he was seeing me for the first time. He looked down at my feet for a couple seconds.

"Hey man, what kinda boots are those?" he asked me.

"I have no idea," I said. I glanced down. My go-go boots shone in the overhead lights. I'd spit-shined them on my way out. The rhinestones sparkled.

"You could kick some serious ass with those big boots," he said. "What size are they? You got some big motherfucking feet." I wasn't sure if the guy was paying me a compliment; I'd never heard of anybody kicking ass with go-go boots, but I figured what he really meant was something like "big feet, big you-know-what." It wasn't the first time somebody'd cruised me at the Krispy Kreme.

"Look," I implored, to nobody in particular, my arms out, crucifixion-style, "all I want is a cup of coffee!"

"I'm really sorry," the clerk said, peering around magenta jumpsuit lady, "but I can't take any orders until this customer gives me sixteen forty-five. Gotta complete the transaction."

The cute guy got back on his cell phone, started up again with the person he'd been talking to the first time around.

"Well, did you tell her?" he asked, then paused. "Look, man, the same Jesus that took care a you is gonna take care a her. You'll be all right soon as you push that cracked-out, sorry-ass bitch through the door. Just do it, man." He looked around the restaurant, then caught a load of my feet. "There's this dude here at the Krispy Kreme's with some big-ass lady's boots, and it got me thinking about those shoe ads and how they say 'Just do it.' Just put that bitch on the street, man. Just do it. Let go and let God." He slammed the phone shut again. "Just do it!" he yelled to the place, sounding like a preacher on Sunday morning.

In the back, I could see through the order window, see the baker leave her conveyor belt of donuts; she stuck her head out the side door to see who was making all the commotion in the restaurant. She looked at me and went back to sorting, shaking her head as she threw hot donuts in boxes.

"All's I need is forty-five cents," magenta jumpsuit lady was saying. "Who's got forty-five cents?" I was mad now—the damn lady *couldn't* count.

"I do!" I said. "I'll pitch in two bucks, if it gets me coffee."

"Now hold on, just a sec," the cell phone guy interrupted, his hand on my shoulder, pulling me to face him. The cashier glowered at the near miss, the cash interruptus. Cell phone guy lowered his voice. "Figure she's strung out?"

"Yep," I said.

"Now, a minute ago, I thought you were some kinda kick-ass dude, when you told that bitch to pay for her donuts. But you know, it's not gonna help if you pay for her food. It's called *enabling*."

"*Hell-OOO*," I said, rapping my knuckles against my own forehead. "How long you been clean?"

"Been nine months," he said. He had nothing on me. I turned away.

And with that, the front doors to the place swung open and a cold wind swept in. A teenage boy sauntered up to magenta jumpsuit lady. He wore a stained "Tupac—RIP" T-shirt, and his glasses sat on the end of his nose. One of the lenses had a lightning-shaped crack running through.

"Mama," he said, "what's goin' on?"

"*Oooh*, I'm *trying* to pay for these *goddamn* donuts," she hollered, "but I need forty-five *motherfucking* cents!" She held her head high, like a dog bellowing at the moon.

Her boy peered at the floor, embarrassed, shuffled his feet in his mismatched bedroom slippers; he sighed, and his breath, its sound so soft, yet so audible, overtook the entire restaurant, as if a wind from some underworld had blown right through. I knew that sigh. I remembered it. Something knocked at me.

"I'll pay for your food," I heard myself saying. "Have anything you want." Cell phone guy glared at me.

"It's sixteen forty-five, then," the clerk said. The boy looked down again. His mother shook her head wildly, "No, no, no, no," and thrummed her fingers on the counter. She would not turn to look at me.

"Mama, just let him pay and let's get on home." She slumped. I paid. "Thank you, sir."

The boy kept his eyes down, and they stuffed a dispenser full of napkins into their box of donuts. As the doors swung closed behind them, I finally got to order my coffee. Cell phone guy ignored me, stood way over to the side over by the half-and-half containers and stir rods and Sweet'N Lows.

"That was a nice thing you did, hon. Need anything else?" the clerk asked me softly, her tone different now. She touched her hand to mine for a moment.

"Huh?"

"You're ... crying," she whispered, pointing her long gold nail to her cheek. She slipped a napkin across the counter with some sugar packets.

I wasn't tasting my weak coffee as I turned and watched magenta jumpsuit lady and her son slip into their car, their box of free donuts steaming on the seat between them. Their old car thumped around the corner, and I kept my gaze fixed for a long while, fixed on the window and on my own wavy reflection in the glass.

Leonard Kress

Boginski Finds a Bride

Boginski went out walking under the El one freezing cold Sunday afternoon. He had nowhere else to go, nothing else to do. The night before he had been kicked out of the White Eagle Club for bothering one of the waitresses, Zosia, a sweet, timid girl, a miner's daughter, just over from Katowice. Boginski kept grabbing her skirt, actually ripping it, trying to get her to sit down at the table he shared with four other young men, none of whom spoke English. That didn't matter to Boginski, who understood the gist of their conversation; he just wanted to buy drinks for someone. They were merchant marines off a freighter from Gdynia, in port a few blocks away. Boginski wouldn't have gotten himself ejected from the club if he had just apologized and kissed Zosia's hand like the sailors did—without licking it.

Now he was hungover and broke and he no longer thought that Zosia would be eager to sleep with him just because he was a citizen and she needed someone to sponsor her for a Green Card. He realized this as he wandered up and down the avenue, taking long, nervous strides under the El platform. He wondered what had happened to all those straight-from-Poland girls who were so desperate to marry Americans. Like the ones his mother used to talk about, always trying to set up an introduction, the ones who treated their men right and spent the whole day cooking and cleaning, bearing children. He could handle that, he used to think, even all that cabbage and beets. The babies and mothers-in-law and cousins brought over for extended vacations. The kind of wife who wouldn't even think of talking to another man, except maybe the priest at confession, and one who could certainly never leave him. Because, well, where could she go? Those kinds of wives would never learn to drive a car, that would be his job—car-ass princesses, he thought. He passed two Polish girls, doubled over and giggling like little kids and walking along with linked elbows, their laughter like a gust of wind tugging his scalp. Both of them wore long, embroidered sheepskins and he couldn't tell where their blond curls ended and the wooly collars began.

Boginski followed them for two blocks, keeping his distance. Then, to keep from following them farther and to escape the wind—to keep from having to endure their blowing him off—he entered what was once St. Stanislas, the old Polish church connected to the school he went to, even graduated from, before he gave up school for good. He wasn't sure who owned the ramshackle place now—the rectory and classrooms demolished years ago. It had changed hands several times in just the last year, and the sign out front announced only *Jesus = Lord*, and nothing more. He thought that maybe he'd ask about the roof, whether they'd be willing to pay him to replace missing slate shingles, blown off by the last storm. The preacher, or whatever he was—Boginski had a hard time understanding how someone who wasn't a priest and wasn't celibate and didn't wear black robes and wasn't fawned over by a group of young boys and old ladies could be a man of God—already knew him because he'd seen him high up on the roof of the abandoned lace factory next door, dismantling the old, wooden water tower, lowering it rotting piece by piece to a Dumpster below. The preacher had watched him for a good half-hour and even brought him out a Styrofoam cup of coffee. No priest had ever done anything like that. Boginski had signaled for him to place it in the hoist so he could raise it up to the roof and not have to listen to the guy yelling up questions that got lost in the fury of the elevated train. Miraculously, only a few drops spilled.

But when Boginski stepped inside, he decided to just hang back by one of the carved mahogany pews. There was a service going on, even though it was late afternoon already, and for the first time in his life he didn't feel totally out of place in a church. Even though every single goddamn statue of the Virgin and the martyred saints and Jesus himself had been removed, some leaving huge, ragged, human-shaped craters in the church walls, like a cartoon character's hasty escape. All the stained glass was gone and the lead frames that once held it stuck out in all directions like insect feelers. Boginski didn't know what made him remain inside and didn't question himself about it. He could see that everyone here was an outcast. He remembered hearing that the church was being rented by a bunch of Gypsies, and maybe, he was hoping, he might have stumbled onto some wild, drunken celebration, full of music and tambourines and dancing girls, flapping their long, flowered skirts up and down. He tried to picture what that would be like, but all he could conjure up was the biker bar down the street with go-go dancers. His mother used to sew costumes for the girls, strange as that was to him—thinking of his mother gossiping with them and getting them all tangled up in her tape measure, as they stripped down to bra and panties. He never saw any of the girls in the house, but he did recognize the patterns of beads and sequins on some of their costumes (sunflowers which were shaped to cover their breasts before the real show began) when he dropped by. Once or twice he tried to use that connection as a pickup line, but it never got him anywhere. The girls quickly backed off, knowing that anything at all that linked them to domesticity would break their concentration—that once their thoughts began to revolve around needle and thread and fittings, it wouldn't be long before they thought about their own kids and their ex-boyfriends, and probably even their own parents. And then it would be impossible to dance and thrust their crotches into the faces of strangers ....

Boginski quickly realized that he must have been wrong about the Gypsy congregation. All he saw were a few dark-haired kids flopped out on the floor. He decided to stay anyway. A woman wearing thick glasses was poking dreamily at a small electronic keyboard, the kind rock groups used to use. But soon she was shaking her head, swiping and pawing at the keys like some relentless itch and choking out some religious song. The whole congregation was on its feet, singing and screaming along. There was nothing synchronized about it, though, and they kept bumping into one another, knocking themselves off balance like merry-go-round-drunk children. There was a bum who shoved his way to the center and started to blow on a harmonica. His hands were fluttering like startled finches. He huffed wildly, gasping to get as much air into the reeds as he could and jerking it across his slobbering mouth like he was loosening lug nuts. When the birds flew off, he shyly placed it back in his torn pocket, and a woman in a tight red dress took his place. She was barefoot—Boginski could see her high heels right where she'd kicked them off, on top of her rumpled coat. Her arms were raised straight up to the ceiling vault, her elbows sharp and hyper-extended and swaying back and forth. Her slender fingers were loose as sewer kelp, and her red nails were flashing.

Boginski was staring at the backs of her thighs as the hem of her tight dress crawled up her legs, up and over the dark band of her pantyhose. He could have stood there gaping for hours, the only one of the congregation doing that, when, all of a sudden, some man grabbed him and dragged him over to her. Other men joined the rush, and once they reached the woman, they circled around her and clasped hands. Fingers on the left and on the right of him pressed powerfully into his wrists, strong enough to stop his pulse. Not one man laid so much as a finger on her as she collapsed to the floor, sobbing.

Boginski only realized that it had been the preacher himself who dragged him into the unbroken circle after he shook himself out and marched over to the podium and signaled for quiet. The organ faded after a little trill, and gradually everyone sat down. Boginski noticed that the dark-haired kids had all migrated to the back of the church and the woman in the red dress was still crumpled on the floor. Only Boginski seemed to notice that her long, blond hair lay splayed out around her face or that her collarbone held glistening beads of sweat or that her pink toenails had pierced their way through the tips of her pantyhose. A fallen angel, Boginski thought, feeling sentimental and mistaking the congregation's scent of filthy coats and unchanged underwear and greasy hair for the incense and dripping wax of his Childhood Church, St. Stanislas. The church where he had been baptized and taken first communion—his tongue long and steady and stiff as the priest laid the wafer upon it. The church where he stole gulps of communion wine along with everyone else, boys and girls alike.

Boginski wondered if she might be of the prostitutes who picked up her johns by hitchhiking under the El. He suspected that her face was all rough and broken-out under its icing of makeup, that her traffic-light blow jobs were lucky to bring her ten bucks a blown wad. He remembered the stupid jokes the visiting Franciscan brother used to tell in Religion class—*How many angels can sit on the head of a pin? Answer: Nun.* Boginski never really got the joke, but then again, he never got much of anything from school. This new angel, though, and this church, inspired him to riff on the joke: *How many angels sit on the head of a needle? How many angels give head for a needle? How much angel dust fits into a needle?* He wondered if the brother would get it.

The blond woman pulled herself up to her knees and tried to smooth out her wrinkled dress. She remained kneeling, her hair flopped up and over her head, hanging over her face like a shroud, like a girl down the shore, drying her wet hair in the sun after a long afternoon dip. It took the preacher several minutes to calm his congregation. When its previous frenzy was reduced to random coughs, sniffles, and sighs, he persuaded his wife to leave the organ for a few moments to speak to the congregation. A draft from the wings shivered her dress as she moved to the pulpit. When she removed her glasses she had the soft, puffy face of Boginski's mother, the same blazing blue child's eyes, that susceptible look she had before the cancer invaded. Boginski could not look at her and shut his eyes. He thought he heard the woman explain his mother's five-fingered outlook on life, complete with accent. "One you born, two you work—or if you no work, you sit," meaning prison. "Three you pray and four you walk," meaning you find a girl. "Five you die." Boginski had heard this over and over again throughout his childhood, just as his neighborhood kids heard *This little piggy* .... When he opened his eyes, though, she was still buttoning up her sweater.

"Last night," the preacher's wife began, "last night I just about reached the end of my rope."

Boginski pictured her hanging from the belfry like in some horror movie he must have seen when he was cutting school. Swinging in the breeze. "I'd had enough," she said, "E-NUFF! I realized I was simply serving too many masters. My children." She paused to let that sink in and Boginski peeked out at the little dark kid hugging the crumpled lady, who was raising her head up, beginning to re-acquaint herself with the surroundings, raking her fingers through her hair. He felt himself surrounded by mothers and he felt himself blessed by them.

"My husband," the preacher's wife continued, glancing down at him, all smiles and nods in the first row. "The poor. The battered. The addicted," she continued. "Too many masters. Not to mention the Lord."

"A-men," the congregation shouted. Even the whore in the red dress was nodding her head, and Boginski fought off the picture of her sucking someone's cock, his cock.

"I who was once pure praise, I who was once pure praise and here I was, screaming and hollering. My words fouler than some harlot streetwalking under the El."

Boginski shuddered. Who was this lady with his mother's face, he wondered. It could have been her twenty years ago, chasing kids from their corner porch stoop, cursing at them in Polish, calling them things like "dog's blood" and "whores," even the boys. And waving a broom, dumping buckets of cold water down from her bedroom window when their laughing and bickering kept her awake. "Get the *hellella* outa here!" she'd snap in her immigrant English. And now he worried that this lady might be about to strike out at him next—in a way that his mother never could? He straightened up in the pew and took his heels down from the one in front. His hands dug into his own thighs. Now that it was too late to apologize to his mother for the ways he screwed up his life and for the ways he failed to save her, he was more prepared than he'd ever been to hear his faults catalogued to his face. He believed he could face a deathbed litany. He scanned the room for a confessional, but they had all been ripped out. *Bless me Father for I have sinned …. I stole a bolt of silk to buy cigarettes …. I stole my sister's ring to buy beer …. I stole my mother's sewing machine to buy speed …. I broke into the rectory ….*

"Heating system shot," she continued. "BB pellets through the new windows. New drips daily …." Boginski scrunched his shoulders down a little. He thought he heard his mother's voice again, from that day in the hospital. She was in such pain that she kept asking the Blessed Mother to take her. Boginski had kept fussing with the morphine drip, trying to explain to his mother about the ten-minute lockout, when no matter how frantically she pressed the button, no drug would be dispensed. "The Blessed Mother will take me," she'd whispered, "she will be kind and take me." Boginski remembered yelling at the nurse before he left. "Ten CCs just ain't enough to do shit!" He knew all about these morphine drips from the time he'd been hospitalized for a motorcycle accident. Luckily for him his girlfriend at the time was an ex-nurse and knew how to bypass the lock without the real nurses finding out. When visiting hours were over and he was kicked out, he pleaded with the nurses to save her.

"Last night it hit me hard," the preacher's wife went on. "Door locked. Me with a precious moment of peace to draw my bath. No sound but the glorious rush of water, steam rising up all about. I lowered myself in. Crying. I anointed myself."

Boginski was sweating now. It dripped down his forehead and branched off to stinging his eyes. He felt it coming all over, like a sparked blowtorch that he couldn't trim down. He squirmed and rubbed his back against the pew to stanch the flow.

"It was then I heard it," the preacher's wife said, slow and certain of her words. "The hissing water like a voice. I heard it. The tingle of soap and shampoo. In those tiny, popping bubbles, I heard it …."

"Praise the Lord!" shouted the congregation.

"In the porcelain pillow holding the tendrils of my hair."

"Praise, praise, praise!"

"The Lord is eager," she sang out and then went silent. The final syllable moaned on inside the huge, porous, almost-empty sanctuary. Boginski moaned along with it, making no effort to suppress it. "Praise. Praise," they hissed together, Boginski and the preacher's wife, like bleeding radiators.

Boginski felt ready to endure anything. He felt himself ready to mount the back of the preacher's wife, to ascend up over the slut in the red dress, to rise with her up over the tar tops of row houses and mills, above the El tracks and the bracketed, leaky wooden towers holding holy water. Up and back to that terrifying, familiar face—

"The Lord is eager for his bride," the preacher's wife cried out.

Kevin Boyle

Emigrant

When the sun goes down after the woman died
That day at dawn, and the ocean lies between
You and the woman who died at dawn while you
Slept dreaming of her dying because you knew
From what had been said that she would not last
The night—fluid in the lungs and cancer there
And everywhere between her neck and pubic bone—
You pull the shades down as if you are pulling down
A symbol, and you pull the shades down on the windows
That face east as if you were pulling down the curtain,
And you light the fire in the fireplace
And light the candles on the mantelpiece
As if the winter solstice day that she died on
Were a symbol of diminishment and then resurgence,
Brio, verve, and then you begin to drink
The whiskey of her country, light as oak wood
With the sun on it, and burning the way
They'll burn her body, and finally you become
Almost like a tree. Wasn't it Derry that meant
Oak in Irish, and isn't she in Derry, and aren't you
So far away that when dawn comes you'll move on
At once and get right back to it, seeing
No symbol where no symbol was intended?

Kevin Boyle

The Word of God

People might think I'm lying when I say
A boy—maybe ten or twelve—asked me
In Ireland if people died in America
As well, because their brother died that winter—

He was only eight—and maybe three or four
Of them waited by the river, stones in hand
For skipping, all looking up at me and waiting,
Those beautifully full Irish clouds passing.

Jen Town

My Love in the Manner of Soviet Espionage

The day made movements to the west,
like a ship, lacquered and flag-waved.

I wanted a hearty borscht and a babushka,
and one of those matryoshka dolls.
I slipped my bare feet into violet shoes
and the mirror said I was ready.

And there was Helga, Hilda, and whomever,
kneading with their forearms into
bread that grew like love

and rose like a bubble
to the surface of the late afternoon,
which gleamed like a serving dish
in the poem, which is neatly folded
and scented, laundered with lavender.

But there were colder times to come,
of course. On the tundra, the wind
was having a field day. Someone called out
in a language hearty as stew. All I wanted
was to sit in some dark corner
and whisper to you my Russian love phrases.

But first I had to walk stone streets
until my feet swelled; I had to find

inhospitable dark alleys. I had to swig
something fiery and tear bread into tiny pieces
while I waited for you with a slip
of a message you'd burn after I'd gone.

Kirby Wright

House of Lies

I sat on the floral-print couch between my big brother, Troy, and our mother. We were waiting for Dadio to get home. Nobody talked. Troy gnashed his gum and blew a bubble. We were both in eighth grade because he'd been held back. I looked at the reflection off the glass door in the living room—we all looked worried. It was as if we were waiting for the judge to hurl a guilty verdict. I looked strange sitting between two blonds, as if I belonged to another family with my dark hair and eyes. The only times I felt connected to them was when my father was in the house, since I took after him in looks. Troy ached for his attention. I'd always wondered if my brother resented me for looking like Dadio, especially after our Moloka'i grandmother said, "Mistah Kirby's da spittin' image of his fathah."

I wanted to run to the beach. But I knew facing the music was better than my father hearing directly from the principal. I wondered if Troy's punishment would exceed mine since he was a year older and Dadio expected him to set an example. I was glad Jen, our kid sister, was over at her friend Heidi's. I was certain there'd be fireworks.

I'd started referring to my old man as "Dadio" after hearing a beatnik use it in *Beach Blanket Bingo*. It made him seem cool and less threatening. I called my mother "June Spoon," the nickname her father had given her in Boston. I knew using it made her feel young and closer to him, even though he lived four thousand miles away in Chicago's Pick-Congress Hotel. She was wearing a yellow cocktail dress that matched the color of her bouffant. She thought she was a dead ringer for Marilyn Monroe, but less trashy. She even had that Marilyn beauty mark on her cheek.

My past with Dadio was troubled. As a toddler, I'd hidden in the bamboo patch to avoid the belt and watched him scramble like one of The Three Stooges scouring the back yard. Fire ants bit me into the open—Dadio yanked off a shoe and whacked the top of my head with the heel. After my hernia operation at nine, he told the nurses I was faking it when I limped through Queen's Hospital. Sometimes I imagined him as the portrait of the iridescent-winged devil in my New Testament.

I'd left the front door open. I figured an open door would pose one less obstacle after a hard day in the salt mines. Things went easier if you prepared for Dadio's arrival, such as placing *The Honolulu Star-Bulletin* on the dining room table and filling the ice bucket.

Tires churned outside.

"Ready or not," Troy groaned.

I knew it was the Olds by the rumble of the big block and the wheezing of its out-of-tune carb.

"Is that him?" June Spoon asked.

"Duh," Troy muttered.

The engine died and shoes grumbled the asphalt. The front door slammed shut and feet shuffled through the foyer. Dadio peered into the living room. His face was drained of the blood that usually gave him a ruddy complexion. His cheeks were as gray as his slacks. He held a leather briefcase in one hand and a gray suit jacket in the other. He clenched his jaw. His glasses seemed fused to his head. He'd invested $100,000 in an oil well tax shelter scheme with the other lawyers at his firm and the IRS was investigating.

"Hello, Dear," June Spoon cooed, "did you have a nice day at the office?"

He entered the room. "Who the hell's leaving this front door wide open?"

Nobody answered.

The top two buttons of Dadio's white dress shirt were unbuttoned and his sleeves were rolled up over the elbows. The knot on his black tie was fat from being loosened. Two decades of litigation had taken their toll: his back hunched, his teeth were nubs from chewing pencils, and his once-proud UH swimmer's chest had become a pair of sagging breasts. He dropped his briefcase on the asbestos tiles. "What's wrong?" he demanded.

"Well," June Spoon answered, "the boys had a little trouble at Punahou."

"Oh?" he asked, staring at me suspiciously. "What kind of little trouble might that be?"

"You're to phone Dr. Johnson first thing in the morning."

"What for?"

"He suspended Troy and Kirby."

"For the luva Pete. How'd this happen?"

I spoke first. I told him how we'd decided to skip woodshop to study for midterms. I avoided mentioning we'd used a scoop net to troll the lily pond for coins and used the loot to buy candy at the Snack Shop. Troy said he didn't need woodshop anyway, since he didn't plan on carpentry work for a life profession. He tried flattering Dadio by claiming he wanted to be a lawyer just like him. I suggested Dr. Johnson was getting revenge because I'd broken it off with his daughter Lucy.

Dadio yanked off his glasses and chewed on the stems. His face flushed red. He tossed his jacket on a mahogany chest with a framed invitation to my parents' Brookline wedding. "Tell me the real reason you both cut class," he said.

"Woodshop sucks," I admitted.

"You learn nothing," Troy tossed in.

"Two poor excuses," he scowled, "by a coupla stupes." He paced the tiles from the mahogany chest to the TV and back again. His oxblood shoes sounded like the ratta-tat-tat of small caliber fire. There was a look in his face between disgust and worry, one that reminded me of Richard Nixon. Dadio stopped in his tracks. "I don't blame Doctor Johnson for suspending you both," he glared. "Now get in your rooms."

"What for?" Troy asked.

"You know what for."

"Dear," June Spoon said, "the boys are sorry for what they've done. They won't do it again."

"You believe that?"

"They're getting too old for spankings."

"June," he snapped, "butt the hell out when I'm disciplining them."

((

I sprawled out naked on my bed. I touched the wall—screams moved in waves through the redwood. Troy was getting it. I was next. Dadio took special delight in double-header beatings with a belt. Troy was his warm-up. He'd already worked up a healthy sweat by the time he reached my room. "Fuck this," I whispered. I sprang off my bed, pulled on my BVDs, tee, and trunks. I snuck down past the wedding photos in the hall and loitered outside my brother's door.

"I'm sorry, Daddy," Troy pleaded, "I'm so sorry!"

It was the same mercy cry I used, but one that turned into a "I hate you, Daddy, I hate you!" chant muffled by my pillow after he'd left my room.

I crept past June Spoon's bathroom and spied into the kitchen. She was pouring bottled teriyaki sauce into a Pyrex dish lined with chicken thighs. Troy's door creaked open and Dadio hurried toward my room. I slipped into the foyer, stumbled into my slippers, and darted out the front door.

I jogged Aukai Avenue and up Elepaio. The sun closed in on the Diamond Head Crater. Mrs. Applestone was walking her cockapoo. Shadows from the shower trees spilled over the streets and sidewalks. A yellow VW bug puttered down the hill—it was Heidi's mother. Mrs. Bathen was driving Jen home after her Liddle Kiddles tea party with Heidi. I ducked behind a hau tree and saw my sister in the back seat with her friend. I waited until Mrs. Bathen hung a left off Elepaio and the bug vanished.

I reached Kilauea Avenue and headed east. I was worried about Jen. She'd escaped hearing the screams today but she was usually in the house when we were getting strapped. I knew the fallout was damaging her in a psychological way. One day, she believed, Dadio would come for her and make his workout a triple-header.

I got winded on Kilauea. I hot-walked to Waialae Avenue and held out my thumb. A Kalani School bus belched by spewing exhaust. Half the sun was below the crater and the streetlights along the highway ignited. Men in aloha shirts and suits zipped by in cars. A Dodge van with a red-bearded hippie at the wheel pulled over. The van's panel had a mural of a curling wave at Pipeline.

"Where to, little brother?" the hippie asked.

"Makapu'u."

He flipped open the passenger door. "All aboard."

We drove through Aina Haina and into Hawaii Kai. We rounded Koko Head Crater listening to Janis Joplin on KKUA radio. He talked about crashing the gate at Woodstock and doing Orange Sunshine with a girl who'd later become his wife. "Righteous vibes at Woodstock," the hippie said. He told me the concert gave him the courage to leave his foster parents and hitchhike over the Continental Divide.

We passed Sandy Beach. The road looped east to south and we climbed a pass between hills of lava. I got out near the Makapu'u lighthouse.

The hippie gave me the peace sign. "Be mellow, little brother," he said and drove away.

Hang gliders floated the sky above me. The ocean below was aquamarine but it switched to deep blue beyond an atoll known as "Rabbit Island." As a boy, Dadio had nearly drowned swimming out to it on a dare from his Uncle Sharkey.

I eased down a lava path glittering with glass shards. The lantana gave off a wild smell and clumps of naupaka were heavy with berry-like seeds. Beer cans, bullet casings, and McDonald's cups littered the underbrush. I reached bottom and kicked off my slippers. The sand felt good. Bodysurfers were heading for the parking lot. I followed a zigzagging high tide marked by broken shells, driftwood, and limu. Plover scuttled the shore. I was mad at myself for forgetting my wallet. The beach ended at a lava pinnacle. I squatted and gathered the shells, stacking them to make a tiny shell house in the sand. I used a strand of limu for a welcome mat and a hau leaf for the driveway.

A man in black trunks rounded the pinnacle. A net was draped over one shoulder and tabbies protected his feet. He studied the surf. Silver sparkled in his jet-black hair. I knew he had Hawaiian blood by his complexion and rugged features. He swung the weights on the net's skirt off his shoulder and rested them on his forearm. He gathered the catgut webbing, twisted back, and released. The net bloomed in mid-air and splashed in the water. He waded out, gathered the weights, and carried a net of squirming fish to shore. He emptied his catch into buckets. He lugged the net and two buckets, taking half-steps in the soft sand. "Hey, haole boy," he called, "you campin'?"

"Yes," I replied. I stuck a bamboo sliver through the roof of my shell house to make a chimney. A gust blew the hau leaf driveway away.

"No mo' sleepin' bag, anythin' li'dat?"

"No."

He came closer. There were holes in the canvas tops of his tabbies. His trunks were turning gray from the sun. "No can stay out heah," he told me, resting the buckets on the sand. "Get spirits."

"I don't believe in spirits."

"Wot yo' name?"

"Kirbz."

"I'm Uncle Freddy. I get two bucket owama, you like help carry?"

"Sure."

"Come den, Kirbz. We go make fish fry."

I got up, put on my slippers, and grabbed a bucket by its handle. We headed for the parking lot. The fish inside my bucket flared their gills trying to breathe.

I rode shotgun. Freddy drove his pickup past Sea Life Park and cruised the lava shore. He pointed out a turtle pond built for the ali'i. We leaned into a curve and the buckets in back slid. A truck in the opposite lane tooted. Freddy waved. He said he "worked construction" in Waikiki and confessed to losing his wife to cancer. He had one boy.

Freddy pulled off the asphalt. The tires grumbled over a gravel road flanked by tall hedges of orange hibiscus. The hedges ended. The gravel became crushed coral and a Portuguese man in greasy jeans gave us the shaka sign. We veered between two lois with rows of taro and bounced through a yard of centipede grass, pitted red dirt, and pili. There were chicken coops and kennels. It stunk of manure. Vines covered the telephone poles and yellow lilikoi dangled off the lines like ornaments. We pulled beside a beige house and Freddy cracked his door. "We go, Kirbz."

Poi dogs charged off the porch. They surround the Datsun and barked ferociously.

"They bite?" I asked.

"Only haoles."

I swung open my door and the dogs smelled my slippers.

"Mind yo' mannahs," Freddy groused. He tossed a handful of fish and the dogs raced off over the lawn.

I grabbed a handle and swung out my bucket. I shadowed Freddy past a plywood table loaded with hooks, wire leaders, lures, catgut, and rusted reels. He draped his net over a laundry line and led the way up a stairway shaded by timber bamboo. He took off his tabbies on the porch and stuck them on the railing. I put my slippers beside the tabbies.

"Come meet my boy," Freddy told me, swinging open a screen door.

I carried my bucket into a front room that smelled like cooking. The aroma of Chinese black bean combined with the scents of garlic, curry, and saffron. The floor was a patchwork of curling linoleum, strips of Astroturf, and lauhala mats. Glass balls hung off the ceiling in cord nets. A boar's head and deer skulls were mounted above a TV with rabbit ears. The top of the TV served as a shelf for an 8-track and conch shells. A cane table displayed family photos and a collection of poi pounders, ulu maika stones, and koa bowls.

A husky boy was sprawled on a love seat. He had his nose in a World Book encyclopedia and wore a green Crater Festival T. "Howzit, Pops," he mumbled. The book hid his face.

"Sonny," Freddy said, "Maks get planny owama."

I followed Freddy into the kitchen and placed my bucket on the stainless steel counter next to his. He returned to the front room. I watched the gills of a weke flutter as it sucked in air.

"Get guest," Freddy told the boy.

"So?"

"No ack pilau. Try come, Kirbz."

I stood in the kitchen doorway. Freddy sat on the arm of the love seat. He nudged the boy's shoulder. He lowered the book. The boy flared his nostrils, as if trying to smell me. He gave me the stink eye. This boy looked familiar. I remembered the most feared student at Star of the Sea Elementary, the one who'd been a pro wrestler in my play.

"Da Destroya?" I asked.

"Chee," he smiled, "you dat keed from ol' days school."

"Pipeline Bloodsuckers!" I cheered.

He rolled off the love seat, stomped the linoleum, and bared his teeth. "I like fo' drink yo' bloods!"

"Unreals," said Freddy. "You wen go same school?"

"Shoots yeah, Pops."

Freddy chuckled. "Small kine worlds."

"Wot you doin' heah?" Da Destroya asked.

"Nothing."

"No lie. Gotta be reason fo' haole come Waimanalo side."

"Sonny," Freddy interrupted, "call Cyril an' Buffalo dem. See if dose buggahs like come ova fo' grind."

"Wahines too?"

"Da mo' da merriah," Freddy answered. He barefooted a strip of Astroturf back to the kitchen like he was walking the plank. I could hear buckets being emptied into the sink and pots clanging.

"Get big changes, Kirbz," Da Destroya said solemnly. "My real name stay 'Lawrence.'"

"Law-rence? Like Lawrence of Arabia?"

"Dat's right. Wot school you go now, Kirbz?"

"Punahou."

"We play Punahou next Friday. I stay da Crusadahs fullback, second string. How come you no like go Saint Louis?"

"My father wanted Punahou."

Lawrence nodded. "He like Kirbz fo' be wit' haoles."

"Quit yakkin'," Freddy called, "an' staht cleanin' house!"

Lawrence swept. I unfolded card tables and propped them up on their skinny legs. We pushed the tables together to make one big one. Lawrence snooped in the kitchen and returned with lauhala place mats, paper napkins, and red plastic plates. We set a table for ten.

"I go out," Lawrence told me.

"Can I go, too?"

"No need. Gotta kennel da dogs, den light da torches fo' vampiahs."

I checked out the photos while Lawrence was doing his chores. There were some unframed ones taken at beach barbecues and picnics at Kapiolani Park. Others were graduation photos and teenage boys in military uniforms. The ones in frames were taken at Christmas—Lawrence and his parents wore either red or green and the backgrounds included wreaths, indoor trees, and garlands with red bows. Lawrence's mother looked pure Hawaiian. There was an angelic look in her smile, as if she knew a spiritual realm was waiting after her time on Earth.

I returned to the kitchen and found Freddy melting butter in an iron skillet. The gas flame sputtered. He washed the owama but didn't gut or scale them. He tossed the fish in a pie plate and rolled them around in flour. They sizzled in the hot butter.

"You don't clean them, Uncle Freddy?"

"No need. Get only small kine crab and limu in da opu."

"What about the heads?"

"Dat's da bess paht, Kirbz. Planny ono meat stay inside."

Freddy put me in charge of flipping. He folded taro leaves into a big pot of steaming water. He splashed sherry in a sauté pan and heaped in black beans. A tiny pan simmered a soy-garlic-watercress dipping sauce for the fish. The rice cooker clicked off. I liked Freddy's style. He kept things simple, cooked fast, and made plenty. Lawrence joined us and took a turn flipping.

Freddy flung the fridge open. He pulled out a sealed jar of black meat and yellow suckers. "Opihi," he said, "dis da kine."

An engine chugged by outside and doors slammed.

"Go see who dat," Freddy told us.

"No need help, Pops?"

"Everythin' undah control, Sonny."

I raced Lawrence through the front room and he beat me to the screen door. He swung it open. Cyril, Freddy's brother, shuffled in wearing moccasins. He was about Freddy's size, but younger and with sideburns like the singer Tom Jones. His family followed him in and I met his wife Anna and their little girls, Evelyn and Nadine. Cyril handed Lawrence two six-packs of bottled Primo and Anna gave me a gau gee cake in firecracker-red wrap. Cyril took off his moccasins, wedged them between a conch shell and the 8-track, and eyeballed me. Lawrence explained we'd gone to the same school "small keed time" and he'd been in my play pitting Fiftieth State wrestlers against vampires. Cyril claimed that some of the ali'i drank blood for power.

A motorcycle rumbled through the yard and I bolted with Lawrence to the porch. A chromed-out chopper with a teardrop tank roared past the coops. A burly man with a crew cut was the driver and his passenger was an Asian woman with long hair. She clutched his waist. He accelerated toward a torch on the far side of the yard and looped back to us.

"Who's this," I asked Lawrence, "Evil Knievel?"

"Buffalo, my muddah's wastoid bruddah."

"Who's the chick?"

"Violet. Fresh off da boat from Manila."

Buffalo pulled alongside a gray-primered Dart. He jammed the kickstand out with a black boot and climbed off with Violet. He had muttonchops and wore white overalls. Violet had on a blue crocheted bikini top and gray cords. Her legs were long and her breasts reminded me of mangoes. She had great hip action. I tried not to stare as she sauntered up the steps behind Buffalo.

"Howzit, Buff," Lawrence said.

"Still hangin'," he replied.

"I should say so," Violet giggled. She had big doe-like eyes. Her choker of abalone shell fragments glittered in the torchlight.

Buffalo took off his boots and stuck them on the railing. He walked the deck in white socks and crossed his massive arms when he reached me. "Who you?" he glared.

"Kirbz," Lawrence answered. "He stay cool."

"Last time had haole in Waimanalo was police."

"Hey, Buff," said Lawrence, "we go arm wrestle."

"Shoots," said Buffalo.

Violet opened the screen door and we joined the others in the front room. Cyril was showing his girls how to roll ulu maikas. Violet took off her cork heels. Anna gossiped with Buffalo about making a stand in Waiahole-Waikane before the taro farmers were evicted.

"Got free hand?" Cyril asked me.

"Yeah."

I grabbed the gau gee cake and followed Cyril as he carried the Primo six-packs into the kitchen. Cyril popped a cap and gave Freddy a beer. The flame simmered under the skillet. Freddy gulped beer and stirred sauce with a wooden spoon.

"Hui!" someone called on the porch.

"Ol' Man Brum," Buffalo greeted, "you sneaky buggah!"

A wizened man entered. He was the guy who'd given us the shaka sign. He handed Violet a stack of white pie boxes tied together with pink string.

Lawrence and Buffalo started arm-wrestling on a mat. Anna and Violet cheered them on. Buffalo's biceps bulged and veins popped out of his forearm. After a five-minute struggle, Lawrence submitted.

Violet wandered over to the cane table and studied the pictures. Her hair fell over her shoulders down to her waist. Her skin seemed to get darker as night set in.

Cyril popped in an 8-track. Tinny speakers played the ukulele-and-guitar intro to "Moonlight Lady." Lawrence sat beside Evelyn on the loveseat and played a uke. Nadine showed Violet some hula moves as Gabby Pahinui sang about a woman with qualities as beautiful as the land and sky.

"Loosen da hips," Nadine instructed, "no shame."

Violet's hips swayed. She had a natural rhythm and soon had the basic moves of the kaholo and ami poe poe down.

Cyril elbowed me. "Nice kine Flip, eh?"

I nodded.

"No let Buff catch you spockin' his wahine."

"Bring Brum's pies," Freddy called from the kitchen.

I plucked the pie stack off the table and hopped from mat to mat back to the kitchen. I put the stack beside the jar of opihi. Anna was massaging poi in a glass mixer. Freddy forked a hunk of pork out of a Tupperware container and stuck it on a glop of cooked taro. He placed the pork and taro on a ti leaf, folded the ti, and secured the little package with string.

"Wow," I said, "laulaus, too."

"Goin' broke da mouth," Freddy promised. He placed the laulau beside a half-dozen others perched on a mesh of chicken wire over a steaming pot.

Anna tossed me an ice cream scooper. I scooped kimchi from a jug and dropped the scoops into koa bowls. Evelyn wandered in and supervised my scoops.

"You get ice cream, Uncle Freddy?" Evelyn whined.

"Wot? You like sweets?"

"I like."

"Only get pie an' da gau gee you wen bring."

"You get squid?"

"You like dat?"

"Only my faddah dem."

"No mo'," Freddy said. "I go catch tomorrow."

Nadine came in and played junk an' a po with Evelyn.

"No fool around," Anna scolded.

Freddy stacked Golden Harvest serving plates with owama and laulaus. "Hele mai 'ai," he said.

Anna and the girls carried out plates, Tupperware containers, pots, bowls, teacups, bottled beer and wine, and canned soda. Buffalo and Cyril brought in benches from outside. The table filled with the main courses and was complemented by white rice, kimchi, red chili peppers with rock salt, sliced green mango, and dipping sauce.

We sat on the benches. I squeezed between Lawrence and Freddy. Buffalo sat directly across from me. He had one arm draped over Violet's shoulder.

Buffalo filled his plate with laulaus and rice.

The men guzzled Primo. The women sipped Boone's Farm Strawberry Hill from Dixie riddle cups. The girls drank ginger ale while Lawrence and I slugged down Cokes.

Lawrence grabbed a fish by the tail, sunk it in the dipping sauce, and swallowed it whole.

The 8-track of Gabby ended. Nobody got up to pop in a new one.

"No be shy," Freddy scolded me. "Eat planny."

Lawrence handed me a wooden spoon. I dug rice out of the pot and slapped it on my red plate. I grabbed two mullet and dropped them on the rice. Freddy tossed a laulau between the fish.

Cyril dipped steamed pork into the dipping sauce for fish and devoured it.

"Gross, Pops!" squealed Nadine.

I crunched off a mullet's head. Freddy was right about it being ono. I folded the body into my mouth. The bones weren't sharp and snapped like raw pasta. A rooster crowed in the yard. Dogs barked. I could hear a big truck grunting on the coast road. I looked at Violet— she looked back.

Buffalo flicked his bottle cap—it whizzed by, narrowly missing my face.

"You local?" he asked me.

"Yeah."

"Portagee?"

"No," I said. "My great-great-grandma was piha kanaka maoli."

Buffalo nodded. "You get chance, brah."

"Yo' faddah do wot?" Cyril asked.

"He's a lawyer."

Buffalo shook his head. Cyril finished his Primo. I understood why they hated lawyers. The big firms worked against Hawaiians getting homestead plots and most were helping landowners evict locals from farmable land in nearby Waiahole-Waikane. I knew I had to break the silence. "You know," I told them, "My Great-Uncle Sharkey trained fighters at CYO Gym in Kalihi, back in the good old days."

Brum smiled big, revealing an upper row of silver teeth. "Sharkey train my faddah," he said. "Only reason Fearless Frankie neva make champ was cuz his bruddah wen die plane crash. He stay hewa fo' go mainland."

After dinner, Lawrence and I headed for the porch to unfold a stack of metal chairs. Anna and Violet carried out zabutons. I leaned against the railing with Lawrence. The torches flickered in the yard. The women and girls camped on the zabutons while Freddy served custard pie topped with sliced papaya.

Freddy brought out ukuleles, two acoustic guitars, and a banjo. He placed them on the railing. Brum took a ukulele. Cyril selected a guitar. Buffalo lit a cigar stub with a Bic lighter and held it in the corner of his mouth before grabbing the banjo. Nadine complained about the cold so Freddy covered her with a quilt. The men made a circle with the chairs and played Hawaiian music. I had trouble with the words but I could understand the blue tone in their voices and the sad notes off the strings. It took me back to the auwe dirges I'd heard at kama'aina funerals on Moloka'i. The men played hard and steady, never stopping to drink or talk story. The poi dogs howled. Moths circled the torches. One moth got too close and spiraled off into the night with burning wings.

The music ended after midnight, not long after the first torch died. Violet hopped on the back of the chopper. Buffalo screeched away, his tires kicking up a cloud of dust on the coral road. Cyril and Anna carried their groggy girls down the stairs to the car.

"Latahs," Cyril called.

The Dart clunked over the pitted lawn.

I helped Lawrence fold the chairs and restack them. He unfurled sleeping bags and we put our backs to the deck and stared up at the stars. A half-moon with a yellow tinge floated above a breadfruit tree. I could hear pots and pans clanging inside. A dog whimpered. I'd phoned home before dessert and told June Spoon I'd return the next morning. "That sonuvabitch," I'd heard Dadio say in the background. I thought about the Wrights in Kahala. Part of me didn't want to belong to them anymore. But another part insisted I return, if only for Jen's sake.

Lawrence stretched. "How come wen you run, Kirbz?"

"To avoid a beating."

"Why yo' faddah like geev you dirty lickin'?"

"For cutting woodshop and lying to the principal."

"Big deal. Tell 'im fo' lighten up."

"I don't like him."

"I no blame you."

"Sorry about your mother."

"My faddah wen tell?"

"Yeah."

He tucked his hands behind his head. "Kirbz," he said, "you evah try talk God?"

"Sometimes."

"I ask planny questions but dat buggah neva wen tell me nothin' yet."

"Maybe He does," I said, "in other ways."

"Maybe so. Or maybe He stay shy."

I thought about fate and coincidence that early morning in Waimanalo. I'd never imagined ever seeing Da Destroya again, yet here we were contemplating the Heavens and talking about God. I felt closer to him than to Troy. I wondered how much of the love I might have had for my brother had been wrecked by Dadio. I wanted to go back in time and extinguish the hate Dadio had learned being raised hanai in Kaimuki.

I sat on the stairway watching chickens peck at rice. A poi dog napped under the plywood table. There were half-eaten fish and rice balls on the lawn from the leftover pig-out enjoyed by the dogs. Freddy was still asleep. He'd taken the week off from construction to patch the roof and give his Datsun a valve job. An orange tabby brushed my leg. The trades made the bamboo shiver. Leaves fell like confetti.

A green Malibu with a blue roof light tooled through the yard and pulled alongside the house. The poi dog under the table yawned.

Cyril got out in HPD blues. "Howzit, Kirbz."

"Where's the Dart?"

"Back home. Dis da town car."

"You're really Five-0?"

"Steve McGarrett takes his ordahs from me," Cyril chuckled. He popped the Malibu's trunk and dug around inside.

Lawrence boogied out in a white short-sleeved, khaki pants, and a blue tie. He smelled like rubbing alcohol from the Vitalis in his hair. He carried books under one arm. "Mo' bettah hele, Kirbz," he said, "befoah Pops make us work."

I hustled to Cyril's car and opened the passenger door. "Shotgun," I said.

Lawrence shook his head. "No dice."

Cyril slammed the trunk. "Kirbz out first," he said, "let 'im have it, kanaka."

Lawrence tapped my shoulder with a fist. "Frickin' haole." He pushed the seat forward and got in back.

We headed west for Diamond Head. The Malibu's engine purred. The purr complemented the Hawaiian songs playing in the car. I stuck my hand between the bucket seats. Lawrence scrawled his number on my palm in red ballpoint. He passed *Great Expectations* forward and I inked my number on the title page.

Cyril reached Kilauea Avenue and hooked a left. I felt like a tough guy cruising down Elepaio. I imagined Cyril and Lawrence as my bodyguards and that I could do anything to anyone I pleased. Maybe I'd trash Mr. Applestone's lawn for coughing up twenty dollars less than he'd promised for me waxing his Thunderbird. I might pay Mrs. Machado a visit and reclaim my kitten Sheriff that June Spoon had given away.

Another left put us on Aukai. Lawrence loved the green street lamps, the ranch homes, and the circular driveways. "Wen I can move in, Kirbz?" he asked. We closed in on the husky hala tree marking my driveway. I powered down the window.

"This place," I pointed.

"Dis da kine," Lawrence said.

Cyril pulled in and idled. I didn't want to climb out of the bucket seat. But Jen haunted my thoughts. She'd be lost without me, alone in a world without treasure maps and make-believe strong enough to battle a violent father and a mother who really didn't care. It seemed odd being home on a school day when I wasn't barfing or hacking up phlegm. June Spoon's Barracuda was parked in the open garage. The Olds was gone.

The front door opened. My mother waltzed over the blacktop wearing a pink dress, a strand of pearls, and gold hoop earrings. She clicked in gold sandals and made her way over to Cyril.

He lowered the glass.

"Hello, officer," June Spoon said. "Did my son do something wrong?"

"No, ma'am," Cyril replied. "Kirbz stayed with my bruddah Freddy dem last night. He wen call last night, yeah?"

"Yes. Yes, he did. Well, thank you for driving Kirby safely home."

"My pleasure, ma'am."

I got out. Lawrence joined me on the blacktop.

"Mom," I called, "this is Lawrence, my friend from Star of the Sea."

She clicked around the Malibu. "Hello, Lawrence," she said, "it's so nice to meet you."

"You get nice place, Missus Wright."

"Well, you should visit us sometime. We'd love to have you."

I knew June Spoon was buttering him up to counteract any negatives I'd said about home life.

"Anytime Kirbz like come Waimanalo, OK by me."

"That's so nice of you, Lawrence."

The police radio crackled—a lady dispatcher requested backup at First Hawaiian Bank.

"Gotta hele," Cyril said from the car.

Lawrence climbed into the passenger seat.

I shut the door behind him.

"Hey, haole boy," he said.

"What?"

He held out his hand and we did our vampire shake from the play. Cyril reversed out and burned rubber.

I walked to the curb. The Malibu turned left at a stop sign and vanished. I felt the kind of lonely I'd known standing at Aloha Tower watching my pal Joey leave for California on the SS Lurline. June Spoon joined me. The trades rustled her skirt. She seemed heavier and older in the sun, as if some secret thing inside kept her preserved.

"We were very worried about you, Kirby," she said. "Only God knows what might have happened."

"How's Jen?"

"Fine. But I almost kept her home from school today because she didn't sleep most of the night. Promise me you'll never do that again."

"Do I get the belt?"

"I told your father that you and Troy were too old for spankings."

"We are, June Spoon."

"Well," she said, "he agreed with me."

The sun ignited her crow's feet. I felt bad for her because Dadio had never encouraged her dream of becoming a singer. He said singing in public would make him look bad as "a professional man." It must have hurt my mother to keep her passion for song bottled up her entire marriage.

June Spoon drove her Barracuda to Kahala Elementary and picked up Jen. My sister was happy to see me. We hunkered down on beanbags and watched the Checkers & Pogo Show. Jen had her brown hair cut short like Twiggy's and her eyes were even darker than Dadio's. I joked about swimming to Moloka'i and back during my "adventure."

Troy strutted in and stood beside the chest. He was getting pudgy from being addicted to soda and embarrassed me whenever he took his shirt off in PE. "Your brother's a fat retard," Collin Fong had told me. Troy pursed his lips, tucked his hands in his armpits, and flapped his elbows as if they were wings. "Puck, puck, puck," he chortled, "guess who I am and win a prize."

Jen raised her hand. "Big Bird!"

"Wrong. Guess again."

"Foghorn Leghorn," I said.

"Nope. I'm Chicken Kirby, the big fat chicken who's a coward for running."

"And you're a fool for staying," I shot back.

"At least I took it, which is more than I can say for you. Where'd you go anyway?"

"Waimanalo."

"Kanaka Central," he chided. "You're lucky they didn't stick you in the imu."

"Get lost."

"Wanna hear something funny?"

"What."

"Dadio swore you were hiding in the garden. He runs out like a madman and turns on the sprinklers full blast trying flush you out."

"Is he dumb enough to think I'd stick around and risk getting caught?"

"Sure. Anyway, he gets in his car and drives around the block maybe five times, like you'd be dense enough to stay on the sidewalk. He comes home for *Mission Impossible* and goes out again. 'Where is that goddamn sonuvabitch?' he asks Mom. He makes her bike all over Kahala looking for you. 'Kirby, oh, Kirby boy,' I hear her calling, like she'd lost her pet poodle or something."

"And then?"

"Dadio looked worried. Real worried. Maybe he thought he'd go to jail or even get sued if you killed yourself eating rat poison or jumping off a cliff."

"What about the cops?"

"What about them?"

"Did he call five-oh?"

"Are you nuts? He doesn't want the fuzz thinking you flew the coop. Imagine if the firm found out? Sayonara, shot at senior partner. Anyway, you're still a chicken for not taking it. He's older now and the belt doesn't hurt so bad."

"I heard you screaming."

"I was faking it."

I realized my brother was right. I was Chicken Kirby. Running was a cowardly thing to do but, at the same time, it sent a message to Dadio that he was losing control.

I thought Dadio might still whack me when he got home. We acted like two strange dogs eager to face off but fearful of getting bit. He played the Ignoring Game. The ground rules were avoiding eye contact and not engaging in dialogue. He grimaced and walked on by when we crossed paths in the hall. It was as though he no longer considered me his son. He went into the master bedroom after a pau hana martini and I heard him push the button that locked the door. He figured he was punishing me by denying his attention. But being ignored was just what I wanted. He didn't come out until June Spoon announced, "Dinner's ready!"

☾

Lamb was the main course. I had my usual ration of two dry chops, a splatter of Birds Eye peas, and a scoop of Minute Rice. The meal was served on stoneware the color of sand. Grains of rice were black from being burned. I sat across from Dadio. Jen was beside me. June Spoon and Troy sat adjacent to Dadio, in the neutral seats that didn't face him. June Spoon glanced at me. Jen kept her eyes on her plate and picked at her food. Dinnertime was agony for her because Dadio criticized her for eating with her mouth open.

Dadio gnawed a chop. His lips and the edges of his mouth glistened with grease. His glasses made his pupils look huge when they floated into the bifocal half-moons in the lenses. "Got you boys back in school," he said. "You return to Punahou on Monday."

"That's wonderful news, dear," June Spoon said. "Don't you think so, boys?"

Troy shook his head like a bobblehead doll. "Goody, goody, gumdrops."

I locked eyes with Dadio. "Did you call Dr. Johnson?"

"Yes, I did, Kirby. He told me you and Troy lied about being way ahead in projects. The fact of the matter is, you're both way behind."

"We only told him the rules," Troy argued. "We never said we were ahead in woodshop."

"But you implied it, Troy. In my book, that's as good as lying."

"Woodshop is home economics for boys," I said. "All you do is saw and file and spin crap on a lathe."

"That's not the point, Kirby. You lied and got caught with your pants down."

"You've never lied?"

"No. There's never a good reason for lying to someone. Take it from me, honesty is the best policy."

"You lied to Harvard," I blurted.

Dadio yanked off his glasses. "What's this?"

"You told the dean your last name was Wilkinson, instead of Wright."

"That wasn't a lie. I didn't get around to changing it, that's all. Who in hell told you that anyway?"

"June Spoon."

Dadio glared at June Spoon.

"All right," she said. "Let's try and be a happy family."

"So," Troy quipped, "according to Attorney Wright, there are various degrees of lying. Some are so harmless they're not considered lies at all. Would that fall into the white lie category?"

"Shut your yap," snapped Dadio.

Troy did the bobblehead move again.

"Don't run off again, Kirby," Dadio warned. "Leaving like that was wrong. Where'd you spend the night?"

"Waimanalo."

"With who?"

"Uncle Freddy."

"Who's he?"

"A big Hawaiian guy," Troy said.

"Let Kirby answer."

"We met at Makapu'u. His brother's a cop."

"Yes," said June Spoon, "he drove our son home in a nice police car."

"Oh," Dadio replied. "This guy's really a cop?"

I nodded. "He said to call him, whenever I want."

"Think you're pretty smart don't you, wise guy?"

"Smart about what?"

"Run away again and I'll lock you out."

Troy laughed drinking his milk. White droplets shot out of his nose and splattered the plastic tablecloth.

Dadio's face flushed red. "What's so funny, Troy?"

"Imagine if the firm knew you locked out your juvenile son?"

"All the lawyers would think Kirby got what he deserved for leaving in the first place."

"OK," June Spoon said, "let's have a pleasant dinner."

My father shoved his plate. Rice and peas flew. A plug of marrow scooted past my milk, bounced over the lip of Jen's plate, and nestled in her peas.

"Pleasant," Dadio huffed, "my okole." He got up. He stuck his glasses back on and retreated to the living room. It was the first time he hadn't asked either Troy or me if he could gnaw on our bones.

I went to bed early. My heart raced. I knew my relationship with Dadio was doomed. I imagined being Cool Hand Luke, the slick prisoner who escapes but foolishly ends up back in jail. My warden knew he didn't have a model son. He had a runaway. I couldn't sleep. I heard June Spoon tell Jen to brush her teeth and get ready for bed. I was worried about my sister, especially how these years would affect her later in life. I doubted she'd marry. Even if she did I guessed it would be a struggle and only hoped she wouldn't end up with someone like Dadio.

The deep voice of the TV anchorman drifted down the hall. He mentioned the Punahou Carnival and eating malasadas. The TV clicked off. Leather sandals smacked the hall tiles and I smelled the perfumed poison of Had-A-Bug. Dadio used an entire can to fumigate the house whenever he got bit. The mosquitoes loved him. I wanted to love him a little, or at least to find some way to get along. But I was certain he'd cornered any love he had to give and banished it to a place deep inside, to a dark box where he stored everything that could possibly hurt him or even make him cry.

Joddy Murray

Zebras Frighten Easily

and in so many directions—
the contrast a fractured
horizontal hold, broken
into lines of cries.
You are steady as ever,
the planet more sure
of itself because you spin
along with it, cells
in you more solidly
transfixed in reverence
to you and spellbound.

Grapes swell in the sun
while the harvester, far
behind, grips a talon
knife between two fingers.

Michael Albright

Foggy Mountain Breakdown

When they let that foreclosed farmer shoot
    the sign of the Midlothian Citizen's Bank,
        I knew that they were meant to be heroes.

A year before the movies got rated,
    this was everything a young boy could want:
        a cigar-sucking blonde with an open blouse,

fast cars to chase, dumb hicks to rob,
    a stupid man shot right through the eye,
        the rapture of bloodshed and the fog of sin

in a bitter and empty movie house,
    exposed to cool blue shimmering light,
        frame by frame in a Technicolor haze.

Not exactly a coming of age, but I learned
    people who do bad things aren't really bad,
        but still die together in slow-motion ballet,

time and life evaporate between flickers—
    the wheels of a bullet-blistered Ford V-8
        rotate suspiciously in reverse

as the car careens forward into the ditch,
    casting out these beautiful monsters
        I'd somehow been persuaded to love.

Wei He

Pulp Fiction

Oh, my girl!
He hits you with an extension cord
You just drained a bottle of beer
You hear your eyes squish when you close them too hard
You know in a few minutes he'll be full of tears
And trying to wipe the hurt off your face
But you don't know in a few years he'll be talking to himself because
    of all the booze

Oh, my good girl!
You never curse in vain
Though you start believing you're God's second thought if he creates
    everything
You start having many feelings at a time
Like something that's been misplaced
Like a Chinatown in America
Like those French fries and ketchup all over your face

No, no, my girl,
You better shut up your sweet mouth
And bury those thin bruised lips
Re-dye your hair in a spring color
Come with me
Let me put you in a poetic situation

My girl, my girl,
Just swallow my words as if they were potato chips
Wrap yourself up with his not-so-clean blanket

I'm turning you into someone, quiet and holy
I'm turning you into someone, quiet and holy, right now

Julie Henson

Psalm for the Good Girl a Year Ago

About last February: you might test
        the girl's hippocampus. Label results: short-

versus long-term: girl *Resilient*
        girl prophet, the cisterns, girl, over

flown the nest girl surprised
        at history repeating in proverbs, *girl*

"where the knuckle cracks, the knuckle bleeds"
        and other words to the wise. Stop pumping gas

in subarctic temperatures, for instance. Oh, Girl, *get a clue*
        & other catch phrases: *God bless the girl child & What's*

love/memory got to do with it? What if it's just
        told for lesson. Allegory:

Girl tells fairy tale: Tenth Street & the house where
        the three boys lived

and one they called Little Baby Jesus
        and he never got his own room. Or OK. Girl

autobiography: "where one goes to find coins and lose them"
        and "the time you pulled an eyelash off my contact

before the roller coaster." The Great Girl Desolation
     of Our Current Era: how seven brides wanted

seven brothers who wanted seven brides who have
     changed their minds by this point, want only cisterns

want cow troughs, want vessels of water—
     girl ringing every drip.

Jane Huffman

Cleopatra III

Do they love you like we love Audrey, Marilyn, Daphne?
Do they carry you on their shoulders, dress you in palm leaves
and horsehair? Do they splay your name in the streets on canvas

banners? Or do they whisper it, vowels unwieldy on their tongues?
Do you have white horses with white manes to pet,
to braid in fishtails on long Sundays with copper beads?

How do you answer when they ask you about your brother?
The vow you wear on your head like a crown of dandelion sugar?
Do you string popcorn on dental floss every year on the day

that the war ended? What does Antony say when he hears
his name? Does he suck it through his teeth like the cold?
Does he braid it into your hair like strands of black magic?

Will he find, in the grave, when he reaches to stroke
the nape of your neck that nothing more exists than lies, names
protruding from your skull not like snakes but like rhyme?

Jill Kronstadt

Fault Lines

When the music is over Laurel yanks the tape out of the deck so that it uncoils like a snarl of yarn, and then she throws it out the driver's-side window. It was an album of love songs, the falling-in-love music and making-love music and end-of-love music. The battered gray convertible, old enough to have a four-track, hurtles down the road. She puts another tape into the deck, Roy Orbison, the top down so that the wind fills her and snatches up the riffs and drumbeats and notes and spiraling lyrics. Next the jazz album her husband Don hates and then the blues album her daughter loves. She tosses out her husband's Nancy Wilson and Johnny Cash. The speakers spew the music into the wind, and one after the other, between cigarettes, she throws the tapes behind her onto the road.

She has an earthquake inside her. It started somewhere behind her left eye and then loped outward until the space between her bones and skin rippled with electricity. For weeks before she left, she felt pregnant with an unknown landscape that swallowed the kitchen and the bungalow, even the fields and barns where Don was foreman, buzzing at a frequency she could intuit but not hear. At night, when she could not sleep, she took the car and slinked back through the door before dawn. Every morning before he left for work, Don moved silently through the kitchen to let Caty sleep. He divided hot-plate-boiled coffee between two mugs, always lukewarm, gritty and heavy on her tongue. *Eat something*, he'd begun whispering. The concern on his face was worse than a fight. The day before she left, the earthquake surged out of her and the floor tilted upwards and down, the walls heaving like an animal gasping for breath. *Are you all right*, Don asked, *You're acting really strange*, and though she jumped at his touch, she knew not to tell him what she saw.

Don's hands on her shoulders, holding her still while she bucked like an unbroken mare in a tether. She remembers backing away from Caty, her keys digging into her palm, the slam of the bungalow door behind her. *I can walk away from my name.* She has no idea whether the words stayed inside her head or flew through the air.

The last thing Laurel remembers is three-year-old Caitlin's wide, brown eyes, filled with dumb faith, Caty in her nightgown, walking barefoot towards her through the gulping silhouette of the doorway. Caty's fist poking a spoon at her Cheerios, raising it so the hollow of the spoon caught the light and became a thin-lipped silver mouth howling, *Mommy, Mommy.* A scream, her own or Caty's, that followed her as her back slid down the wall to the floor. Laurel remembers Caty crying, but her memory is ripped in pieces, all out of order. Her daughter's arms around her, trusting and heavy, as though her mother were as solid as the knuckled hills that ringed the valley, the valley that was the first thing she threw away. She remembers driving with the sun in her eyes until the road finally steadied under her. In between, nothing.

Now, driving away from home, she is on the 15, headed toward Barstow. In the seat next to her slumps the duffel bag she can't remember packing before she left, and she keeps pulling things out of it: a fuchsia pump with faint laugh lines traced on the forefoot, a crushed half-eaten bag of stale Cheetos that she finishes at eighty-seven miles per hour and then sets aflame with her lighter before letting it fly out of her hand. She sucks the Day-Glo salt from her fingers while the schism between guilt and love shimmers in the heat over the asphalt ahead of her and weaves over the dotted line in the center of the road. The electrical poles are the throbbing of her heart, and after the tapes are gone it is as though the radio is the only thing keeping her alive.

Her tongue has the texture of caterpillar, and salt burns the corners of her mouth. Don's voice snagged on its note of pleading. *Laurel, where are you going?* A sweater flies behind her like a kite, followed by a glitter miniskirt that hurls itself down. The duffel, seemingly bottomless, yields bikini tops, jeans, nightgowns, short-shorts, T-shirts, a pair of cowboy boots, a down coat of Don's.

Amid the clothes her fingers pick out the surprise shape of a bottle of Ten High. She holds it to her ear and shakes without taking her eyes from the road, the sloshing telling her she still has booze, and she leans down to slide it under the passenger seat, the ball of her foot still pressed hard onto the gas pedal. She reaches into her purse to find her checkbook, the Visa, the scrawled slips of paper with addresses for Caty's playdates, phone numbers without names. All of it in the road.

The road begins to spin. The ragged landscape whirls around her and comes to a stop when the hood of the car noses into a shallow ditch. "Shit!" she says. Her face jerks toward the horn, and when her forehead collapses into the steering wheel a long wail carries away from her into the empty fields and into a clutch of scrub oak. She buries her head in her hands and the wail continues. She can't tell if it is coming from the car or her own lungs. With her eyes closed she can't tell if the sweet-smelling dampness on her hands and face is sweat, vomit, or blood.

When she opens her eyes again the sky is bleeding scarlet into falling dusk. Her clothes feel clammy and smell vaguely of vinegar. She fumbles above her head for the lightswitch, pulls the visor mirror down with shaking hands, and digs deep into her purse for a stump of lipstick. She squints at the image of her face, then licks her fingers to rub out the haloes of mascara below her eyes. She smears on the lipstick and smudges some on her cheeks for blush.

She pulls a cigarette and her lighter out of her purse and yanks open the door handle, sucking in her breath at the pain in her wrist, and kicks the door till it groans open. Luckily the windshield is intact except for a long, horizontal crack that follows the line of the horizon. She holds on to the door to pull herself to her feet. The air smells sweet with hay and the dry, herbal scent where the car has broken the branches of the oleander growing in the ditch.

She looks out over the stubble of hay under the darkening sky. The sky is a hand that squeezes her head like a blob of bread dough. Despite the makeup, one of her eyes feels gummy and smaller than the other. It is painful to breathe. She lights the cigarette and walks in a slow circle around the car, her right knee aching. She remembers the bottle, gulps a few pulls for the pain. In the headlights, she sees that a dense hedge of oleander has broken the car's skid into the ditch. She rakes her eyes over the crumpled bumper and hood and decides the car is drivable.

Don will be feeding Caty instant mac and cheese for dinner, moving with the economy and quiet he has around the horses. The slow cadence of his gestures will soothe Caty. She is surprised to realize that she is aware of this calm, which is a part of him and not a part of her. She wonders if Don realizes yet that this time she's not coming home. He cannot possibly have imagined that she is a woman who does not deserve to weep from homesickness, a woman who does not deserve to be forgiven: a woman who would leave her child.

The knowledge claws its way out of her gut, filth-colored and putrid. She can think of nothing more vile than what she has already become. Un-mother. *Caty doesn't know I've left her,* she thinks. *There's still time. I could go home again, and nobody would know I didn't mean to come back.*

She feels the earthquake approach again, miles of desert heaving in the distance. Like a dog or a horse or a bobcat that can feel a temblor coming, she has gained the power to sense what no one else can hear. She pulls the keys out of the ignition and worries the one for the bungalow off the key ring. She throws the key as hard as she can into the darkest part of the hayfield.

The lies she could tell instead of leaving pour unbidden into the space the key has left. *This guy stole my purse while I was pumping gas, and he looked so scary I didn't call the police. It was the weirdest thing —I let this lady borrow it to open up a package, and she accidentally threw it in the Dumpster with the cardboard box, and the hell I was going in there with the rats just for a key.* The lies are the compass that points toward home.

She thinks of Caty, terrified by the feel of cold air on her skin last winter, braced on the threshold of the bungalow when Laurel needed to go to the grocery store. Caty's arms spread wide to be picked up, tears running down her cheeks. She did not cry or scream, but a piercing whine wavered around her. *Caty, dammit, get the fuck in the car.* In the end Laurel dragged her by the wrists, Caty shrieking and digging her heels into the damp earth all the way down the path. As Laurel strapped her into the car, Caty suddenly went still. When the car started she made no sound but little gulping breaths and she moved nothing but her eyes while Laurel sobbed the whole way to the store.

Now, with her car at the edge of the hayfield, she cries again. She is more loathsome than she has ever been, but her tears are the same tears as always. There is no bottom to her ugliness and no way to stop herself from plummeting. She wants the night to be over, but her lungs keep sucking air. The earth shudders into her and she swallows some more booze to keep it down. She wants to disappear, but she can't help but be somewhere.

If I drive all night, she thinks, *I can be home by morning.*

She gets back into the car and drops the gearshift into reverse.

She has made it out of the Mojave and halfway to Barstow when the engine stammers, bucks, and then goes silent. She switches off the headlights to save the battery and squints west up the road, where she can see the silvery fuzz of a town far off in the distance—Yermo, probably. This time, she doesn't cry, but sits down on the dented hood of the car and waits.

When she sees the headlights she slides the wedding ring into her jeans pocket and steps out onto the road. It takes her a few tries before someone stops. He's driving a late-model Plymouth with a God's-eye hanging from the rearview mirror, and the gravel on the side of the road pops under the new tires when he slows down and stops his car in front of hers. He looks like he's in his late forties or early fifties, and he juts a knobby elbow out the window when he turns to her.

"Car trouble, ma'am?"

Laurel slides off the car hood and swivels her head away from the man's gaze. She lurches in her heels even though the Ten High has become just a warm blur going cool and clear at the edges. His hair is cut short, not quite a crew cut, and his face, like the God's-eye, is diamond shaped.

She lets tears fill her eyes and streak down her cheeks. "Out of gas," she says.

"You sure?" the man says. "It looks like you had a little bender, too."

"Oh," she sniffs. "That wasn't actually me." She watches his eyes as they take in her grubby clothes and the bruise on her forehead from the accident, and then her breasts and thighs, and she makes sure he sees her limping as she approaches his car. "Can you give me a ride to Barstow? Or Yermo. I just need gas. I can hitch back."

"Sure," he says. "Get in." He leans to push open the passenger-side door and starts up the road before she has a chance to buckle her seat belt. "Might have to take you back to your car, too, though—can't have a lady out by herself in the middle of the night."

"You have no idea how grateful I am," Laurel says.

"I'm Troy."

"I'm Sarah," Laurel says.

"Pretty name. Where you headed?"

"I have family out north of Quartz Hill."

"Kind of late to be out driving alone, isn't it?"

She shrugs. "I really appreciate the ride." She has no idea what time it is and doesn't want to ask.

"Looks like maybe somebody hurt you," Troy continues. "You think?"

"Maybe," she says. "Maybe you can take care of me tonight."

The car still smells new, the seats slick and lemony, and she feels dirty enough to wish she had a towel under her. They are both silent awhile, watching the lights of Yermo get bigger and clearer. She notices a guitar case behind the driver's seat. "Are you a musician?" she asks.

"Yup," he says. He keeps his eyes on the road, but she can see his sideways grin. "Just finished a gig, in fact."

"Really? Would I know you?" She forces her face into the shape of a smile. She notices his hands on the steering wheel, the fingers unnaturally long. She can feel a headache emerging from the bruise on her forehead.

"I doubt it. But one of these days—well, Sarah, one of these days you might."

"Are you from around here?"

"Nope. Los Angeles." He uses the Spanish pronunciation—*Ahn-hay-lace*—drawing out the syllables so that he almost sounds like he's mocking himself at the same time he's trying to impress her.

"Will you play me something on your guitar?" she asks.

A sign shoots past her window: "The Yermo Lions Club Welcomes You." Troy turns right at the next intersection. Laurel can see a gas station farther up the road, but he pulls into a parking lot with a sign, *Lee's Tavern*. Dust rises up to the windows. The lot is mostly full of cars with license plates from California, Nevada, Arizona, and Utah: tourists going to and from Vegas.

"Later," Troy says. "Play before work."

"We should go play in Vegas," she says.

"Seems like you're the kind of girl who might make me do things I don't want to do." He has a smooth voice, like a car salesman's, or, she supposes, a singer's.

"Yes," Laurel says. "I'm exactly that kind of girl."

"Well, well. In that case, care for a drink before we drive off to slay the dragon?"

"That would be nice," Laurel says.

They push through the smoky doorway. A mix of locals and tourists, mostly men and a few women dressed in clothes too tight and low cut for their figures, clumps near the bar. "What's your drink, sweetheart?" Troy asks.

"Whiskey sour," she says.

"That's a lot of drink for a tiny little thing like you."

She giggles, because she can see he likes it. "Aw, Troy, are you going to snitch on me?"

"You seem like just my kind of girl," he says, pawing his arm around her waist and down to her butt. He returns with the whiskey sour and a pint of beer for himself, and they climb up on a pair of bar stools.

"Mind if I smoke?" she asks. She reaches across the bar for a pack of cardboard matches stamped *Lee's Tavern* and thumbs through her purse for a cigarette. "Oh, shoot! I'm out."

"I've got it," Troy says. He gets up and goes to the back of the dance floor, where there's a cigarette machine with pull handles, and returns with a pack of Winstons.

"I just can't believe it. You're like my guardian angel, saving me from the desert and taking such good care of me." Her palm finds his knee.

He picks up her hand and holds it in his. He fingers the slender ribbon of white at the base of her ring finger and looks at her without speaking.

"It's not what you think," she says.

"I'm not a big thinker." He pulls her hand toward his lips and all at once they are kissing, whiskey mixing with beer on their tongues. They go on like that for a while, his wide, spidery hands moving over her, stopping just short of anything that might get them kicked out.

"Have you ever done this before?" she asks. "I think I need another drink."

She sucks down another whiskey sour, then another. Her thoughts start to jump again, like a skipping record, and she drinks faster to slow them down. She and Troy end up outside behind the bar for air, writhing together out of sight between a Dumpster and a chain-link fence. His lips brush her throat and slip under her bra. She feels her jeans and panties roll down toward her knees like she's a teenager. Out of the corner of her eye, she sees headlights flash across the fence. She pulls Troy into her mouth and then between her legs. He makes a sound like hiccups as he pushes into her. She moans the way Don likes it and, after Troy comes, she hangs on his shirt to pull herself back up to standing, her eyes still closed.

When they are done Troy holds her face between his hands. She burrows into his chest and starts to cry. "I'm sorry," she whimpers. "I think I'm drunk."

Troy strokes her hair, his arms still around her, ropy and bony. "It's OK, it's OK," he says. "I'll take care of you."

Sobs rise out of her for the hundredth time that day. Knowing that she has succumbed to tears again makes her cry harder, till she is pounding Troy's chest and squirming against the hold of his arms. "I want to go home," she manages. "I just want to go home."

When he lets her go her hands fly to her face. Troy pulls up his pants and then pulls up hers. He buttons her blouse while the whole time she cries like Caty. "I'm sorry," she says.

"It's late," Troy says. "Let's get a room."

"I could go."

"All the filling stations are closed—there's no point in leaving now."

She shrugs. "I guess," she says.

He leads her back to his car, snakes around a couple of blocks, and turns into a parking lot in front of a motel whose neon sign still pulses *VACANCY*. Laurel presses her face against the window, her gaze going west into darkness. Now that she cannot possibly drive home tonight, she feels the outrage of displacement flare through her limbs; she imagines that only the solidity and density of Don's body, her cheek settled in the space between his shoulder blades, could bring her back to stillness.

"Wait here,"Troy says, and before she can answer he is already striding toward the office. She sees that he is already tired of playing the hero, but that maybe, if she needs him enough, she can make them last till morning. She gets out of the car and arranges herself in front of the passenger-side door. When Troy comes back to the car she smiles and reaches for his belt buckle. "Sorry about before," she says. "I'm just so grateful for everything you've done for me. You've been unreal."

"The pleasure is all mine," he says. He jingles the room key in front of her chest. When they get to the room he tosses it on the dresser. The room is small and grubby, dominated by a flowered bedspread pulled over a concave mattress. The headboard is covered with chipped, sloppily applied paint, haloed with grime above the pillows, and Laurel notices a constellation of burns in the bedspread that make her want another cigarette.

They take off their clothes again, their skin jaundiced under the yellow motel room lamps. Her bruised knee and ribs flame like gaslights, but she doesn't feel them. In the motel, without the bar noise, she can hear Troy's teeth grinding as he fucks her, the cadence of the bedsprings and the wobbling headboard.

Afterwards, while she pretends to sleep, she hears him turn the shower on in the bathroom, as though he wants to wash her off him, and when he comes back to bed they do not touch.

In the morning, fingers of pain jab up her spine and clutch her neck, shoulders, and knee. The right side of her rib cage feels pried apart; the cerulean-tinged desert light, when it squeezes between the flimsy blinds, makes her vibrate with nausea.

When she opens her eyes, Troy is gone.

She drags herself upright, wraps the sheet around herself, and limps to the bathroom. She glimpses her bruised, swollen eye in the mirror just before she heaves into the toilet. Bolts of pain shoot through her face and ribs when she starts to cry again, so intense that she stops after a single strangled yelp. The room key is missing. She picks at her filthy clothes, tossed on one of the chairs the night before, and then gingerly dresses. Then she turns her face toward the window and lets the sun burn through her eyelids until the room seems to fracture like a kaleidoscope with no center. Beyond it is a jittery image of the road leaping through the windshield, her car refueled and aimed toward home. She tries to make a plan that will put her inside the image she imagines, and each time, she ends up in a Yermo motel room, unable to rise from her chair, with Troy's smell still on her hands.

She does not know how much time has passed before the door clatters open. Troy looks like a different man in daylight, bonier, with pink-rimmed gray eyes and thin lips that he licks before speaking.

"Huh," he says. "I didn't think you'd still be here."

"I thought maybe you weren't coming back."

Troy slaps a newspaper down on the rickety table and sits in the other chair. He places a large Styrofoam coffee in the center of the table and unfurls the paper so that it fills the space between them. Automatically, she reaches for the coffee, and just as smoothly, he lifts it and drinks.

"We didn't have as much fun last night as I thought we were going to," Troy says.

"What do you mean?"

"Nothing in particular. Just an observation." He shakes the paper and bends it backwards. "Quite a shiner you've got there."

"It's fine."

"Someone might think you're in some kind of situation."

"I guess I am. I probably should be on my way pretty soon."

"Go ahead," he says, gesturing toward the door. "I'm sure you can get the front desk to call a cab. Oh, I forgot. You lost your wallet."

"Sorry," she says. "I don't mean to rush you."

"Don't worry—you haven't rushed me at all." He sips the coffee again, and a swirl of steam rises from it when he puts it down. "So, where's your husband?"

"Are you married?" Laurel asks.

"My wife's back in L.A."

"Does she know?"

"Know what?"

"Know that you do this."

"Does your husband know?"

"Oh, God," Laurel says. "Yes. Yes, I think so."

"Hmm," Troy says.

"Do you think he'll take me back?" Laurel asks.

"You'd know better than I would."

"I have a daughter. Four years old." Her voice wavers.

"Fuck," Troy says. "Please, enough with the waterworks." He puts the paper down and stands up, leaving the half-empty coffee cup on the table. She doesn't dare try to touch it again even though its aroma shoots her through with desire to drink it black with rum and aspirin, and after Troy collects his things he dumps the rest of the coffee into the sink.

He looks at her briefly, and then his glance skitters away from her. "Let's go," he says.

At the gas station, Troy fills his own tank and a gas can he keeps in the trunk. The outline of Yermo hovers in the rearview and then disappears in the distance. They don't say anything else until they reach Laurel's car, still hunched by the roadside where they left it.

Troy gets out of his car, pops the trunk, lifts the gas can, and starts feeding gas into Laurel's tank while she watches. They stand without touching. Laurel looks west in the direction of home. It's almost midday; she can tell by the shadows pooled at the feet of the sagebrush and cacti. When the gas can is empty, Troy lets it drop to the ground, and the metal echoes when it hits the empty road.

"Thank you," Laurel says.

Troy doesn't answer, just looks at her with no expression, his eyes two gray holes in his face. She backs toward the side of the car, cold spilling through her veins. He pushes his body into hers, hard, and claws his fingers behind her head to pull her mouth into his. She listens for the earthquake but hears only desert, silent and still, and the sound of her own whimpering. "Don't hurt me," she manages. "I just want to go home."

In response, Troy shoves her into the side of the car so that it lurches against her weight, but then his hands fall back to his sides and he steps away. "I've done enough for you already," he says.

The words are a relief exactly like pain. Laurel doesn't move. She looks down at her feet and waits until the shaking begins, shuddering through her body until even the car trembles. Troy walks into the center of the road, picks up the gas can, and puts it back in the trunk of his own car. She hears him slam his door, and then his car's tires screech on the asphalt as he makes a U-turn back toward Yermo.

Laurel watches the taillights recede and then disappear into a dip in the road before she gets into the car. She rolls open the window, pries the Ten High from under the seat, and lights a cigarette, letting wisps of smoke curl around her as she empties the bottle in sips. West is Barstow and Quartz Hill and home and the valley; east leads back to the Mojave and out to the Nevada state line. She digs her fingers down into her pocket and fishes out the wedding ring, rolling it between her thumb and forefinger without putting it on. She does not want to be here, stopped on the side of the road between Barstow and Death Valley, when dusk returns. She does not know which direction will take her away from herself.

I will never see Caty again, she thinks, testing the thought to see if it holds, as though she's standing on a sprained limb. The car is already pointed toward home, and she could still follow it there. Every cell in her body wants to return to the valley and the weight of Caty's body in her arms, but she doesn't know if she can carry the weight of forgiveness.

When she puts the key in the ignition, the engine looses a metallic sigh and then turns over. All her options have narrowed and converged on a single pinprick of possibility, so that in the whole, endless expanse of desert there are no more directions but *away*. She throws the ring out the window into the desert before she can change her mind.

She starts the car, swinging it in a half-circle until it faces east. She flips the radio dial as she drives, but nothing comes in except fuzz. The car tumbles forward until afternoon becomes another night, and by the time dawn appears as an arc of gold edging over the hills, a ligature too slender to be felt, her eyes are so dry that the road swims and curls in front of her. As the car hurtles through darkness the only thing left with her is a long howl of loneliness, which she means to cast off like everything else, but whose fierce grip carries her and clings to her like the memory of the child she has left behind.

Donald Illich

Misdirection

It doesn't have to be a crime.
You could replace
your spouse's light yogurt
with regular flavored.
Or give someone wrong directions,
so she ends up
in the warehouse district.
Even set up a fake store
where people can buy make-believe
products, each one
—horse jam, octopus wine,
butter made of politicians—
more ridiculous than the next.
It can be a little trick,
a kind of misdirection.
Like love—
you can stay with a person
a full forty years
and say at the last
that it wasn't true.
All the joy and pain was plastic,
all the laughter and tears
were lies. Watch
your graves split apart.
Watch the sorrow
on the gravedigger's
smile.

Ana Merino

Indifference

Over the pain of being
and not being liked,
I set the table and wait for dinner.

Each bedroom sounds
like a jungle
or a storm.

But in the bathroom
the mirrors don't hide,
they spit.
Each corner has its nest
and there the spiders
weave their webs,
but in the patio
I delouse children
and crush the nits with my nails
like a big-game hunter
with long fingers
and dirty hair.

Over the pain my hands complain
and I forget, I don't exist;
Even with a blow I don't open my mouth.

Translated from the Spanish by Toshiya Kamei

Charlotte Pence

Ozymandias and Ye

Everyone agrees that Ozymandias can go screw himself.
"Look on my works," he says, and we do, satisfied
with shell slivers and wind. How easy it is to dislike him,

even though Ozy is a stand-in for many of us, minus
the kingdom and rubies and whatnot. I, too, puff and bellow
about my busy life. I, too, wobble underneath the strain

of computer cranings. I, too, leave trunkless legs and
sometimes believe otherwise. Yet if I died from a paper cut
made lethal by methicillin-resistant *Staphylococcus aureus*,

then this might become an important poem. Important
enough for past pets to resurrect. The cat would yodel
my praises, hermit crab would extrovert, the dog, meow.

For isn't it our nature to overinflate? We who have built
nothing, why aren't we something grand, like rain or grass?
Why so sand? Beaches have their whiskey shakes. Water its

virgin/whore thing. Everything disrupting our attempts
with theirs. In the meantime, Ozy remains like the rest
of us. Just another poet who can't write a love poem.

The Missouri State University Literary Competitions

Moon City Review is a publication of Moon City Press, an independent press housed in Missouri State University's Department of English. To help commemorate the journal's origins as a student journal, we are proud to publish, via an open competition, one piece of fiction and one poem by members of our student population.

This past year, the poetry entries were judged by Debra Kang Dean, author of the full-length collections *Precipitate* and *News of Home*, as well as *Fugitive Blues*, winner of Moon City Press' 2012 Blue Moon Chapbook Competition. Dean chose Hannah Farley's poem "Harrisburg, One Week Later" as this year's winner. Of Farley's poem, Dean notes, "Scrutinizing the American Dream, 'Harrisburg, One Week Later' is not pretty, but it is beautiful in its enactments." She adds, "In a flat voice, to borrow a phrase from James Wright, it appeals to multiple senses, and, using minimal punctuation, renders a scene simultaneously real and surreal, its lines trailing off, except for one: 'The other was gone.'"

The other poets who were named as finalists include the following students:

Elizabeth Alphonse
Terry Belew
Anthony Isaac Bradley
Jessica Brenneke

On the fiction side, this year's competition was judged by Phong Nguyen, whose story collections include *Memory Sickness* and *Pages From the Textbook of Alternate History*. Nguyen selected Tyler Barnes' entry "Limbs for the Loved" for the prize. Speaking of Barnes' story, Nguyen declares, "'Limbs for the Loved' is intense, intelligent, and strange. It is full of metaphor, yet persistently physical and real. The story propels the reader forward like a bullet train."

Our other student finalists in fiction are as follows:

Kaitlyn Cooley
Ryan Hubble
Tay Marie Lorenzo
Carla Melton
Kathleen Sanders
Danyelle Steinkamp

We are proud to present our students' work to you in the following pages, as we are proud of the work all our students do here at Missouri State.

Hannah Farley

Harrisburg, One Week Later

A flag hung over the field of horses with a broken Walmart background
posing as a façade
scrutinizing the American Dream

There was no sound after the storm broke but
the toll of smoke detectors
somebody forgot or couldn't turn off

People walked reverently as if in church
searching for the lost souls
the tornado tore away from them

The government cleanup called it Zone Seven
but to us it was Water Street
where three of us were taken

One side of the street remained untouched, a museum piece of life before
white picket fence as straight as the railroad tracks across town
swing sets still cradling their tiny, wide-eyed occupants

The other was gone
Christmas lights and baby bottles clung together in the clogged gutters
No one had much use for them now

Neighbors and strangers pulled together
searching for some light in the darker places
Children buried a smashed, dead bird

Tyler Barnes

Limbs for the Loved

When you felt yourself slipping, tripping over the platform, towards the metal tracks, it didn't feel like the world was being ripped out from under you—you would say you'd been bobbing above and below water for a long time, you're used to the feeling. When the burning white headlights of the bullet train came speeding toward you and they became your sunshine, your first thought wasn't, *Who's going to take care of Addy now? Who's going to keep her on her feet?* Rather, random pictures and sounds that wouldn't have amounted to anything other than the story of routines, un-events. When you felt some lunatic's hands push you in the way of the train, you thought, *I'll die a virgin.*

Now, you wake up in the soft, cold hospital bed in a room full of beeping sounds and you're covered in gauze and wires. When you wake up, you have at least four new middle names. Their names are Blood Transfusion, Skin Grafts, Right Arm, and Right Leg. A whole arm and leg! All part of the new, experimental transplant program to see if whole limbs from kind, caring donors could function for someone in need of replacements. The doctors and the surgeons and the nurses who walk into your room throughout the timeless day tell you how incredibly lucky and special you are, how thankful you should be to the donors who were able to provide you a chance of new life after the horrible train accident ruined your "tick-tock, check on your sister, tick-tock, don't wonder if she's worth it" routine.

You've been unconscious for days. By now, you imagine Addy's been kicked out of the building, she's on the streets, relapsed again and starving without you to bring home groceries. But your recovering drug addict of a sister whom you've declared to save because she's "more than her addictions" and for whom you've selflessly given up any hopes of your own future, doesn't seem so important in that lonely white hospital room. In that place where the only sound comes from life monitors and heavy breathing, you're free to think thoughts you don't ever allow yourself to think—selfish thoughts like applying to college and getting a better job somewhere far away and finding someone to love who isn't usually just casually boozed out of her mind.

Here, your only company comes from the freshly off-the-ice corpse pieces keeping you alive and whole, so maybe the thoughts come from them—from the new blood swimming in you or from your canvas of discolored skin grafts or from your brand new, slightly used right leg and arm. They all come from different bodies donated to science. A part of the experimental program to see if donated organs or even whole limbs could be transplanted to a patient whose own body was in such complete disrepair. You signed up to be a potential patient in the trial because it was going to pay you a little each month, and if you were ever in need of surgery then, well … at least it would be free of cost.

"All the scars and stitches," the doctor says to you when you very softly and kindly ask him for a mirror, "they'll all go away. Don't worry yourself over it; no need to see what it all looks like right now." And inside your head that's covered in stitches and staples and scars and gangrene flesh, you say, *I was hit by a train … some maniac pushed me into a train … I was torn to shreds by a train and now I'm a sewn up pile of biohazard waste and I just want to know if I look human.* Maybe Blood Transfusion is thinking like that. Whoever it came from must have had anger issues because you don't think like that. Things get better, ;hey look up. Eventually Addy will be the sweetheart kid she used to be. Eventually you'll find a girl who can give you a chance, eventually you'll experience life outside of the beaten-down side of a town.

You start wondering whose forearm had they taken from the "bodies donated to science"pool to circuit into your mangled stump? … Christ, what had you looked like on that operating table while the doctors played Operation and Jigsaw with an icebox of meat pieces? Where are your irreparable limbs now? Likely thrown down the wastebasket. Incinerated. Could they do that with cheese-grated limbs and organs?

You're a new family of dead people. Welcome to your new travel buddies, your nameless body parts who died to resurrect you. Is this what resurrection is like? Because it feels lackluster. When the nurse unlocks the door to come in and check your vitals and I.V., make small talk and whatever other stuff nurses do, you mutter, "Do I look like Frankenstein?"

"Actually, Frankenstein was the doctor, not the—." And you think to yourself, *The what? The dead guy? The lonely, tragic, innocent but purposeless corpse put back together from other corpses?* Yeah, you've looked up the plot to *Frankenstein* on Wikipedia, too. But you wouldn't ever tell her off like that. She's only trying to do her job, she's only trying to help you with her bubbly indifferent smile and apologetic teeth, so you wouldn't be that kind of an ass. You're a nice guy, there's just a part of you that's burning with ire; it's burning with wrath and you can feel it pulsating in the fingers that aren't yours. But she's a sweet girl, with her humble lipstick that didn't try to draw too much attention. She's the kind of girl you could run away with. But she still passes you by just like everyone else does and when she closes the door behind her, it leaves your soft, sensitive skin grafts in painful jitter.

You don't ever talk about these fantasies because you're a good kid, a respectful kid who lives without making a mess of things, without screwing up other peoples' lives. But Right Arm and Right Leg and Skin Grafts, they live with you now. They want something to do, something to live in, and God knows they wouldn't be satisfied with the half-life of a too-nice, too-quiet, routine guy desperately trying to take care of the ruined (no, don't say that) sister who *used* to be his sister. What had you been doing that night by the train? It had been late and when it gets very late and when Addy finally falls asleep on the dirty carpet, always next to an empty bottle of liquor, then sometimes (just *sometimes*, is that so much to ask for?) you like to walk down the street, sit on the bench, and watch the trains pass. It's vibrantly frightening and alluring to watch the people fly by and imagine them ending up fresh and alive in a whole other world.

Now, parts of you are being power-washed off one of those trains.

You walk home when no one comes to pick up your stitched together, meat-puzzle body. But that's OK, who was supposed to pick you up, anyway? Addy doesn't have a car, and even if she did there wouldn't be any way in hell she would have her license. Dad died last year—God knows that didn't help your efforts to keep Addy off the wagon—so he's not coming. Mom left before her little girl had enough time to memorize her face. Your landlord? Your coworkers at the gas station? Ha. Ha. You can still laugh, internally. Good to know your donated limbs share your humor.

The hospital gives you a pair of crutches to walk home with because your new leg, which feels like it used to belong to some rickety old man, is still taking an adjustment to walk with. All along the way, the sunlight is shining too bright over the black street and the low, sunken buildings, shining over the sidewalks that stretch and roll and wind forever but never actually go anywhere. All along the way, into the graffiti-soaked downtown where you can hear the noise of the train rumbling not too far off, you wonder how many people are staring at you from the street or from their rusty cars or from their dirty, red-bricked building windows. You wonder how many of them are wondering what happened to you, why your right arm and leg are different colors and why patches of your skin are stretched and yellow and wrinkled and scarred. You wonder how many of those women will never talk to you.

Those people are just like you; you know that. You know they'll never ever be able to rise up out of this place. They'll never have what you *want*.

In fact, there's a homeless person who lives outside of the convenience store. His bed is the hard bench by the wall away from the side of the road, where people take their smoke breaks. He'll never have the life he should want; he'll never have the life he should deserve. The guy's a veteran, you think; you haven't talked to him even though maybe you should. You think you've seen him wearing dog tags over his marked and punctured brown coat. Every time you see him, he looks more and more like the person who just wants to be left alone, like a wounded animal, and you've seen him limp one of his legs around like it were lame. Just let him have some peace; you don't ever ask his name or where he's from or what he wants from life or what he needs from life or where he would rather be than here, but you know that the bum with a bum leg could use some love in the form of someone putting a twenty-dollar bill in his hand. But you only see a handful of twenty-dollar bills every biweekly paycheck.

You think about him because you see him as you walk near the gas station. You see him limping, but casually limping like he was so used to the pain, around to the wall with the bench at its side. You're right; he does have a bum leg, his right leg? His right leg. For only a second, you hope he sees you limping towards the store, too, so he can know he isn't alone. You're a good guy. You care so much about other people's pain.

By the time you make it home to the apartment, your donor's right foot feels like its bursting out of the stitching in your shoe which is half a size too small. Things can't be perfect. You hope whoever gave you this leg had a good life even though you know they probably overdosed on pain pills and left their body parts up for adoption in the medical donation pool. You wonder if they ever actually thought about how one of their limbs would end up sewn on a train-accident survivor. People are supposed to give an arm and a leg to the people they love, but would this guy have loved you? Would you have been worth it? The bum by the gas station could have deserved a new leg.

The landlord sees you as soon as you walk in the door to the apartment complex; he's waiting there at the front desk with a fan blowing the hot air through his thinning hair. The walls are a drab, musty yellow color, the kind of paint color so old it's blissfully unaware of how old it is. When you first moved Addy in with you, she said the office color was something she had vomited once. Mr. Martie didn't like her much. He doesn't see who you see: your little sister who used to tell you and Dad about her new career dreams every other week; your little sister who had gone from wanting to be an actress to an artist to a teacher to a microphysicist to boozehound to a radio talk-show hostess to a drug addict to a physical rehabilitation worker back to a drug addict; your little sister, whose reasoning was that life was just rooted in too many decisions, too many "life purposes," and too much stress; your little sister, who would go missing for a night every once in a while and for whom you would comb up and down the dark streets while hoping she hadn't gotten herself into too much trouble. She used to be more than who she was. She used to want to mean something, but Mr. Martie doesn't see that about her. She doesn't see that about herself. The idiots she sleeps around with every now and again don't see that, hell. And all you want is for her to have another chance at being that little girl she used to be, who played with little old, dirty green Army men and who nabbed empty cardboard boxes off the street and out of Dumpsters so she could build forts in Dad's living room.

Mr. Martie warns you every time he sees you helping her back in through the door late at night that if she stirs up in trouble in the building, your lease is done for. But the poor guy can't help but be bitter. You know that. The bulletin boards above his desk computer are full of thumbtacked brochures for all the places he'll never go, like Florence and Dublin and Rio de Janeiro. Sometimes you wonder if he ever waits at the train stop to watch them all pass by, too—you wonder if he ever contemplates just letting everything go. He has to want that; everyone wants that. You don't talk to him often so you don't know where his family is or if he wants one or what he wanted to do with his life before he got sucked into dead-yellow-rat's-nest-apartment managing, but you know he deserves for someone to buy him a train ticket.

It takes a few seconds to open the door when your new right arm switches between feeling like an arm and feeling like a rubbery octopus tentacle, but when you open it, Martie's there behind his very early 2000's computer screen to remind you rent was due yesterday and that Addy didn't answer when he knocked on the door. He says, "You all right? You don't look so good." Next he says, "JESUS CHRIST what happened to you!? Your face ... what's wrong with your arm? You're shuffling with a limp, what happened!? ... Your skin ...."

You tell him about the train, how you've been in the hospital for the past few days, how the blood in your body isn't entirely yours anymore and he says several amazed swear words before he lets you know, with a frustrated sigh that, well, he needs the rent soon, but he leaves it at that and then looks back down at his computer like you had disappeared into a black hole. It wasn't really charity or sympathy, but it was kind of like pity. Pity charity is the best kind of charity. It doesn't force you to give up your blood, flesh, and sweat; it doesn't force you to have to know the person or to acknowledge their existence forever, rather just to know that what they are sucks compared to what they *could* be. You've been swimming in that all your life. It doesn't taste bitter; you're used to it:

"Oh, that's your sister? You're so brave for taking care of her. Oh, you weren't able to apply for college? College isn't everything; don't let it get you down. Oh, you've never had a girlfriend? Someone will see what a nice kind of guy you are soon." The kind of charity your delusional, inattentive grandma would give. It feels nice even though inside your head you're begging, "Grandma, shut up. You don't even know me."

You're the guy who will never get to grow up and you're the guy who no one will ever know. You're OK with that so long as Addy ends up in a better place; you're OK with that so long as that bum outside of work gets picked up off the street. Someone has to care if all the world can deal out is pity.

Remember to pity that guy who was ripped apart by a train; remember to condemn his sister without knowing the bright little girl she used to be.

So what if you wait by the train stop and imagine a life of your own every so often? A life with chances, like school outside this shambled, mud-drenched neighborhood with a cute girl like the nurse. A life full of mountains just a train's-reach away and even a life with a Mom who could lend him money for a ticket. Those were just fantasies. You know that the train will never pick you up. Just look what it did to you already.

Addy's waiting in the living room. Not waiting on you, just waiting for the daylight to pass. She doesn't even say anything before you see her head full of matted, unwashed hair bob up from the behind the dirty couch. It's a dark room that gives off the air of a ramshackle project building with its dingy piss-colored curtains pulled over the wide window, which leaves everything shrouded in a hazy, sleepy glow. It's always like this. "Where've you been?" She asks you like a child in dismay at the fact that parents have to leave sometimes. You tell her that you've been in the hospital—you tell her while you try not to acknowledge the one, two, three mostly empty liquor bottles in the living room which provided just too much trouble to finish or to be thrown away. The distant, blotted yellow light trying to breach the hot cave from outside is even more absorbed in the smoke from the cigarette she set down on the coffee table ashtray. Every time you see that tray out, every time you see a new carton of smokes you try to hide them somewhere (you wouldn't just throw them away; that's cruel), she always sniffs them out like the stash of thrift store toys and Happy Meal prizes Dad would give you each on your birthdays. "God, are you serious? You couldn't have called or something?"

You remind her she never answers her phone when you try to get a hold of her, anyways; she promises if she knew it were an emergency and not another one of your big brother "Don't do this, just come back home for the night" things, then she would have answered. You want to strangle her with the logical fallacy stumbling through her rancid breath, but you don't because she only shuts down whenever you whip out your high school diploma formal argumentative skills. Instead you tell her how you've been in the hospital for the past few days after a crazy person smashed you into a train and after the surgeons sewed some new skin and some fresh, new, slightly used limbs onto you. She laughs at you, then she rushes up, laughs some more, the kind of laugh it sounds like she squeezed out to drown all the churning noise in your guts.

Over the crunchy carpet she darts towards you, standing right in front of you. She could have hugged you like she hadn't done willingly in however many years. Instead, she runs her hands over your face, over the tickling skin that isn't really yours even though it refuses to go away; then, over the right arm that's just a little bit too short and very much a different color; then over the metal bracelet that's connecting the veins between the two miserable bodies; then she drops to her knees and runs her hands up and down the leg and all the while she's mumbling, "This isn't yours, this isn't yours, this isn't yours, why the hell did they do this to you?"

She falls back and you try to catch her but your leg can't quite support you like you want it to yet, so you tumble with her. She goes for one of the bottles that turned out to not be so empty after all but you grab it out of her hand with your yellow right fingers, and just the slightest brush against her sends her recoiling and spitting out what she had drunk. You want to scream at her, "Look at me again! Touch me! This is what could happen to you! What do you think I wonder about whenever you spend half the night crawling around downtown high out your mind? Because I'll tell you, now I'm gonna have nightmares that the same lunatic who did this to me is going to push you in front of that train, too. Wake up, Addy! Do you have any idea what you're doing to yourself? Wake up! Get clean, get sober, get a job and hang around people who I don't have to worry about wanting to get you wasted or to rape you or to push you in front of a goddamn train!"

But you just say, "Look, this is a new start, Addy. OK, it sucks, God, I know it sucks, but you've gotta help me … *please*, you've gotta help me. Stop all the drinking and the smoking and running off at night to God knows where, please. Just stay here with me, OK? Just stay here with me. I need you, OK?"

Slowly, she says, "OK." You screw the cap back on the bottle of vodka while she silently, lethargically moves to throw away the empty bottles under, around, and on the coffee table and frayed plaid couch that was her bedroom. But she never takes her eyes, her quivering, nervous eyes off of the parts of you which aren't really you. She looks at them like she doesn't know them. She looks at *all* the parts of you like she doesn't know any of them.

You don't ask her what she's been doing for the past few days. Right now, you don't want to hear her say, "Nothing," so instead you just clean around the little apartment, throwing away trash then sitting on the couch with her in silence, waiting for something to change but the sunlight is still muted and leashed.

Eventually, with all the room in a lull and while she's there, still looking back and forth between your skin grafts and the shadows in the corners of the room, you say, "Remember when you were like six or seven years old and you would throw those *awful* temper tantrums and slam me out of our room while Dad was at work? It was after one of us had shown you how to lock the door. And so to try and make it better and ya know, make you let me back in our room, I would bring you a bunch of potato chips and Oreos from the cabinet, hell, I would get out all the peanut butter and jelly and tell you I would make you a triple-decker PB&J if you would let me in. But it didn't matter what I tried to bring you, even if I offered you your toys that were thrown all over the living room outside, you would never unlock the door for me. Whenever you got like that, I could plan to hang out in the living room until Dad got home. Do you remember?"

She nods her head, no.

She didn't understand when you told her that you were going to step out for just a little bit. Telling her that you just had to do something wasn't good enough, but there was no point explaining what you were going to do when she wouldn't have understood. She asked you how you could tell her how much you needed her and how much you needed her to sober up right now after you just got back from being operated on in the hospital, if you were just going to turn right around to go do something else.

Just when, well, not really progress, but something had been made, you ruin it. Wait. No, no, no, you didn't ruin anything. This isn't a bad thing. You're about to do something good. With that half-empty bottle of vodka wrapped in a brown paper bag in your hands as you walk by the corner of the gas station, you know you're doing something good.

"How ya doing, sir?" you say to the bum with his bum leg, sleeping on his bench by the store as the sun is receding and the evening is turning a drowsy purple. He just looks up at you, surprised. He asks if you know him, and you tell him you don't but you brought him something that might make his lonely night a little better. He scoffs and turns away at the sight of the bottle and he tells you to leave.

What do you mean, leave, you try not to say. "Boy, I don't drink. If you knew me, you'd know that. And before you reach into your pocket to give me some change instead, don't. I don't want charity from people who don't care who I am." You tell him you don't drink either, you were just trying to give it away and you thought it would cheer him up. "You don't even know my name. Don't ask for it. If you wanted to help me then you would have asked for my story a long time ago—any one of those times you've walked on by me. You don't help people by handing them a bottle, dumbass."

You don't know what to say, so you throw the bottle away and your courageous mission to help out the bum becomes a hobbled walk of shame back home. How did that guy expect anyone to help him if he wouldn't take charity like that in the first place?

Maybe you did ruin it, because Addy has one of her boyfriends hanging out on the couch when you get back home. That bum with the lame leg might as well be standing in the doorway telling you that you know him as well as you know your sister—because she cares about you enough to wait five minutes to invite one of her greasy-haired, tattooed boys over instead of waiting another twenty-five for you to get back home. You want to explode with all the wasted efforts you've ever tried on her, with all the care and attention you gave her, none of which ever mattered.

You were brought back to life, piece by piece, watching the trains fly by and dreaming of a better life, a life of your own where you didn't have to live in what used to be—in the sister you used to have who didn't give a damn about wanting to be who she was supposed to be.

You ask her why you weren't good enough, why she had to be the reason that you want, more than anything else in the world, to be on a train going somewhere far away. You tell her you would give her your own, rented arm if it was worth it to her; if she would take it and buy her way into a new home, into a new life, like the one she could have had when she had so much potential back when she was a little girl. She says you never knew her. She says you work for her but she never wanted money; she says you keep her in line but you never say a word to her; she says you don't care who she is, just what you want her to be.

She says that she did what you asked; there aren't any drinks or cigarettes around the apartment except for the one her boyfriend is smoking, a greasy, sleazy man who looks like he should have been hanging out in a back alley. She says she loves the kid, who sits there quiet with his jaw hanging open, and she says that she loves you, too, but you don't love her. But screw all of everything you've ever given up on or ever *needed* her to be; she loves another countless one-night stand because he *got* her, or whatever.

You don't explode. You never explode. You're always quietly imploding, with all the God-given and donor-donated flesh and bones and skin crashing down inwards on you until you walk as heavily as a black hole: the greatest mass of limbs and anger and as empty as the void that unanswered love is. You walk out and leave the door open. She can take care of it; nothing you did ever really took care of little Addy anyway. How much of "you" is really left to give her love, anyways? Would she have loved the soul Right Arm or Right Leg or Skin Grafts or Blood Transfusion came from? Would they have been who she needed? Here, take them. Stand by the train and scrape up the mangled parts you need because the human body is always worth more in parts than it ever will be whole. But you don't say it. You just walk out the open door and into starless oblivion medical-hazard wastebasket world.

You were never really a part of that world, more so just a helping hand. You pass the gas station on the sidewalk and the guy isn't there tonight. You can see the train stop far in the distance, but you can't see anyone waiting there. Maybe no one can afford to. It's a shame the world wants souls to fill it, to move it, to love it, when all everyone has is bleeding, drying skin. The New Life Prosthetics Institute doesn't want donated souls; they want organs and limbs and blood and eyeballs to clamp onto amputee victims via metal, circuited bracelets. Addy wants what you don't have to give. The Institute's catalog, calling for all kinds of body parts, never listed the price of a soul. A functioning right arm was worth $150,000, and that was enough for a girl to go to rehab, go to college, to go on a honeymoon with whoever she married. That was enough for a bum to buy a new leg for himself, enough for a rundown apartment manager to take a very long vacation.

From your memory of reading over the catalog when you signed up for the experimental program in the first place, they never gave instructions on donating a soul to someone in need. You only have what the world gives you, and sometimes you can quite literally be made of charity.

And that's what you're thinking when you blindly walk your way into the hospital and tell the clueless twenty-something-year-olds that you're here to see the coroner's office before he leaves for the night. You say that you can show yourself down. If they're calling security then they're doing it quietly while your clunking footsteps echo their way down the basement and you're practically dragging your leg behind you.

Indeed, security doesn't seem to be a huge deal here, because you walk into the coroner's office with the push of a door. And there you are, standing in the very off-limits, very illegal-to-stand-in autopsy room while the doctor is shouting surprised obscenities. You tell him your will already states that upon your death, everything will go to Addy (not that he's paying close attention beyond his panic). So you lay out on one of the cold, empty slabs in a room full of cadavers. You spread out your limbs; you spread out the love the nameless donors gave you and you offer it up to someone else.

Maybe little Addy can love them more. Imagine all the train tickets she could buy. Imagine all lives she could live. Give back more than what you get; take two of everything. You tell the doctor you're ready to be donated to the medical foundation for a better life. Go on, begin the dissection already!

Tatiana Forero Puerta

Orphan Love

—for Vannesa

Sister, you see right through my neon jellyfish
diaphragm to the core. We have differently
placed scars, identical cuts. We share
the same chocolate-almond eyes,
same dirt on our freckled noses,
same dead parents.

To live without suffocating
your center with my love, squeezing
you until I bruise you, protecting
the scabs in the process, is impossible.
We are misshapen, also we bloomed.
Raptly so. You are my sun.

What will be of us when we become
someone else's mothers? Will I be
your children's grandmother? Grand-
father? Will it get any easier—loving
the unseen? Or will we love through them
as one passes through a tunnel
with an inkling that we are guided
by the ephemeral.

We conjure pet names for each other,
bluffing on our memories. I see traces
of them on the ridge of your button
nose: material for more stories.
      We can only guess what our parents
      might have whispered as we slept.

Grant Clauser

Séance

Because circles are infinite
we hold hands, let the want
of our bodies rise around us
like mayflies rising from a river.
Because voices are made of waves
that travel space until they break
up against a dam, we ask for signs
that prove the world isn't flat
where ships tumble and never return.
Because once, at a train station
there was a face in the crowd
that looked like you, and her eyes
reflected light the way
a beaver pond holds the whole sky
in its mountain gaze.
Because I wanted to reach out,
touch the water and your hand
but my grip was weak,
the promise of voices rising
over the heads of the crowd
until even the sky wasn't enough
to hold it all, like waves
forcing themselves beyond the beach
to take what doesn't belong
to the sea.
So here we are, dragging
your name across the dark

bank of the room,
sifting through Styx's flotsam
for a whisper, a wind,
something to make it rain.

Changming Yuan

Frogs in the Fog

For the past half-century, I have never seen
a single frog in this city, not even in the whole country,
but there are four big-mouthed frogs leaping around
afar in a rice field of my native village, four frogs
squatting under the rotten bridge on the way leading
to my junior high school, four frogs playing on a big
lotus leaf in my heart, four frogs calling constantly
from the dark pages of history invisible at midnight,
four frogs meditating under a puti tree transplanted
in a nature park, four frogs swimming into a fishnet
like bloated tadpoles, the same four frogs whose
monotoned songs resonate aloud in different tongues
with different pitches, yes, the four frogs still there.

Kate Belew

Go Down to the River

The crocodile crosses the street.
No, the crocodile crosses the swamp.
No, the crocodile crosses me off his list.

I go down to the river
one afternoon. The crocodile
invites me down to the edge

of the river, the rainy season. The crocodile
says it's time we have a talk,
old friend, let me put your head in my

mouth. He smiles at me. But I have
grown older since our last conversation.
I know better than to wet his gums.

The crocodile says you have been
opening your eyes at four a.m. to my voice.
The crocodile says I want to chew your feet

off to keep you with me. The crocodile
is a doctor playing Operation with
a blindfold. He will butcher me

for the hell of it. There will be no regret
at the edge of the river, the rainy season.
The crocodile is my discontent,

my vertigo, and he is also my cheating
tendencies. The crocodile goes to Afghanistan
and comes back ten times more angry.

The crocodile is how I feel growing
up to be my father. The crocodile
is what keeps me

in bed until I go down to the river.
His massive scaled body like a hand
on the mouth of the river.

Mitchell Krockmalnik Grabois

Sacrament

My village's only common property is a single pistachio tree that belongs in a nursing home, but we give her twenty-four-hour care in the spot in which she has always stood. We live on a diet of thistle stems and burdock roots, and thus we have all begun to hallucinate. The children are dead or dying, but we see them playing. A pistachio is a sacrament, the shell His body, the nut His blood.

An upside-down rainbow, a smile in the sky, a rare event: God is pleased. He feels: *This neighborhood is mine. I know the sudden dips and speed bumps and the best place for a jar of Obsidian Dark.*

Most of the time God is displeased, but people misinterpret Him. They see a rainbow, all glowing colors, and they miss that it's a giant frown. God asks Himself: *Why did I set up this game with one of the rules being that I cannot communicate directly?*

Britt Haraway

Lilly the Kid

The kid had curly hair like yours that deviled up on the sides when it was hot outside. She picked the sour oranges in the corner of the yard and scratched herself pretty good on the limbs but didn't notice. One-year-old thin skin I'd put the sunscreen on. It went on thick and left white streaks down—her face a tired clown. She liked to roll the oranges and then forget about them. Then, she would sit in the dirt. She'd look up when planes came by, and she'd walk with her finger pointed out down around her hip, like a gun fighter, in case she saw something new or familiar. She was at the hurricane tree, the one we'd had to trim crazy after Hurricane Dolly. The tiny branches grew out awkward from the big round trunk. You told me it would come back, but I'd said just cut it down. And now our baby is in the shade of its new branches, out like a bush. Burning. Telling us things. The baby grabbed some long gray bark that had fallen and tried to jam it back on the tree. She'd aimed right at the long brown scar, right where it must have been. I wish you were here to see her try. We could watch her keep her greedy pointer out and loaded.

Pablo Piñero Stillmann

The First Man in Space

Like all of his other accomplishments, the first man in space, floating above our planet, rationalized this feat into irrelevance: It had all happened because he'd blurted out the word *rope*. Sadly, history too has undervalued Ian Donatien Fouroux's inaugural trip into space for reasons that are all too familiar for those living below the equator.

Fouroux's only two friends were Camila and Tito Mazzilli, a married couple, both of them renowned physicists, whom Fouroux met during his brief stint as a hashish dealer. The Mazzillis would often have him over for supper at their house, in the outskirts of Buenos Aires, where the three would eat steak and potatoes, drink generous amounts of wine, and get high. Fouroux, who was normally bored by social activities, spent countless hours at the Mazzillis' going up and down his list of cosmological queries. *What do you mean time and space feed off of each other? Has the universe always existed? Can you explain the twin paradox to me again?* (The exact nature of Fouroux's relationship with the Mazzillis remains murky. A recent biography of Camila cites anonymous sources to posit that the three were involved in some sort of intricate BDSM fantasy game, while an article written by a grandchild of the physicists argues that they only befriended the lovable loser out of pity.)

After a particularly heavy night of eating and drinking, the Mazzillis took their friend out to the shed to show him a project they'd been working on secretly. It was a transparent sphere with a single leather chair inside. In front of the chair was a yoke, and atop the yoke, they'd installed (what was then) an ultra-modern screen. Peppered throughout the outer dermis of the sphere were small yet powerful motors.

"That is either the ugliest or most beautiful thing I've ever seen," said Fouroux. "It brings to mind the cruelty of both life and death."

Tito lit a joint dipped in hydrocodone. He was so moved in so many ways by his and Camila's "child," as they referred to the sphere, that he could never be in its presence without some kind of anxyolitic. "It began as a joke," he explained. "But my wife and I are too serious for jokes."

"It can go up into and travel through space," said Camila. "We've done the math. It works."

Fouroux, who never doubted a word said by the Mazzillis, went up to the sphere and touched it with his open hand. He fogged the glass with his breath and drew a happy face with his finger. "And the fuel?"

"Excellent question," said Camila. She walked over to a dark corner and picked up another, smaller sphere. "It goes in this."

"It's not big enough," said Tito. "I mean, it's as big as it can be, but not big enough to carry the amount of fuel necessary for a round trip."

"We can send it there," said Camila, "but we can't bring it back."

Then, like possessed by the spirit of someone with self-confidence, Frouroux took a sip of wine and said, "Rope."

A thick silence floated into the shed. Then Tito: "A couple of hundred thousand kilometers of rope?"

"Why not," asked his wife. She was the daughter of one of Latin America's richest men, so she was used to asking that question. "You put the sphere out there and then you pull it back with the rope."

Tito and Camila would've had no problem carrying this out in the open, with permission from the government—they both considered themselves apolitical—but the military state would make them wait at least a year while they prepared the launching ceremony and neither of them had the patience. They were fortunate enough to have a good friend (one of Camila's ex-lovers) in the soon-to-be-defunct Ministry of Supraterrestrial Exploration, Martín Ronconi, who sneaked out the machinery necessary to launch the sphere to a soccer pitch near the Mazzollis' house.

Tito and Camila, who had been fighting about who would get to go up to space since the sphere had begun to become a reality, knew they'd made the right decision as they watched a smiling Fouroux, in his fire-retardant suit, screwing on his helmet.

"You know," said Camila to the impromptu pilot, "in another universe you are a cosmologist."

"And in another universe," said Tito, "you are a preacher."

"In another universe," said Camila, "you drive a taxi. You are a playwright, a dentist, a military dictator."

"In another universe," said Fouroux, his words echoing inside his helmet, "I am about to become the first man in space."

The sphere launched at around two in the morning and we know very little about what happened next. We do know, though, that the farther away Fouroux got from the soccer field, from the outskirts of Buenos Aires, from Argentina, from Earth, the more he realized how inconsequential and incredibly crucial everything was. We know that he must have felt his soul expand until it pushed his heart and that at some point it became crystal clear to him that all this time he'd been in love with Camila.

Paul Arrand Rodgers

020. Raticate

Raticate's sturdy fangs grow steadily. To keep them ground down, it gnaws on rocks and logs. It may even chew on the walls of houses.
—Pokémon Ruby/Sapphire

Until I broke the right canine, I chewed on anything that fit into my mouth. The first things that fit were chosen for me: My father's index finger, my mother's nipples. But my mouth was always growing. I went to school and gnawed on pens until my mouth was full of ink. I went to the movies and crunched unpopped popcorn during all the quiet parts. I ate grass. My teeth knew the smooth contours of playground gravel. At night I went mad with boredom and chewed on myself. When I had gum in my mouth, my mother said I was like a cow with its cud. Really I was a rat, trying to keep my fangs untangled.

Paul Arrand Rodgers

124. Jynx

It seductively wiggles its hips as it walks. It can cause people to dance in unison with it."
—Pokémon Red/Blue

Browsing the porn at Jay's Food Shoppe, you ask what kind of woman I'd like to sleep with. It's 1998—we are ten, and I say that I like sleeping over in your room. You tell me that we are growing up, that one day we'll have to sleep with women. This is something you're looking forward to. You roll a magazine up in your hands and stuff it down the front of your pants—your choices were always easy.

I'll have you know, I did my research. It's two in the morning in 1999, and my family's dial-up modem is loading images of a naked woman, pixel by pixel. Her hair comes in first, blond and curled. Her eyebrows are plucked to a high, surprised arch and she's wearing mascara. She's smirking. She has a hand up, one finger to a glossy lip; its nail is painted a girlish shade of pink. Her chin appears, and it gives way to the neck and the shoulders. She's wearing a mesh camisole with a plunging neckline, but this doesn't matter because her other hand is in view now, and it is pulling the camisole up, and there are her breasts ... and I feel nothing. You're always telling me how great it must be to touch a woman's breasts, but here I am staring at them and all I can feel is a hollowness in my guts; the fact of this hollowness like the fact of her breasts, there and undeniable. I study the crude printouts of pop stars that you keep stashed in a binder under your bed: Britney Spears, Kylie Minogue, Destiny's Child, the Spice Girls. I put the binder away. When I finally figure out my shape against the blur of the world, I'll realize that there was nothing wrong with liking these women without liking them, no shame in dancing to a cassingle of "Bills, Bills, Bills" in my basement room. Until then,

I continue to torture myself. Television: Dana Scully, Xena: Warrior Princess, RuPaul. Stop there, move closer to the screen. There is RuPaul, interviewing another woman on VH1, so tall, so gorgeous. I ask my mother about her. I learn about drag. On the Internet, I load a picture of her in disbelief. She had hair. She had *shape*. A man.

2001, Madonna releases a single that asks men if they know what life feels like for girls. I listen to it frequently, thinking that I do. Because of RuPaul. Because of Prince in *Purple Rain* and Bowie in *Labyrinth*. Because you asked me what kind of woman I'd like to sleep with, and the not-woman I found led me to men. I thought all women desired men and I believed that desire repulsive. I'm writing in a journal in 2008 that I think I want to date a man. It is 2009 and I am in a gay bar, trying not to look at the man getting a blowjob in the corner, the man peeling off his mesh shirt on the dance floor, the man looking at me the way one looks at the most pitiful object at a local art show. In 2012 I am on a train back from a wedding in Boston, writing about how I gave a volunteer from the Human Rights Campaign some money because I thought he was cute, about how hot I thought one of the men at the reception was. Then I get high with my seatmate and write her a love letter. I'm in a car with a woman in Detroit; she's telling me that "Autumn Sweater" is her favorite make-out song. She plays it and I am unmoved, and she asks me if I'm sure my online dating profile should say I'm bisexual. I change it. Then I see you at a party and you ask what kind of women I like to sleep with. Friend, if RuPaul wiggled her hips for me now, I'd move mine in unison.

Matthew Ferrence

Blooding

A fox teetered down the dirt track road. It staggered toward the ditch, swung back to the middle, paused. This was a rare sight when I was a boy, a fox so close to the farmhouse. We rushed to the kitchen windows. It was a red fox, though colored more like the mine-tainted water of the nearby creek. Clumps of hair hung loose on its body, sheets of skin exposed. Driven by the relentless itch of mites burrowed into its skin, the fox had torn its own pelt away. It carried mange and, not soon enough, would suffer infectious death. My father fetched his rifle. Yet by the time he'd loaded and headed outside, the fox had disappeared into the fields.

In the rear of the Sportsmen's Club exhibit building, crowds gathered near the two live exhibits. In one, whitetail fawns lay curled in spotted balls. I watched them through cut pine bows and hexagons of chicken wire. Nearby, a raccoon paced in a small cage, back and forth and back again. I loved this long cinderblock building more than any of the others at the county fair, here where I could stare at animals that, normally, only appeared on the farm as peripheral flashes, as shadows darting into corn rows, as ethereal midnight screams. We exited the building past a worn taxidermy mount of a dirty orange fox, the animal's flayed skin contoured around a base of styrofoam and wooden sticks, its moist eyes replaced by shining resin beads, within which the reflection of the raccoon paced back and forth and back again.

Mostly eleven-year-old boys crowded the Sportsmen's Club building. On a spitting November day, we huddled over paper exams from the State Game Commission, scribbling answers to state-crafted questions.

Is it safe to lean a loaded shotgun against a fence while you stretch over the wire?

List the categories of traps that may be used to lawfully capture furbearing mammals.

We'd been trained for two consecutive Saturdays. "Leave the land better than you found it," we had been told. Always follow "fair chase rules." Repeating these slogans accurately would help ensure a passing grade, followed by authorization to purchase hunting and trapping licenses as soon as we turned twelve.

Course instructors tallied our scores. A white-haired instructor stepped forward, and we fell silent, anticipating our coming success. The instructor filled the room with his gravel voice. We were an embarrassment, he told us, performing poorly enough to earn only contempt.

He called a name. An Amish boy, a bit older than the rest of us, stood slowly. I remember the size of his eyes, wide and glossy and near tears. The instructor growled out his score, low, paused, shouted *failed*. He barked more names, pleased, it seemed, that this first boy had unexpectedly stood in shame. Other boys followed suit, slowly rising as their names were called, the legs of their metal folding chairs rasping the concrete floor. *Failed*, the volunteer said. *Failed. Failed. Failed.* A third of the room was standing, boyish faces flushing red, heads weighted toward the floor.

After moving to the Laurel Highlands of Southern Pennsylvania, I often saw a fox on the golf course, a small red who watched me from the knoll of the ninth fairway. Not far from that spot, the Rolling Rock Club maintained breeding pens for their stock of pheasants. Through the summer, the birds grew to full size, then were released in distant fields, where they would be hunted by members of the club carrying expensive shotguns and decked out in Orvis gear.

That autumn, pheasants appeared in droves on the golf course. These survivors had dodged the hunt and now returned to the place of their rearing only to be blocked by the tight weave of protective netting enclosing the pens. The birds roamed nearby, calling through the mesh to their brood.

The fox figured out how to hunt the dumb-bred birds. He hung out near the pens, too, where I often discovered splashes of feather and bone, the remains of nighttime feedings.

In late autumn, the orange-blazed hunters from the Club moved through the fields beyond the pens. Their dogs flushed confused birds that took to the wing, some bouncing off the pens' netting, others circling over the field where shotguns raised and filled the air with pellets.

On some weekend mornings, I heard the echoes of Rolling Rock bugles. Riders gathered, members of the club donning dress jackets, fuzzy helmets, and high leather boots. For nearly a hundred years, the Club has organized fox hunts, packs of trained hounds braying before a phalanx of horses. The riders used to run the foxes until they were weak enough to catch. A rider experiencing a first kill was rewarded with a ritual blooding, smears of iron-rich fox blood flooded with oxygen from a fear-pumping heart stretching across smiling faces.

No more fox kills these days: and this, I imagine, is said by some with great lament. Tradition has fallen away. Instead, it is the fox I saw on the golf course who smears his face with blood, tucking into a fallen bird, crunching bones in the darkness when bugles do not blow.

On New Year's Day, a fox lay in the fresh snow by the farm driveway. My father chatted with the trapper, who had just recently set a string along the upper fields. Against the white, the orange of the fox seemed to glow, a smooth pelt, thick, free of disease. This was a large male, strong and well fed.

I saw him as I returned from the store, where I'd fetched yogurt, cream for my morning coffee. Just a glimpse: the two men, hands in pockets, hunched slightly in the cold as they stood beside the driveway, the dead fox, a splash of rich red blooding the snow. The fox's mouth hung open, and if not for the blood I could imagine it as peaceful, if not for the blood trickling fresh from the recent kill. I did not know and would not ask whether the trapper released the steel jaws after driving a bullet into the fox's brain or if, to preserve the pelt, he clubbed it swiftly.

A fine pelt, my father would tell me that night, would probably bring five or ten dollars. In his voice, I would detect the conflict of that bounty, the few dollars measured against the memory of running his own trapline. Cold mornings. Hot wood stoves. Spending money. Freedom to wander the back woods of his own Pennsylvania childhood.

A few days later, my sister's dog would wander into one of the trapper's sets, ensnaring itself in jaws that my sister could not easily release. Her six-year-old daughter would race down the hillside, back to the house for help, her tiny mouth open and red, panting, so red, against the new snow.

Rob Talbert

Field Trip

I once saw a drag queen smear
red lipstick on the face of a lion.

The cops came running to drag him away,
dress caught up around the knees

and him yelling about his father. The Texas sun
beat down all pissed off as usual;

the zoo gave us ice cream to lighten the mood.
That kind of thing stays in the mind

like a beating in an alleyway, only to resurface
years later but while I'm still young,

watching a girlfriend stare into a makeup mirror,
or coming home early from school and catching

my father wearing only a slip. *Explore the Night*
was dark and cold and filled with creatures

quietly watching. In *Aquatic World* an employee
struggled to explain why a shark

was eating its young. There is always a cage.
A pane of glass. A *Sorry, no.* A strip of caution tape.

Field Trip

A room you can enter and a room you can't.
Love becomes a sugar-pumped child, unchaperoned

and running through a hotel, trying all the doors.
From the school bus I watched the wheat

stream bright and golden and waist level
past the window. I thought about the lion,

and I imagined him freely plunging
through the field. Sprinting away from some stripped

and shredded carcass. His stomach full of raw meat.
Lips a full rouge.

Kelly Davio

Pantoum for Someone Else's Child

Biology tells me I should want this:
a chubby infant, cannonball snug as he naps
on my belly, we two a faintly breathing heap
as his mother lists, arms freed for a moment.

My friend's baby, chubby cannonball that naps
in my lap, doesn't care that he's not my son,
that I'll leave this house with my arms free
of his milk-fed weight, none of my genes his.

He's not my child, but evolution doesn't care,
says, *Wouldn't this be nice?* Forgets my hazards,
these faulty genes of mine that could be his,
the lurking danger that spins in my DNA.

Wouldn't this be nice? evolution says. Forget
that one chance in five of death on arrival.
Ignore the lurking codes that twist my DNA,
that would unwind the springs of his legs.

That one-in-five chance: worse odds
than one bullet in a crank of empty chambers.
I unwind his legs that go springing at my ribs
while his feet punch me from the outside in.

Evolution abhors an empty chamber, scoffs
at the image of a faintly breathing heap
in an incubator. Biology kicks me
from the outside in, tells me I should want this.

Kelly Davio

In the Infusion Center,

we appear overnight, odd
numbers scattered about,
looming in manner of toadstools.
Heads furred, stems rooted to chairs,
budgeless. Here comes the nurse
and there the needle,

thereafter the gurney
and curtained room.
Prickle of nerve and bloody meat,
hair popped loose of follicle.
The janitor huffs about our feet,
vacuums up our evidence,

our body bits gone to slag, to heap.
Hot grinds the sun on fish tank,
we note the clownfish and loathe him.
Pretty tail, so sparkly fin, we don't endorse
his peeking orange. Give us the suckerfish,
devourer of the green-grown slime.

Alex Vartan Gubbins

The Art of Recognizing
Signs of Suicide

Specialist Worthy speaks a slow drawl
in sequence with the drone of wearing
ball bearings on a truck that passes
our windows on the way to gate check.

My eyes are buried in how he fidgets:
fingers dress right dress, up and down
his seams, nails shine like plastic
in each flinch, pause, another cinch.

They'll chapter me out he says. Guess
I'd be excited too if my battle buddy
stopped me from going through with it,
barrel in mouth, smooth steel on enamel,

like how a tired dog cherishes a bone.
Scuffed knee pads tell the story of how,
when in need of haven away from heat,
he dives then rolls, bullets a foot above.

Everything rests on how solid he plants
his feet to the earth, springs up like a
jack-in-the-box, aims at a target he knows
nothing about.

Melissa Frederick

Dead

For ten days it was the same day. I opened my eyes to daylight. Through the blinds, the light was mostly gray. I could picture the sky furrowed with thick clouds, the kind that hinted at snow. From October to April, Iowa was all snow, at least as far as I could tell from two years of living in the state. Sidewalks became mazes cut through knee-deep white, and to get anywhere fast, you had to leap over trench walls and hope you didn't get stuck. Side streets never got plowed—people just drove over new snowfall until roads were packed smooth. In all directions, the world lay colorless. Land and sky mirrored each other, like the front and back covers of a book.

I remembered all these details from my formerly three-dimensional life, when sitting and walking and eating and sleeping formed a continuous sphere of movement. Once that single persistent day began, however, my body insisted on staying flat. Bed became a constant. I had no desire to leave horizontal surfaces, not even to prop myself up with pillows. Being upright felt wrong somehow, like straining against a tether threaded through my skull. So I slept most of the time and shuffled to the bathroom when I could and stared at fake grain lines on the wood-paneled walls of my bedroom. At age twenty-four, I settled into an existence as a layer of Iowa snow, cold and inert.

The wood paneling that surrounded me, as I lay curled on my queen-sized mattress, had to have been installed in the 1970s, an economical splash of class in what was likely meant as a den or study. The rest of our little rented Cape Cod had been updated: furnished kitchen, extra bathroom in the basement, free cable (courtesy of the company that never shut it off), and two spacious bedrooms with cream-colored walls and bay windows. My housemates, both named Erin, took those. Because I was last to show up at the beginning of the school year, Erin and Erin had helpfully set up my bed in the dingy disco-era makeout room. It made no difference, though. I wanted the world to leave me alone. There was no life outside my breath, my stiff neck and throbbing head, the faint brown threads that drained down the walls and sometimes collected in pools or formed little, irregular beads. Often, I'd find myself searching for patterns, where branching veins bent at the same angle, where strange-shaped islands repeated.

Ironically, the artificial wood that enclosed me knew more than I did about my body's process of self-suffocation. All around me the map had been plotted, some twenty-five years before I arrived in Iowa. Long, meandering veins. Floating clusters caught in the act of adhering to bigger ones. An image of a log jam recurred endlessly in front of my face, but my eyes were too dull, my mind too muddled, to recognize what I was seeing. Meanwhile, a vein behind my ear continued to close.

My mother and I had furnished my room in a hurry and on a budget. In the handful of days before she flew back to Pennsylvania, we picked through warehouses of desks and bureaus cast off by other university nomads, bought cheap folding chairs, and arranged and draped a few clean, sturdy boxes with the Middle Eastern-looking blankets I'd collected because I was the bohemian type. For some reason, though, we hadn't bothered to slap together a nightstand. This meant that my digital alarm clock sat on the floor—not even on a pile of books, which would shift and scatter with the tides of my studies. Instead, the long plastic brick lay wherever I happened to chuck it after I switched off the alarm.

In my sick bed, a clock on the floor was a problem. To read the numbers accurately, I had to dangle my head over the edge of the mattress and sometimes contort my upper body so I had a good line of sight. I never made the effort to reach out and move the clock. The floor was a long way down. Even so, I felt a need to check the time constantly, giving myself arbitrary countdowns like some sadistic cross between a test proctor and an aerobics instructor. *In ten minutes, you will get out of bed. At 2 p.m., you will get up to eat. Wake up now. It's going on 4 p.m.* The reality, of course, was that I wound up keeping a vigil around the glowing green numbers while my day dissolved. Tracking time became a hobby. I felt comforted by sensing a schedule shaping my leaden existence. Plus, it didn't hurt that knowing the time gave me a narrative arc to follow when my mother called. "No, Mom, still not feeling well. I slept for about twelve hours last night. I woke up at ten forty-two."

At some point during the line-tracing and clock-watching, a pack of songs wormed their way into my brain. Like musical headaches, scraps of tunes would pulse and linger. These were songs I didn't even like or listen to very often. Although I loved many tracks off They Might Be Giants' *Flood*, the one from that album that stuck was a gloomy, droning march called "Dead." The melody was insidious—piano pounding, John Linnell's vocals at their most whiny and pinched—and came with lyrics that I always found abrasively quirky:

> I returned a bag of groceries
> Accidently taken off
> The shelf before the expiration date.
> I came back as a bag of groceries
> Accidentally taken off
> The shelf before the date stamped on myself.

Dead I was not, but I often wished I could at least kill off the brain cells that kept that song lodged in my cranium.

One sequence of lines thrummed away mercilessly, over and over, like a mental picket line: *Did a large procession wave their torches / as my head fell in the basket / and was everybody dancing on the casket?* This was the wad of gum on the carpet, the hairy clog that wouldn't yield no matter how much I plunged the bathroom sink. At times, I heard those lines so much my internal ear kept switching the words "basket" and "casket" until I forgot which was supposed to come first. It didn't matter, anyway, when I drifted off for the umpteenth time, my face mashed against my Kalona Star quilt. Caskets and baskets tend to travel horizontally. At that point in my life, there was nothing I wanted more than to be carried, trundled, rolled.

Daylight brought distractions. My first-floor cave sat next to the front door. Lincoln Way, a major artery in the town of Ames, ran right past our shallow yard. The combination of traffic noise, scraping boots and shovels, and undergrads hollering like they were on some kind of fox-hunting expedition took the edge off my alienation, my sense of malfunction. I could listen to my two fellow grad students slip out to catch the bus, get to classes they taught or took, hit the library as they worked on their theses, continue in the perpetual motion of their lives. Meals and health center visits also occurred here and there, when I convinced myself I could face verticality for a couple of hours. Details of my forays out of bed varied, but not significantly. All the medical personnel at the Health Center were convinced I had a "persistent virus." They insisted I drink fluids and sent me home. During an ER visit, I was told I had an ear infection. I got a prescription for antibiotics and took in some extra fluids before I left. Having a pill bottle in hand felt like progress.

I drank as much fluid as my stomach would hold. I ate Oreos and buttered toast. I sucked warm, diluted Jell-O off a teaspoon. If I could keep that down, I'd get two teaspoons. I took Zantac for indigestion. I puked on the side of the road. The Health Center nurses got sick of seeing me. One told me, depending on how persistent my virus became, I might have to put off graduation. It was the end of February.

Erin and Erin checked in on me periodically. Once, while I was awake, they opened my bedroom door a crack. I was lying on my back, and I turned my head at the same time their faces appeared, dark-haired Erin behind blond Erin, two friends exploring an abandoned attic. Both women gasped then giggled. I laughed with them and assured them that even though I still felt sick, I wasn't feeling any worse. I didn't need anything. I was fine. They said a few awkward good-byes and left me to contemplate caskets and baskets. I have no idea what they expected to find, nor what they thought they saw when they nudged open the door.

I came back as a bag of groceries / accidently taken off / the shelf before the date stamped on myself. Lying on my stomach, listening inwardly, I couldn't decide if that last syllable was "self" or "sack." In Iowa, a paper or plastic "sack" came with what you bought at the supermarket or convenience store. *You want a sack?* the cashier would ask. After you said yes, and he fluffed one open and stuffed in your Advil and gum, you'd thank him, and he'd say, "You bet." In Iowa, nice was the only polite emotion among strangers.

((

Invariably, the most traumatic moments I encountered on my journeys out of the house (apart from leaving my snarled nest of blankets and quilts) happened when someone decided to administer IV fluids. That's when the blizzard of needles would hit. One stick, two sticks, three sticks. I was told I had tiny veins. Tiny, collapsed veins with virtually no liquid running through them, someone should have mentioned, but I suppose the medical professionals were trying to keep me optimistic. Four sticks, five sticks, six sticks. In the ER, a parade of EMTs came through to start a line, because they'd had experience with difficult patients. EMTs could thread those delicate, cappellini-thin IV catheters while keeping their balance in an ambulance hurtling through crowded intersections, probably during snowstorms, too. The EMTs I met, however, stopped after two tries and gawked. Legend was accruing to my body like stigmata.

End of the day at the Health Center. The doctor on duty wanted me to give a urine sample to see if I was dehydrated. I couldn't. She ordered IV fluids and told me as soon as I felt like it I should head for the bathroom with a specimen cup. Then we would know whether or not I had enough liquid in my system. Freezing, tucked under a flimsy, institutional blanket on a gurney, I didn't have the strength to point out the irony.

Everyone left the room except for the long-faced nurse tasked with searching my limbs for a usable vein. She hovered near the gurney, taking stock of my body with big, dark, sorrowful eyes.

"You might want to start thinking warm thoughts now, Melissa. This might get difficult." Plastic began to click and crackle as she gathered supplies from a drawer. Even in the face of another barrage of needles, I began to relax. Under the dim light, shored up by metal guardrails, I felt safe. I had found an island, an accretion of mud and branches and debris in the middle of a flood. I knew it was a temporary situation. The Health Center had no beds to hold students overnight. I had only a virus, some fatigue and dehydration. At some point, the doctor would release me, my refuge would disintegrate, and the fierce current would carry me back into chaos. But for that moment, while the nurse prepared to puncture my skin, I was grounded. I had faith. No qualms over a few pinpricks, or even a whole quarrel of razor-tipped arrows, was going to rob me of my minutes of peace.

After only two sticks, I had a working IV line taped to the side of my foot. The nurse let out a long sigh. "Someone must be watching over you, Melissa." Her dark eyes glimmered with the danger she felt had passed.

At night, when Lincoln Way went silent and only the street lamp in front of our house sent in a weak finger of light, the battle inside my head began. Far-off explosions would erupt like thunder. A nearby force would open fire. I had no control over any of it. I was a soldier in the trenches, unarmed and invisible. I couldn't even cover my ears to keep out the noise. Even though the war wasn't mine to fight, I had to witness the ordeal, listen to the constant shatterings and crashes that never ended in the darkness of my skull. I wasn't even a soldier. I was land.

The next day was the same day. My eyes opened to daylight. I shifted around my bed. I traced lines with my eyes. I sat up long enough to eat Oreos. In the hours I believed in progress, I would call my parents in Pennsylvania and give them the good news: I got up long enough to watch TV. I changed my clothes. I drank some orange juice with breakfast. Later, after the orange juice wound up mixed with sputum in a toilet, I'd sink back into the day's familiar routine. I lay down on dirty sheets. I heard my housemates spraying the surfaces I'd touched when I left my room. I persisted.

Did a large procession wave their torches / as my head fell in the casket? Or was it "basket"? In my mind, I monitored the sounds of the words as they made their circuits around the hidden chambers of my ear. Heavy words. Words in jackboots. Words that plodded, clustered, clumped, slogged, clogged, and finally stuck. Too many words, whose mass disrupted the healthy circulation of thoughts around my brain as efficiently as an axe to the neck. Like the lines on my wall, these perceptions were not metaphorical. They were part of a disease process, feral, ferocious, and as yet undiscovered.

Later, I learned terms associated with my condition: hypercoagulation, cerebral venous sinus thrombosis, antiphospholipid antibody syndrome, systemic lupus erythematosus. These words left no room for ambiguity. They couldn't be swapped. For the rest of my life, they would burrow into my every joint and blood vessel and

135

muscle fiber until they explained my existence. But back then, on that endless day, I had no access to the power of those words. I was trapped in the meaningless spiral of baskets and caskets.

Every once in a while, I would cry. *Now it's over, I'm dead and I haven't done anything that I want / or I'm still alive and there's nothing I want to do.* It was the sheer unbroken monotony of my body's disrepair that wore me down. When I was younger—a fearful child, a maudlin teenager—I pictured death as a stalker, a fierce enemy meant to be dodged and outwitted. Prostrate on a mattress in Iowa, I wondered if death approached in this subtler way, a brutal half-reality that stuck with you until you consciously made the decision to find the exit door and slip out. A day without end, then nothing.

Deep down, I knew why I couldn't stand that They Might Be Giants song. It terrified me.

I'd like to think if I'd really understood I was dying, I would have fought harder, screamed at more doctors, insisted on serious treatment at a hospital and not a crappy university health center. But that mundane, syrupy-slow descent into dissolution resembled nothing I'd ever envisioned, let alone prepared for. I had no strategy, no defenses. I didn't even have the conviction to break the Midwestern code of civility, track down the Erins, and say, *Help me.*

Casket or basket? Self or sack? Someone, please, let my body break.

Roy Bentley

WD8RBB

You were a ham radio operator, WD8RBB your call sign.
When you died, neighbors took apart the antennae tower
like stories about someone having outlandish circus sex
with a willing stranger. The tower sold for a good price.

Deep into grief for my mother, once I heard you praying
as if someone were listening in a paradise whose call sign
only the unborn and the true believer commit to memory.
After, you might start coughing or go into the bathroom.
Minus distortion or atmospheric interference, a message
of dire warning seemed to flash from a rubble of throat.

We had eavesdropped, you and I, on the Thrilla in Manila
on a Trans-Oceanic Zenith beside your amateur radio gear.
That drama traveled to us by the refraction of radio waves.
Existence and oblivion are pugilists, Ali-Fraziers contesting
the likelihood we're here and gone. Remember that family
who lived down the street when I was a kid, the Kostas?

They acted, rain or shine, as if being alive is the problem.
I recall them acknowledging—with all their mad pointing
and yelling in ballpark-angry American English and their
native Greek—that talk is not just talk or silence silence.

Ken Letko

Jack

what I need
when I have
a flat tire

when apple juice
goes bad
applejack

without a jack cut
no cribbage player
can score perfectly

jack of spades
you're one eyed
and well groomed

jack of hearts
you too
are one eyed

but sometimes you
separate the king
from the queen

blackjack you're exactly
twenty-one and ready
for a wild night

blackjack you've seen
some street fights
broken teeth and noses

monterey jack
you're so mellow
you just melt

what the shift boss
says I don't know
jack-of-all-trades

you know none

Salgado Maranhão

Poetry

My legs got lost
in your forking paths,
in the free love of your beat,
and, monk of madness,
I coupled with chaos,
remaking myself on the edge of the cliff.

centuries on end in the waiting room
of your temple
in search of some promise,
of some uncertainty in your future,
centuries turned to slime,
reduced to Z,
gigolo of leftovers,

all so that once in a while
you show me the face of God.

Translated from the Portuguese by Alexis Levitin

Salgado Maranhão

The Link

pointless for me to go back
to the ruins of our promise:
the latex kiss,
the heart of ice.

love is safe
       in the infinitive,
without a draft,
without a daily log.

I have neither doctrine
nor idols of bullshit
host of poetry.
I sink my claws

       into a breath
of light and time,
in the company of the wind
gathering together footprints.

Translated from the Portuguese by Alexis Levitin

Shane Stricker

The Kingdom of God Is Within You

I got tired of hearing Tommy James Cecil saying it was worth it. Like when I'd stolen some liquor from my brother's freezer and watered it down and Foster'd noticed it was watered down and he'd called me out on it and told me he was gonna whoop my ass and then—before it got good and really sunk in that he was really gonna do it—my ass was almost done and whooped.

At school on Monday I told Tommy James Cecil about the ass-whooping I took for watering down that liquor and he laughed in that sort of snorty way he has and he started into what all we'd done on Friday, about the realty signs we'd stolen, laughing about me hanging off the wood Century 21 sign until it snapped and I fell ass first to the cold, hard ground. By that time he was all ate up with laughing about me trying to hold my pants up with one hand, carrying the sign with the other, stumbling and falling until I was back in the truck, taking another drink of what got my ass whooped later. And he done forgot already what all happened Friday except for the sign stealing, but he was laughing and I had even started laughing and we stayed like that until he told me it was all worth it.

Every time he said that, I walked off feeling about stupid and like I was gonna punch something at the same time. But I never really did punch or kick a thing at all except where there's a patch in the wall from when I thought Roxanne Parsons was pregnant. She'd called me up and my momma answered and I'd taken the cordless back in my room and hollered at Mom that I had it, but I could still hear her breathing on the other phone so I yelled square in the receiver that I had it and she didn't act like she'd done a thing wrong in the world but just said she didn't hear me before and said bye to Roxanne and hung up for real. But I knew she liked to listen in to what me and Roxanne was saying to each other cause I'd get in my room and be talking dirty, saying things about that sweet stuff I hadn't seen but one time before and I'd hear a cough and a click and I knew she'd heard what I'd said cause the next morning she couldn't hardly look me in the eye as she took my toast from the toaster and dropped it, then a stick of butter, and then a knife onto the table in front of my place.

Mom hung up and Roxanne, who sounded positively cheerful, in full-on bliss mode with my mom, started crying like she was being skinned alive and maybe she felt like she was, too, but how she'd put on such an act for my momma made me wonder what kind of an act she'd pulled on me. Roxanne was talking so fast and through the tears and sniffling it took me a second to catch up to what she was saying, took me a second to figure she was saying she missed her visitor, that she was knocked up. Thinking about that act she'd just put on for my momma, I couldn't help but picture a needle going through a condom. And I asked her how late she was, not knowing what in the hell I was talking about—as if had I gotten a number I would have known whether it was all OK or not—but I didn't get a number. Roxanne just said late, all capitals, LATE, and I would have understood the tone even if I'd not spoken the language.

And about a week after that, after awkward looks, look-aways in class, awkward passes in the hall, awkward interactions with Debbie Marlow in chemistry lab—cause Debbie and Roxanne's best friends—it got to the point with Debbie Marlow that she was telling me to man up and started talking all this wedding-marriage stuff so that I couldn't even get the Bunsen burner lit and she had to do it for me. After two days of all that, and not talking to Roxanne at all, she calls and says she's told her mom and dad and that they want to meet with my mom and they want us to come over there, to the house. Her momma was cooking, she says, and did my mom like mushrooms cause her mom was making beef stroganoff? My mom didn't like mushrooms from the day she was born and I had bigger fish to fry than that at the moment and I said I guess that meant that she was keeping it and hell hath no fury like a girl, woman, who's just told her daddy she ain't his little girl no more and called her baby daddy to tell him dinner's at seven—not ask him, but tell him dinner's at seven—and he says that, THAT, capital, every letter: THAT.

But that's not even when I kicked the hole in the wall because I hadn't even told Tommy James Cecil that Roxanne was pregnant yet, had told zero, zilch, no people she was pregnant and I didn't put my foot through the wall until after I'd told my mom, until after I'd told Tommy James Cecil, until after I'd had dinner, beef stroganoff, with Roxanne's mom and dad knowing not twenty feet away is where I'd impregnated their daughter with them sitting right over there on that couch in the family room watching *Quantum Leap*.

And Al was talking to Sam about saving the whole history of treatment for the mentally retarded as I busted the nut that must have gotten up there and swam in. And I'm sitting there, at Roxanne's family's table, wondering if she heard Al, too, or if it was just me and then knowing it would be rude to ask something like that even if her mom and dad and my mom weren't sitting there. And Don and Becky Parsons and Janie Jenson all got along just fabulously, my mom talking about how tough it was being a single mother when I was little and about how my dad had run off to Des Moines, Iowa, with some skanky-looking nineteen-year-old when I was only two, about how I welcomed, WELCOMED, the responsibility that was on the way and Don and Becky trading off telling about how kids our age didn't know nothing about responsibility, nothing about raising babies, talking about us as if we were babies, as if we'd not just cooked one up about as easily as Becky Parsons made beef stroganoff for folks who didn't care nothing for mushrooms, didn't care nothing at all for mushrooms one way or the other. No. Sir.

We didn't want no mushrooms and I sure as hell didn't want to have no baby. Sure as hell was not WELCOMING the responsibility coming my way. Sure as hell was sitting there thinking about waiting for my mom and the Parsons to get back into the steady rhythm of dogging me and Roxanne pretty good so I could scrape some of what was on my plate off into the floor and hope Rags' old ass would get off his bed in the corner of the room and cough his way over until he finally saw or smelled the mushrooms sitting right in front of his face. But I knew my luck in that moment and mine was such that the dog wouldn't like mushrooms or better still, would like them just fine, would love the sons-of-bitches but be so damned allergic to them he'd eat until he got gassy and started farting all over the place before falling stiff dead next to Roxanne's chair and that would about sum up everything I was in the world to my mom, to the Parsons: a daughter knocking-up, senior-citizen-dog murderer. Hell, I might as well have gone ahead and shit in their fridge and turned over their television while I was at it with what I'd already done.

But I didn't scrape nothing off my plate and when Becky Parsons asked if I didn't like it, I'd lied to her, told her I liked it just fine but wasn't hungry and Don reached across the table and told me, not a foot from my face, that I had better damn well get hungry, that I had damn well better eat what I was served because this was life and in life men eat the shit they're served and smile while they're doing it. And he half-stood there, cold-staring me from before I picked up my fork through me damn near gagging on every bite and nothing being left on my plate but brown juice. And I looked at Rags instead of staring up at Don and Rags licked his lips every time I took a bite and no one said shit to my mom when she said she wasn't hungry except Roxanne's mom who told her she understood. Who could eat at a time like this?

At the door, after my mom stepped through the frame, telling the Parsons she had their number and making sure Don and Becky had ours, Don looked down on me and said he'd be seeing a hell of a lot more of me in the coming days before adding, just before the door came to, years. And Mom laughed in the car, laughed, and told me how much she liked them, how they could be friends—her and Becky—if circumstances had worked out differently and when I'd tried to say something about the meal, about the way Don talked to me, Mom backhanded me across the mouth and nose and my face turned red, but I did not cry and she didn't look over to see where she was slapping or what the slap'd done after, neither. She drove on like nothing at all had happened and I had a red mark across my face still when I called Tommy James Cecil, long after my mother'd gone to sleep, and told him I had something to tell him and no, it could not wait and no, I didn't want to say it over the telephone. And the red mark was still there when I opened the window and slunk out, meeting Tommy James Cecil at the corner behind the Walkers' azalea bushes.

I told him Roxanne was pregnant and a little about going to eat over at their house and he asked if she was keeping it and asked all about dinner and what Roxanne's parents had said, what my mom had said, if I'd talked to Foster, that surely something like this had come up when Foster was still living at home, and I had to tell him about us not talking with Foster no more cause he'd just stolen a bunch of VHS tapes and my granddaddy's coin collection, and all the aluminum cans in the garage Mom was saving up for our vacation— garage was almost full, too, bags upon bags stacked concrete to rafters—and a bunch of other things like my card collection and all the mousetraps in the whole damn house for whatever reason. He started laughing like that was the funniest thing in the world, the funniest thing I'd ever said. He kept saying mousetraps over and over, through all the laughing, and I thought I wanted to haul off and hit him then, thought that was about as pissed as I could be until he said, you got to fuck her, didn't you? And now with her fucking pregnant and keeping it, y'all can fuck just like rabbits. I was steaming pretty good and thinking Roxanne wasn't never gonna fuck me again, about how no girl was ever gonna fuck me again, and thinking how bad my luck was for getting her pregnant on the first time and already thinking Tommy James Cecil was an asshole when he fake jabbed at my stomach and told me it was worth it.

Over the next three nights I didn't sleep at all except for a few hours and during that time I dreamed Tommy James Cecil was a great big Pez dispenser, his giant-ass head on a blue base, and instead of Pez he just kept yelling it was worth it and rapid-firing babies at me until babies was all there was, until all there was was babies. I woke up throwing the sheets off of me like they was babies, sweating like I'd been out mowing yards, knowing someone was watching me and it was my mom and she was talking about my conscience—that little man deep inside who was getting the better of me—and I wished and hoped to a god I'd been talking to more and more often these last several days that the little man inside of me was not Tommy James Cecil and thinking that if it was I might as well go ahead and off myself because there wasn't much more I could take and that would just be one thing too many.

The night I did kick a hole in the wall, Mom said she wanted something to eat but instead of going to Cream Castle like she said she was she parked in the Magnificent Pizza Play World's parking lot and asked me if I remembered having a birthday party there and I said I did, but that I also remembered wanting to have it in Cape at

Chuck E. Cheese's and the glance she cut me told me she'd thought about and dismissed the notion of slapping me again and instead of slapping me she told me I was gonna sit there and shut the hell up. Instead of shutting the hell up, I asked her how long we were going to sit there and before I could get out that I was hungry I had another backhand across the mouth and that night we sat there for two more hours, neither of us talking, just sitting there. And when we got home there were nine messages on the answering machine: the first two from Roxanne saying we needed to talk, the next one from Foster saying he and Mom needed to talk, the next saying we needed to change our long distance service immediately if we were gonna reap the benefits of the promotion they had going on up there and that one sounded more promising than the next five from Roxanne saying about the same thing she had on the first two: we needed to talk.

So I took the cordless back in my bedroom and dialed Roxanne up and Don answered and I asked to talk to her. He said he'd see and sat there humming and humming and humming before telling me he'd get her and the humming felt like something I could fall right through and then I heard Roxanne's voice and a click and a breath and before Roxanne could say anything at all I was telling her she needed to stop breathing and she started yelling at me to drop dead, telling me she's not, capital NOT, the one who should stop breathing and before she got finished with her hollering I heard the click again and knew whoever it was on the line had gotten off and I asked her what she wanted and she stopped her yelling. Told me she was pregnant and I told her I got it, she was pregnant, I was the daddy, told her she made herself perfectly clear on that one, crystal, and then she spelled it out for me. W-A-S-N-APOSTROPHE-T. All caps.

And I asked her what in the hell she meant she wasn't pregnant, that we'd told our parents and had that dinner together and I'd eaten a whole motherfucking plate of nothing more than mushrooms, and I'd had to deal with Debbie Marlow almost convincing me it was time to put a ring on it, and I asked her didn't she take a pregnancy test, and didn't it turn up positive, and didn't she go to the doctor to make sure the test was right or, at least, at the very fucking least, didn't she take two or three or four more tests after that first one to make damn certain she was what she thought she was before going on in the living room while her parents were sitting there watching more *Quantum Leap*—cause that's about all there ever was on their television—and telling them she was with our baby?

And I didn't know Roxanne had it in her but she didn't cry louder or sit there quiet on the other end of the phone waiting for me to finish with all I had to say—and I sure wasn't done by a long shot, not by a long way—before she come back that she'd not taken a test at all, that she'd gone strictly off being late, and that, if I really wanted to know the truth, if I was so goddamn good dealing with the realness of everything, she wasn't even sure the baby would have been mine at all but that it might have been Tommy James Cecil's, that he'd fucked her the night before I'd come over, and that the only reason she didn't tell him it was his was because he was a no-good piece of shit who wouldn't have said nothing at all about the baby other than to tell her they were going to St. Louis or Memphis to get the problem solved and she didn't want the problem solved. She said she wanted the baby and now was all broken up that there wasn't no baby inside of her, no baby to make her life stretch out straight like her momma said she'd done for her, no baby to go out shopping for and damn did she want to go shopping for that baby, she'd said, buying up little onesies and toys and diapers and all that other shit people buy for babies and something about the way she said all that made me less angry with her, made me want to go over and hold onto her for a while even though she'd fucked my best friend the night before me and neither one of them had thought to say anything to me about that, even though she'd made me tell my momma she was pregnant.

I guess she did a real number on me, too, because there I was, lying on my bed, apologizing to her for her not having a baby wrapped up deep and small inside of her, for not wanting nothing to do with that baby, for every hurtful thought I'd had and every hurtful thing I'd said, and I even started apologizing for the way I'd acted at dinner with her parents, though I'm pretty sure I'd acted about as right, just walking through the door, as anyone ever had when knowing what they were getting into.

I heard footsteps coming down the hall just after I'd hung up the phone and when the door opened and my mom stood there smiling, I knew I'd been so caught up in everything going on between me and Roxanne that I hadn't listened for more breathing or more clicking and that Mom had heard every cent of everything I'd said and I was embarrassed for all the apologizing I'd done and Mom told me I'd really come around and that she wanted to buy me a double bacon cheeseburger and a chocolate malt from Cream Castle and I told her I wasn't the least bit hungry, that I had some business to take care of. Mom told me she'd go ahead and get me a burger and malt anyway, that I didn't have to go with her, and before too long I heard her car backing down the drive and pulling away and I took up the telephone and pressed the numbers for Tommy James Cecil and when he picked up he was already laughing and telling me he was fucking Debbie Marlow and she'd already called to tell him Roxanne wasn't pregnant and that man, did I dodge a motherfucking bullet on that one, and asked if I wanted to go out drinking that night, that he'd been over to my brother's, over to Foster's house by himself, and said he knew why my brother'd been stealing all that shit from us, that Foster was in such a bad way, blowing shit up his nose, smoking shit, he didn't even care if Tommy James Cecil took a whole pint of Jägermeister from his freezer as long as he left the money for it on the counter.

And right then, I didn't even want to call him out on what all I'd heard, didn't even want to say another word to him about anything ever, and I wondered who was living whose life and if Tommy James Cecil and I might just as well switch houses and he could go on living as me, apologizing all the time for what he'd done and not done, and I could go on being him, telling everyone it was worth it all the time, and he could have my brother and my mom and any girl I might ever have a chance with in the future. And that's when he told me it had all been worth it and I threw the phone across the room and started kicking, just kicking, and before I knew it my foot was through the wall and I stayed that way, shin deep, until my mom came in to tell me the food was there, and she didn't know what to say except that she'd done lost one son already, she sure as shit wasn't planning on losing another so I had better pull my head out of my ass and figure out whatever I needed to figure out. Then, when I was about ready to scream at her, to say she didn't know shit about shit, she told me she was going to bed and there was a double burger on the kitchen counter and a malt in the fridge for me.

Eugenie Theall

Embrace

I sink into your arms
the way a fertilized egg
nestles into the uterine wall—
does what it's meant to do,
takes root. Divides,
multiplies. Squeezes blood,
pumps waste, opens its eyes,
breathes.

Eugenie Theall

Evelyn Nesbit Contemplates

My husband eyes the carbon print, follows the trails
embroidered into this silk robe, overlapping branches,
the curve of my hip, bent perfumed knee, one foot peeking out
like a sidewinder lost in white fur.

Lounging on bearskin, I lean into the back of its neck,
not thinking of him. Have you ever met someone new, a stranger
who didn't seem so far removed and from the moment he spoke,
his voice filled your head?

I remember my vows, but when my eyes close, I am suspended
in a red velvet swing and know only the bear's open mouth,
preserved teeth, eyeless sockets, and that even without flesh,
I'd know the shape of my lover's skull, the straight line of jaw,

the beauty of bone.

Jennifer Jackson Berry

Fair

Leg skin stretched to shine, the boy
waddled to the scale, his father's hand
on his four-year-old back. Compassion
lived in the carnie: *Seventy-nine?* & then *Aww,*
you win! Go pick a prize! She never even
whispered afterward what 79 lowballed.
I recognized the father as my boyfriend
at nineteen, the man six years my senior who
grabbed my breasts, paws swinging
from a four hundred-pound frame, *these are too big*.
He did that kind of damage you can't
really describe. If I were a different person,
I might brag about being tied to the bed
for my first time.
My husband standing beside me
in the crowd around the game
read every story, even ones I never told,
in my face watching that ugly face,
proud his son fooled his first woman
into feeling sorry for him.

John Andrews

Tallahassee Rain

There's a moment you can't escape: the water
filling up streets, the men in the back bar, needing water.

He's taking a piss next to me. *Stare at the ceiling.*
You want to kiss it. Don't look. Just listen to the water.

I'll find this flood folded into a junk drawer, dance
feeling myself up with leftover bath water.

A kiss. Just once on the lips, when we were drunk. Things I remember:
hand-wrapped hips, the kitchen slow dance, the boiling water.

I wish I could kaleidoscope his face. A thousand facets staring back,
cinderblocks around his feet, my hands holding him under water.

Colin always watched from the bathroom doorway. My pants
halfway down my legs, arm outstretched to test the water.

Patricia Heim

Becoming a Woman: A Requiem

My mother's death certificate states that she died early in the morning of August 29, 1963—four weeks after she'd trudged upstairs one Friday evening, complaining of nausea, and threw up in the toilet before passing out on the bathroom floor. Hospitalized, and for want of X-ray computed tomography able to detect the snowballing mass in the left lobe of her brain, she was treated for meningitis-encephalitis before being diagnosed with exhaustion, sent home on pain medication and, of all things, bed rest: She hadn't gotten herself out of bed since the night she'd collapsed, often spoke nonsense, could barely even hold up her head.

When her doctor came by to explain the findings in the autopsy report, I wondered how many astrocytes—star-shaped cells that make up the gluelike supportive tissue of the brain—would constitute a tumor the size of a small grapefruit. How anything in the exquisite shape of a star, conjuring the glittering sky on moonless nights, the diamond-studded morning surf, and the radiance of my mother's smile, could embark on so malignant a course as to snuff out the light of my thirteen-year-old life.

I was asleep that morning when the hospital called, and if I heard the phone ring, either chose to ignore it or thought I was dreaming. I remember, however, that the sun was scarcely up when my older brother, just out of high school, poked his head through my bedroom doorway waking me with a kindness I was astonished he possessed. It made me feel close to him and, yet, uneasy.

"Patsy," he said, "you need to get up and dress quickly. Dad already left." After a pause, he lowered his voice, adding, "Mom's dying; we have to go and say good-bye."

"She's dying?" I repeated, as if challenging reality to explain itself. My eyes stung with a coating of tears, while my muscles quailed and my legs seemed about to float out from under me. My chest felt tight though strangely hollow, as my lungs snatched the air that still echoed with the sound of the telephone ringing. Despite the chirping of birds and crickets, the rustling of maple trees, and that back-to-school redolence drifting through the window on the late August breeze, a shroud of silence fell over everything.

It was a nurse who'd called to summon us, her words—as I heard my father repeating them at the hospital and, afterward, back at the house—impressing me deeply. Like a woman who, after giving birth, recounts her story of labor and delivery to process the experience, bed it down in her bones so she'll never forget. "Mr. Finn," she'd said, "your wife's condition is very grave."

Although I was going into eighth grade, I'd never encountered the word "grave" used as an adjective before. Now someone was saying it about my mother, who had not an illness per se but a "condition," indicating at least she was still alive. I played the sentence over in my mind, soothed by its pithy, lyrical quality, reminding me of the poetry I'd learned these past seven years in parochial school: "I shot an arrow into the air" or "Into the valley of Death, rode the six hundred."

No one in our household spoke so articulately or with any real sophistication. And I think, too, that the adjective "grave" deflected my attention from the noun, while the word "wife" left no doubt as to what, precisely, she'd been to him.

After my brother returned to his room, I stood in my closet, fumbling through my dresses and skirts. Since it was Sunday and we were practicing Catholics, ordinarily, we'd be attending Mass. To see my mother for the last time, therefore, wasn't just an important occasion; it was a religious one as well. Especially in that death, like the Sabbath, had an aura of holiness and solemnity about it. There must be some appropriate attire, only nothing I tried on felt quite right.

My wardrobe consisted of my school uniform and blouses, recent Christmas and Easter outfits, a few which, undoubtedly, didn't fit, and a windfall of dresses bestowed upon me, seasonally, by an adopted friend who lived down the street. I have no idea what I settled on, only that I was in my closet under great duress, paralyzed for what felt like a very long time, frazzled about being late as much as bewildered over what to wear. Although I'd yet to learn algebra, my life seemed to hinge upon solving a complex equation in a few split seconds, wherein X amounted to zero conflict.

There was no right outfit. And in my frenzy to invent one, as Cinderella had done to attend the king's ball, time froze, which must have been to my advantage. If I could stop the clock, I could forestall the inevitable. I suppose I washed myself up and combed my hair, but in my mind, only clothes counted. To cover me, perhaps, in the event I'd feel exposed, lacking the protection of a mother in the world, or to hold me together—I was shivering with a chill that stems from the quick, my teeth chattering—for fear I'd somehow fall apart.

In my powerless state, the right outfit might have also represented freedom of choice. While some things, like death, simply happened, others I still could choose. Sorting through my clothes, like Cinderella her lentils, fostering the illusion I could cull my feelings: arrive at the hospital clad only in acceptable ones, those unacceptable—outrage at my mother for getting sick, elation at the prospect of claiming my autonomy—concealed within the folds and pleats. Our close yet difficult relationship, complicated by the topsy-turvy of adolescence and exacerbated by her illness and impending death, would culminate on a positive note: I wouldn't end up feeling guilty, miss my mother terribly, or ever be lonely.

But I was thirteen, my body a mysterious, unsettling space, quivering like the Earth in early spring. I was in love with possibility and pulled toward the world with an indecipherable longing, yet clinging to what I was leaving behind. Now my mother was dying, and though I couldn't have known it consciously, I needed her blessing: to confer upon me the rites of womanhood, giving me permission to fill her shoes. Not as my father's wife, including presiding over her household and inheriting her things—the idea naturally playing itself out in the back of my mind—but as someone, ultimately, worthy of surpassing her.

What a fine line I had to walk to turn my father's head without arousing my mother's envy. To appeal to him as a woman while to her a little girl, which, in many ways I was and now, suddenly, wished to remain. Despite my magical thinking, I left the house at my brother's urging, wound in a braid of impossible feelings, unwilling to accept what fate had in store.

During the fifteen minutes—which felt like an hour—it took us to drive to the hospital, neither my brother nor I uttered a word. From the passenger seat, I gazed through the windshield at the blue-skied world of people in cars, some with radios blaring, on what to them was an ordinary Sunday morning. *How can it be*, I wondered, *that my brother heeds the laws of traffic, while I hold my breath and bite my lip, pressing an imaginary accelerator to the floor? Why is everyone in our way? Don't they understand that we have the right to speed ahead? My mother's dying. If I don't see her one last time, set things right before saying good-bye, I don't know how I'll ever go on.*

Whatever it was I needed to "set right," I doubt, at thirteen, I could have articulated. Surely, I wanted to repair our relationship, transform myself from an ever-flipping coin of ambivalence into a daughter capable of mourning her mother: a person neither good nor bad but a unique and tolerable amalgam of both—someone I dearly loved in whom I was equally disappointed. Sweeping clear a path, I'd move forward less conflicted, fueled and comforted by the pleasanter feelings and memories we'd shared: her listening after school as I prattled on, in detail, about my day; setting my hair in curlers at night and, in the morning, combing it out in a pageboy fluff; at Christmastime, granting me a day off from school, riding the trolley and el to the Wanamaker's Light Show and, after lunching at the soda fountain of F.W. Woolworth, buying me a Christmas dress; laughing while we watched reruns of *I Love Lucy* or played Old Maid on our blanket at the beach.

I would have liked for her to have taught me things besides how to vacuum, dust, and make my bed: such as baking, sewing, gardening, or needlework, as I enjoyed being creative with my hands—back when I'd played with dolls, I'd cobbled their clothes and furniture with scraps she'd given me or that I'd scavenged from around the house. She might have guided me through the steps for earning my Girl Scout badges rather than coaching me, tepidly, from the sidelines. Or signed me up for a lesson or two: piano, swimming, dancing, or singing—I'd learned to swim by imitating friends who knew how, had been singing my heart out from the time I was three. Something as simple as doing the dishes together—as if I were her apprentice, a woman in the making—would have strengthened our connection, enhanced my sense of ease with both her and myself.

She read magazines but not books, lacked hobbies, applied accuracy and precision to little other than paying bills, ironing, or roasting a turkey, and although while chatting on the phone, she doodled in the margins of the telephone directory—realistic-looking dogs and cats, teapots, cups and saucers, and cupcakes—I never once saw her drawing a picture. At fifty-four, maybe she presumed she still had time.

What I wanted most, however, what I felt missing all along, was for my mother to see me, to notice me, to confirm my existence as a bona fide person. Not as an extension of her, a forever baby meant, like a pet, to keep her company, but as an adolescent entitled to her development, a daughter deserving of her mother's respect. I needed to get to the hospital to find myself in my mother's eyes, once and for all to see that I truly mattered.

My mother hadn't intended for me to feel this way. Having nurtured five sons and two daughters over the past thirty-two years (my oldest brother was nineteen when she had me), I doubt she was aware of her own needs and wants, causing her to be preoccupied, discouraged, and often depressed. My father, an enterprising and driven uneducated man, had been largely unavailable, particularly emotionally. Both had suffered gaps and derailments in their own developments, were limited in what they could bring to raising a family.

My father's absorption in his world of work and the fact that my youngest brother, my only sibling still at home, was a high school senior tightened my mother's hold on me, turning growing up into a formidable task. Since she'd yet to become her own person, rendering her insecure and, therefore, unfulfilled, my instinct to separate, to push off from her and swim on my own, made both of us feel anxious and me, often, guilty. All my life, I'd sensed her ferment, fearing, someday, she might pack up and leave; I half expected she'd vanish if I turned my head.

"Hi, Mom," I'd say, almost in a sheepish tone, when phoning to ask, "Would it be OK if I stayed at so-and-so's for dinner?"

"Well, all right," she'd say, wistfully, "but I made spaghetti (roast beef, pork chops, macaroni and cheese ...), one of your favorites."

"Sounds delicious, Mom," I'd say. "Save me some for later? I promise I won't be long," torn by the thought she'd be lonely without me, "forgetting" my mounting resentment toward her. If she'd permitted me to invite my friends to my room, insisted my dad patch that hole in my ceiling, I might have wanted to spend more time at home.

This reluctance to own and share unwanted feelings made the business of separating worse. In our family, the open expression of conflict was unheard of: strong feelings, negative ones, especially, largely unwelcome. Only my father was allowed to shout (although recently I'd been getting away with slamming an occasional drawer or door). Not because no one cared. We believed stifling our feelings essential to harmony. Consequently, despite that my mom was good natured, someone I usually liked being around—I could brush her hair and cry on her shoulder, curl up with her on the sofa to watch a soap opera—emotional intimacy was a foreign substance, along the lines of an allergen. As my body started to change, I became awkward even with her. She hadn't broached the subject of buying me a bra, hadn't yet prepared me for getting my period.

Furthermore, our temperaments were different: hers, laid back and reticent with a tactless bent and lighthearted streak, and mine, touchy and thin skinned, according to her, but also perceptive, communicative, dreamy, and intense. Sometimes she'd dismiss me with a wave of the hand, as if she found me annoying or even taxing.

"You're too sensitive," she'd said, not long before she died, as I cringed and blushed when, in front of my sister, she plucked from a pile of laundry she was folding the bra I'd secretly bought for myself, holding it up, saying, "Look what we have here," attempting, I suppose, to assuage my discomfort.

As if I hadn't been embarrassed enough, skulking around the lingerie department, stealthily comparing labels, nabbing a "training bra" from the rack after dodging the saleswoman who'd tried to help. I'd meant to wash the bra myself to prevent such an incident from ever occurring.

Eventually her shiny, smoke-colored eyes, her singsong voice, and the sound of her warm body, bustling about the house, would coax me back into her orbit. In her presence, more than anyone's, I saw the world as safe. It's what a mother was; I knew nothing else, ever craving chunks of her that felt hidden from me. When she retreated inside herself, her face vacant, I felt shut out. Without a recipe for knowing and being known, I, in turn, hid chunks of myself from her—together they'd form a prayer that would go on ceaselessly even until now.

She was tired, discouraged, possibly even already sick. Her husband busy and, lately, drinking, her older children lagging in their development (some dropping out of school, others marrying often because they "had to"), her life was a disappointment she hadn't foreseen. She'd told me I was the one who'd make her proud. But how could I do so when she hardly knew me, rarely interacted with me in a way that helped me know myself? When she'd lacked the gumption to stand up to my dad, to set firm rules and limits with us, her children, such as, doling out an unequivocal "No," a list of chores, and a regular allowance? When, despite how elegantly she carried herself, how she got all gussied up to go out with my father, I sensed, deep down, she wasn't proud of herself?

At the hospital that morning, after a nurse invited us into my mother's room, drab, white, and windowless (due to overcrowding she'd been moved to the basement), we encircled her bed. My father, a slender man in his mid-fifties who walked with a slight limp and looked a bit like Henry Fonda, was wearing a suit. I'd like to think he was standing beside me, maybe even holding my hand, but what I remember is how he hung his head and slouched his typically straight back and angular shoulders, seeming to take up a great deal of space while crying, audibly, into his handkerchief.

I fastened my gaze to my mother's motionless face, her eyes and mouth, forever closed, sealing her into a futureless realm, a world in which I no longer existed. Her dark, formerly wavy hair, flattened against her skull, looked thinner and grayer than I remembered. Her body, small and withered, all but lost beneath the sheets.

Here the narrative breaks down and havoc takes over. In the nether part of my chest, someone mute keeps banging on something. It feels like protest: "No, no, no," and the louder it grows the more I wonder if I'm about to go mad. Does the banging girl want out so she can tear up the room? The notes I've written no longer make sense, and a gnawing in my stomach has spoiled my appetite. When I take myself out for a walk, it occurs to me: My mind both accepts and rejects what my body remembers. After more than four decades, how to process the raw bits of wordless experience?

☾

The morning my mother died, since my aunt, her only sister, had recently suffered a stroke, my uncle, an owlish-looking and bookish, priestly sort of man, drove to the hospital alone, toting along his rosary beads and offering to lead us in praying the rosary. Like water lapping against the chine of a boat, our voices rose and fell to the rhythm of prayer (*Holy Mary, Mother of God, pray for us sinners, now and at the hour of our death. Amen*), numbing my mind to the Cain it was raising.

Now I'm scratching my neck; now, loudly, clapping my hands. Now, I'm pounding my fist on my desk. Is the anger because my mother had died, because my hopes had been dashed, because we'd missed the chance to say good-bye? Because I felt helpless, had seen womanhood reduced to sickness and death, for all of these things? Or, is anger, in and of itself, an organizing feature of mental life?

As does a child to the tree on Christmas morning, I'd rushed to the hospital, expecting to find my mother there. Similarly, I'd fancied myself as a gift that would light up her face the moment she saw it. Over the past weeks, while she lay bedridden at home or in the hospital, quarantined, babbling and thrashing about until, at last, a team of nurses tied her down, I'd worried she'd begun to forget me. Yet it was I who, feeling cut loose and exhilaratingly free, had, at times, forgotten her. I'd pined for her, too, hours on end, terrified at the notion of living without her, uncertain if and when she'd ever come home.

She hadn't waited and I'd been so vulnerable, my heart galloping in front of me the entire way over. Then she was dead, and it was as if I'd been dropped or spilled, frantically wanting to clean up the mess. Hot and nauseous, shock waves reverberating through every nerve, I wondered how I'd face the future: a maze of cliffs and abysses that stretched out before me. Despite my resourcefulness, I wasn't equipped. Surely, there were rules I could memorize for navigating life, engraved in stone like the Ten Commandments.

If I'd had time, alone, with my mother's body, I might have caressed her face, reassured by its familiar contours, held in check by the seamlessness of her skin. I might have lain my head against her chest, even fallen to my knees, crying my heart out as if she could hear. I would have told her how much I needed her and how sorry I was for my selfish ways: running off to the pool at my father's bidding while she lay sick in bed, usually asleep or in a daze, and just last week, for stealing her jewelry to be the gypsy fortune-teller at our neighborhood fun fair. She'd caught me red-handed.

"You never help me," she'd said, waking up coherent, taking me aback. With my father—determined to make up for the times he'd ignored her—now constantly by her side, how could I have known she'd wanted my help?

Was it for snitching her jewelry that I'd blamed myself for my mother's death? For exceeding her, filling my purse with the spoils of victory? Or was I simply a thirteen-year-old girl who wanted to be grown up like her sister, her sisters-in-law and, yes, her mother? Who chose to feel like a thief, even a murderer, rather than a child at the mercy of the whims of chance?

Had I been able to, I would have wrestled back control from the indifferent universe, vowing to make everything up, including dawdling in my closet (despite that she was already dead) and my wicked thoughts and feelings; how they must have destroyed her. I would have pleaded with her to forgive me and begged her to stay. Then I might have fallen on top of her, as if her body were a vessel that would ferry me safely to wherever she was going.

After saying good-bye to our dead mother, we went to Mass at an old Gothic-style church—one of the three we'd visited each Holy Thursday. Throughout the service, my father wept. At the end, the pastor consoled us, then beckoned us to an outside grotto where, before a statue of the Blessed Virgin, we recited with him a second rosary. However, I'd had nothing to eat or drink all morning and wanted only to go home and be alone.

I half anticipated finding my mother there, the house cheerfully neat and airy, smelling of pancakes, bacon, and percolating coffee. As though she'd been home all along and, while we were gone, had risen from her sickbed like Lazarus from his tomb, washed and dressed and gone straight to the kitchen to cheer us up with a hearty breakfast.

When we entered the house, my father started to cry and, as he did the next few days whenever I walked by, pulled me close, draping his body over me as if I were a coatrack. He was sorry, he cried, that I'd lost my mother. I was sorry, too, not just for myself but for him as well. Yet he was heavy and suffocating and I wanted to throw him off, as Jesus must have wanted to lose his cross. Shouldn't I be leaning on him? When he sat down to phone everyone we knew, he broke down each time after saying the word "died."

My sister tells me that, for the longest time that day, she couldn't find me. Where else would I have been but lying on my bed, imagining my mother's warm body beneath me? My teenage hate, now miraculously eclipsed by love, had cast her into the fairest light, as the poet's love had Annabel Lee: nothing ever would "dissever my soul from the soul." Amazingly, death possessed a silver lining, transporting me to a peaceful place not unlike a mother's womb.

All afternoon, people arrived laden with food. Beer was poured, voices raised, and before long, we were having a party. Though never once did I see my father laughing. I sampled every cake on the table and helped myself to whatever I pleased. A wave of euphoria dispelled my grief, leading me to consider, as I had when she was sick: Maybe it wouldn't be so bad, after all, not to have a mother in the world.

Days later, my uncle, after signing my aunt out of the nursing home, came to the viewing with her on his arm. A figment of her former plump and jovial self, she wore a somber black dress and polished black "nun" shoes, her salt-and-pepper hair, as always, pinned in a bun on top of her head. I hadn't seen her in months, the flame of recognition guttering in the eyes so like my mom's. After they paused at the casket where my mother's body lay, arrayed in the rose-petal pink gown she'd worn that spring to my dad's inauguration as a Knight of Columbus, I heard my uncle say, "You know who this is, don't you, Anna? It's your little sister, Elizabeth."

"Elizabeth," she repeated, sounding it out, as would a child.

Overcome with dismay, I stole through a back door of the funeral home into the parking lot, where I plopped my head down and sobbed on the hood of a car, still radiating with the warmth of the afternoon sun.

I know what to write next, but it feels tantamount to lifting that car off the ground. How do I begin when, suddenly, I'm weak and somewhat giddy? I remember the episode; I've written about it a few times before, but today it wants to play hide-and-seek. Or am I the one who's playing the game?

The day my mother was released from the hospital, diagnosed with exhaustion, I was beside myself with excitement, the dream I'd spun from waiting and longing about to be realized by the happiest reunion. She was getting better; our lives would soon return to normal. Probably because no one, even a crystal-ball-reading fortune-teller, could have predicted the future, no one intervened on behalf of reality.

At the sound of my father's car in the driveway, I raced to the front porch, where I stood and held the screen door open. It was an intoxicating morning, the scent of freshly mown grass, mingled with the odor of vines and weeds, permeating the cooler, dry air, the nostalgic chorus of daily life wafting from our neighbors' houses and yards. When he cut the engine, however, the spinning world stopped breathlessly still.

Finally, just as the anticipation was proving insufferable, my father, who seemed to have been trying to rally my mother, got out of the car and went round to open the passenger door. After crouching down for another excruciatingly long time, he emerged with his arm wrapped securely about her. Her beige, flat "house shoes" shuffling as he nearly carried her up the walkway, onto the porch, past my raging body and stupefied face.

Once in the living room, having maneuvered her to the couch, my father sat my mother down before gingerly setting himself down beside her, her frame slumping into his, her head flopping onto his shoulder as if she were a rag doll (which, at that point, she may as well have been as far as I was concerned). She was wearing a two-piece, fern-colored, camouflage-like dress, its skirt twisted around her legs like a nightgown during a fitful sleep.

Standing a few feet away, I waited for her to acknowledge me, before saying, tentatively, "Hi, Mom," managing a convincing smile.

When she failed to respond, my father said, encouragingly, "You know who this is, don't you, Betty?"

The silence unbearable, he added, "It's Patsy." For my sake, I reckoned, more than hers.

"Patsy," she parroted, sounding like a two-year-old.

So bowled over I couldn't breathe, I staggered through the dining room and kitchen before plowing through the screen door onto the back porch—the stage on which I'd been known to dance and sing—where I expected to take an exceedingly deep breath. The need to inhale, both equal in force and opposite in direction of the urge to weep, made me feel I was choking to death. Something managed to shift the balance, and I made a horrible gasping sound before bursting into violent sobs. My face in my hands, I crumpled to my knees, lamenting over and over, "She didn't know my name. How could my mother not know my name?"

I was kind enough to my mother after that, though my shattered heart had petrified, and I went about life in a detached sort of way. At least until a week or so later, when she had a convulsion, and my father and brother whisked her off to the emergency room. I arrived home to an empty house—I'd been at the pool with my friends, practicing the back dive, and no one had bothered to leave me a note. Panicked, I darted up and down the stairs yelping, "Mom, Mom? I can't find my mother. Where in the world can I find my mother?" What happened next I don't remember: if my father called, if it dawned on me to call my sister or look up Fitzgerald Mercy Hospital in the yellow pages. Things, eventually, settling back down before I relapsed into my dispassionate state, at least until the morning the telephone rang, and I wanted her back in a desperate way.

Why don't I remember crying after my mother died—other than on seeing my aunt at the viewing? Because, for me, the real day she died was that day on the back porch, when I sank to the ground as my world imploded. The day I understood I'd lost her for good. The day I declared myself a woman, setting "my face like flint," swearing like one of God's fallen angels, "I don't need a mother anymore. If I never need anyone again, no one will ever be able to hurt me."

At my mother's Requiem Mass, I wore the white patent-leather French heels, the garter belt and stockings, and the orange-Creamsicle-colored dress I'd worn for Easter, the covered buttons down the bodice matching the orange-checked collar and cuffs. At the conclusion of the service, while the organist played the "Tantum Ergo," I watched the women from our neighborhood dab tears from their eyes as we processed down the aisle behind the pallbearers, five of them my mother's sons.

The sight of these mothers weeping penetrated the fog through which I still don't remember the cloth-covered coffin decked in roses, the celebrant who'd read, eulogized, incanted, and prayed, sprinkling holy water upon our heads, or even my self-consciousness as I thought, ironically: *Now that I'm a motherless child, maybe everyone will come to love me.*

Curtis Smith

Illusion

The summer of her mother's illness, the girl often accompanied her father to the studio. *Have you seen Ann-Margret?* her friends asked. *Or Raquel or Brando?* Not Ann-Margret or Raquel, the girl replied, and Brando was rumored to be drying out in Palm Springs. But she had seen Audrey Hepburn, her long legs and tight Capris, her wide eyes masked behind square sunglasses. And she'd seen Cyd Charisse and Julie Andrews and Davy Jones. *Davy Jones!* her friends sighed, clutching each other, a pantomime of swoons. The girl didn't say these encounters were only glimpses, the stars often lost within the swirl of their entourages. She didn't tell them she stood taller than Davy Jones or about the paleness of his cheeks.

Morning, and she sat beside her father in the pickup. The radio on, the two of them quiet for the traffic report, and in time, her father allowed her to make the call—Melrose or the Santa Monica. They shared the road with delivery trucks, the newspapers dropped in heavy bundles, the fruit fresh from the valley. Her father pointed out the houses of stars from the old days, the handsome faces who'd floundered in the world of talkies, others who'd sunk into scandal and disgrace. The gardeners already at work on the wide lawns. Men with brown skin, the houses' histories unimportant to their tasks, their thoughts in the moment, the flowers they planted, the arcing streams cast from their sprinklers. Another perfect day.

Her father swore the sun was different here, a passing through a prism tinted by desert and sea. He paused to admire things the girl took for granted—the ocean's scent on the night breeze, the reach of eighty-foot palms. When he spoke of these wonders, the girl imagined him as a boy, the handful of fading black-and-white photos that had survived the trip west, the sidewalks of Philadelphia and not a blade of grass to be seen. A wave through the studio gates, the guards she soon knew by name, a tip of a hat, "Morning, little lady." Speed bumps inside, and with each, the rattle of tools in the truck's bed. Back east, her father had learned his trade framing houses, the staked-out streets of Levittown, the claiming of grassland and pastures. At the studio, he constructed three-walled rooms on air-conditioned sets. Once, the girl asked if he missed making things that were real. He smiled. "And who's to say they're not real?"

Her father procured a visitor's badge, her name misspelled, but she didn't mind. With the badge pinned to her blouse, the girl roamed the lot, the labyrinth of offices and bungalows falling into order a bit more each day. She saw Frederic March kissing a girl young enough to be his granddaughter. She laughed at a clan of loincloth-clad cavemen playing poker in the shade of an elderberry tree. She fancied herself invisible, and perhaps she was, a child among so many adults, her steps carrying her at a different speed than the lot's bustle. Emboldened, she snuck onto soundstages and discovered if she folded herself into the shadows and acted as if she had a right to be there, no one said a word. Here, she witnessed the mechanics of illusion. The false suns and painted forests. The snowflakes that never melted. The actors' luxury of having a second chance to speak their hearts.

The girl and her father met outside the commissary for lunch. "Sorry, sorry," he'd say, for he was often late, his breath short from his hurry, his tool belt jangling, paint splatters on his boots. The girl assured him she didn't mind, which was true. She had the sunshine after all, and the company of so many interesting people. Trays in hand, the girl and her father entered a dining area as long as a soundstage. Tall windows blurred the boundary between outside and in. Fans turned beneath the ceiling, the chatter of hundreds rising then descending in a murmur bright and hollow. They had a favorite table, a corner space beneath one of the windows, the tumbling sunshine captured in their water glasses, rainbows on their trays. Sometimes the girl asked her father to retell the story of how he'd met her mother at this very table. He smiled as he spoke, the tale always changing to keep his daughter entertained, new details about how his usually steady hands trembled as he approached the pretty extra dressed in a nun's habit. How she'd teased him about the sawdust in his hair.

Her studio summer. That's how she remembered those months. The lot's workaday whirl, the occasional star sighting, her drifting between soundstages, scenes that came to her like dreams within a dream. Yet the summer's most vivid memory is from a night at home. Rain, sheets of it, a ragged rhythm on the roof. The girl played with the TV's antenna, her mother in her robe. "There, baby." Her voice thinned and hardened like a stick whittled to its core. "That's perfect." Her father in bed, exhausted from his work on the lot and the chores at home his wife was too weak to finish. The girl and her mother staying up to watch the late movie. A film in which her mother was an extra, a face in the crowd, but in real life, a newlywed and, unknown to her, pregnant.

"It's just a few moments," the mother said. A smile, the pale skin that had once loved the sun. "Don't want you to be disappointed."

"I won't be." The girl curled close.

Her scene deep in the third reel. A love story, the female lead a woman the girl had passed on the lot. Her mother's age. The girl held her mother's thin hand and considered the expanse that separated the sick and the well. The girl asked questions—did she meet her new husband for lunch at the commissary? What was the director like? Was the costume designer the haggard woman who cursed in Russian between puffs of her Lucky Strikes? Outside, the rain, the streaked windows illuminated when the lightning cracked. The girl thought of the soundman's tricks, the imitations that shook her as much as the real thing.

"Here it comes," the mother said. A scene at a crowded train station. The lovers embracing. Would they ever see each other again?

"There!" The girl clutched the sleeve of her mother's robe. The heavy material, her mother always so cold these days.

The girl's mother in the background. Her face, yes, before her wasting. A fancy hat and a long coat. Her eyes on the train, a handkerchief waving in her hand. The leads bid their tearful farewells. The train pulls away. The girl laid her head on her mother's shoulder. Her mother dwindling, still waving as she fades beneath the smoke.

Shelly Weathers

Drafts

I owed my sick March to the bank men who used to be everywhere, waiting to corner stallers. They stood around in shirtsleeves and ties, looking friendly and familiar, like the kind of guys you'd want to know, but you don't. I've personally observed bank men who, seeing a woman watching her kids playing in the yard, would stop to ask for a drink of water on a hot day. As soon as the woman would go inside to get the water, they'd rip the air conditioner out of the front window of her house and run down the street with it while her kids all stood there, feeling like thieves.

I saw it when it happened to us. My mother chased them, arguing, throwing the glass of water at their feet, but they only stopped long enough to wave a paper so full of venom, it caused her arm to wither when she touched it. She could hardly hold her coffee cup or brush my hair after that.

In the fall, my mother, her one good arm working the wheel, maneuvered our dented, gray Impala into a dark corner of a cousin's garage where bank men could not find it the way they had so easily spotted our air conditioner. She begged coworkers for rides to the Woolco where she worked the registers, but all of my miles, school miles, were unaccounted for.

Once, she tried letting me walk. On my way home in the afternoon, I saw a man leaning against the stop sign on the corner of my street. He smiled at me. Debt isn't natural, so I smiled back. He smiled broader and broader until I thought his face would split and peel off his skull. He smiled while he followed me home, smiled while he stood outside for so long, my mother had to sneak through the alley and crouch behind the back porch until after dark. Even then, he stayed, smiling, lighting cigarette off cigarette, spilling orange ash all over the front stoop.

Eventually, my mother climbed through the bathroom window, clutching at the toilet tank for leverage, slithering over the tiles of the wall to the tiles of the floor. I thought she'd break her ribs, crush her hips, but she only pulled down the rolling blind and warped the brittle sill so it yawed to the left and shampoo bottles slid off its end in all the days to come. The draft it let in was my fault. I went back to being sick, if anyone asked. School called and got ugly about it, but they were too mild and counted for nothing against the bank men.

All of March, I watched television, which we owned outright, ate chips my mother brought home from extra Woolco picnic supplies. Displays have overages enough to feed a family if you don't mind pieces of things. A whole month, nearly two, drifted by while I ate chipped chips, slept in, flopped around, and coughed out loud for eavesdroppers. I grew so convincing at flu, some days, I didn't even stand up.

Close to May, my mother caught the car up with money she'd saved while we hid and ate overages, while I played flu. By then I was coughing in truth, having fainting fits, shaking when I tried to run or play. Nights, I soaked the sheets with sweat. She said it proved I could do something right, but I knew I owed it to the bank men, to their unwelcome smiles and their cigarette butts, still trampled down here and there about the edges of the yard like old, unpaid vouchers for so many ill wishes.

Matt Cashion

What to Do When Your Spouse Is Burning

Don't talk.

If you make the mistake of talking, don't say, "Well, this is typical."

Don't say, "Can you relax long enough for me to create a cost-benefit analysis spreadsheet on various resolution strategies that will ensure our highest rate of success in the most efficient manner?"

Don't say, "Hell. Where did I put that thing—the red thing that was lying on the floor of the utility closet for so long it had spiderwebs all over it and kept getting in the way of my slippers, the—what do you call it—red container-thing with the pull-pin thing on top that you pull out and spray that I tested on the hydrangeas fourteen years ago when I set them on fire, heroically determined to have properly working equipment for just such a time as this, though I've admitted it was foolish to burn the hydrangeas. I've apologized a hundred times for that. I'm big enough to say I was wrong on that one. But is the red thing in the garage? Next to the smoke detectors?"

Don't waste time, at *this* time, constructing a time-consuming apology.

Don't say, "I'm sorry I've been such an incendiary device lately. I truly am."

If you make the mistake of constructing an apology while your spouse is burning, do not water it down by attaching excuses. Furthermore, do not introduce language that deflects blame.

Don't say, "It's not my fault." Don't say, "I never learned the basics of fire prevention or fire suppression because my parental models ran for the hills and left me in fire-retardant pajamas that I stopped wearing when we got engaged."

Do not say, "I was too busy for the fifteen years we lived next door to Tim the firefighter/EMT to ask his advice on how best to help a spouse should s/he spontaneously combust. I fully intended to invite him over to build a bonfire out back, at which point I planned to hand him a beer and become best friends, quite a plausible plan had I had time to execute it."

Don't say, "I'd like to respectfully disagree that I have trouble making or keeping friends, which I would have proved once Tim and I built our bonfire and drank a beer and stared into it while I interviewed him on the fire-safety tips he shared with third-graders, although, honestly, one has to wonder whether Tim would even be a good best friend or whether he would offer credible advice because we know his wife was having an affair with the distilled-water delivery man *and* his own house caught fire seven summers ago from a clogged dryer vent (a hazard I inspected every Sunday morning on our own dryer, by the way, though I was too big to brag about it). And when the black smoke poured out of his bottom windows and you instructed me to "do something," my first thought was to call his cell phone, but then I pondered all the reasons (while you dialed 9-1-1) I'd never had the chance to trade numbers with him the way a good neighbor would. I never saw him. If I wasn't in my basement revising the blueprints for my time machine and if he wasn't working at the fire station, he was up early and out late putting fire-resistant shingles on all of his friends' roofs, or installing high-efficiency insulation at his mother's house, or he was visiting third-grade classrooms, and I was pretty busy myself, revising my blueprints, which, yes, I agree has taken too long, but you can't imagine the pace at which time machine technology continues to evolve, the details of which I stopped sharing when you stopped showing interest in my work fourteen and a half years ago. I also washed the dishes. Cooked a meatloaf. Got a vasectomy so I'd have more time for my time machine. Made the bed. Vacuumed. Very happy, mind you, to do those things for you/us, while you worked so hard at that job you hated so I'd have time to stay in the basement, very happy indeed, complaining only moderately I'd say, though I agree it was too much and not at all in proportion with the amount of complaint-worthy shit you suffered at that soul-deadening job with those toxic people, though one time, feeling so tender about your wasting your talents at that place that I was moved to tears, I dropped my pencil and came upstairs to say, 'I'm sorry. I'm sorry you have to work at that place, but very soon I'll take us away from here.' To which you replied, 'It burns my ass that you use the phrase "have to."' Which was not what I meant at all, I tried to say, but you were already smoldering, so I retreated to the basement and picked up my pencil and made this mental note: 'Make a physical note to look for the red thing with the pull-pin thing.'"

Do not say, "Shoo-wee."

Do not invoke your spouse's family and the potential role you think they may have played in making this event inevitable. Do not say, "You know, your father says your great-grandfather was pretty hot-tempered."

Do not—though you may now begin to see the severity of the situation and your role in creating conditions that have made it worse—offer your spouse a hug. You might take a long step forward and hold a painfully gruesome expression on your own face that reveals all the horror you feel at this moment and the devastating loneliness it portends, and you may extend your arms. Then think this: Is saving someone on fire like saving someone who's drowning? Doesn't one need to be sufficiently equipped and properly trained to prevent doubling the number of potential fatalities?

Do not say, "Do you think it's too late to salvage anything?"

Do not say, "Would you like to plant rutabaga in our winter garden?"

Do not obsess over calling yourself a failure while making endless comparisons to the quick-thinking actions of the kindhearted neighbor who will, just that second, appear. The quick-thinking, kindhearted neighbor will rush to the aid of your burning spouse, take the lead position in performing a deft-footed drop-and-roll learned in third grade, then offer a bottled water, an ear, a towel, a vodka tonic, a sincere note of empathy, complete agreement on the sorrowful state of the world and the trouble we have living in it, which creates such constantly flammable conditions. "I've been burned too," the quick-thinking, kindhearted neighbor will say. "Not much fun being burned. It's a wonder we're not all burning all the time." The quick-thinking, kindhearted neighbor, with a sexy light in his eyes, will offer to take your spouse swimming at a secluded spot he happens to know, available to heroes. First, the kind neighbor will insist on rest. He will say, "I'll pick you up if you recover," giving your spouse something to dream about. Then the quick-thinking, kindhearted neighbor will pull a guitar from his anus and strum while singing this: "I'm so sorry I cannot offer you a hug; it would only cause you pain."

While obsessing over this comparative view of yourself as a slow-thinking, coldhearted spouse, refrain from playing, for hours on end, with endless boxes of matches.

Seclude yourself and listen to your spouse's ghost. The ghost will say, "For fuck's sake, grow up and stop playing with matches. It's a pitiful self-pitying and pathetic ploy to cast yourself as a victim you hope someone will think worth dowsing. Force yourself to face a mirror."

Face a mirror.

Respect the mess you've made.

Forgive the fire; it is innocent.

Become best friends with Viktor E. Frankl.

Take time to shred those silly time machine blueprints you've wasted your life on.

Study the nervous system of the fruit fly. Study its aggression gene. There are many genes that play a furtive role, especially in males who compete for the attention of females.

Listen to your spouse's ghost long after you've grown deaf.

Listen to the ghost while you lose your hair, your muscle mass, your balance, your sense of smell, your teeth, your taste, your sight, your hippocampus.

Shake your head and say, "Good golly, miss Molly."

Stare at the ashes inside the urn you hope she would have liked and say good night, say good morning, say good afternoon, say good night.

Say, "Fine. I will turn my new work toward forgiving myself for giving you the final word."

Ace Boggess

Something Important

my mother says "don't write about me
write about something important"

which could mean torn limbs of children
after a bomb attack in Syria

or nature's stormtroopers battering coasts &
attacking through faulty tectonic plates

yet more likely invites some fiction
about the mysteries of blood

that will sell a million copies
like a hardback bible of these escapes from other torments

I once told her I was reading a Michael Connelly book
about a baby-raping cop killer &

she said "good maybe you'll learn something"
which she didn't mean the way it sounded

but as a comment on the economics of popular prose
what is something important enough to write about?

just fantasy sticking its tongue in the ear of finance?
what of wars? or else desires?

maybe it's the ensorcelling perfection of a sunrise
tranquility from fields of unblemished snow

she in silhouette between these things
walks outside to collect the daily paper

her breath crafts concrete poems in the air
for now I find this image is enough

Jason Olsen

Potato Chips

The diner complained about the potatoes;
the cook, tired of trying to please the public,
took the potatoes and threw
them back on his counter, thinking, *You son of a bitch,*
you want these potatoes cooked …,
and he put the potatoes, sliced thin—
ridiculously thin, aggressively thin—
into the fryer and, as the potatoes crisped,
beyond anything anyone had ever tried,
the cook stared at that customer through the slats
in the kitchen door, muttering, "I'll show him.
That bastard won't know what hit him."

Jo Brachman

Suspended

When I see cotton panties strung like prayer
flags on the clothesline, crayon colors
for each day of a little girl's week,
I send up a prayer for the girl
of my jackhammer youth,
who that first night at college forgot
her mother had sewn her name
into everything, thought the serenading boys
signaled a panty raid, who assumed the mind
she possessed was her own.
She tossed out a pair from the third-story
dorm window, not black lace, but new, heavy
cotton, not French cut, but hipster underpants,
her calling card, a surrender of fragile bravado
that first night on an Alabama campus.
The next day in the cafeteria, boys dangled
the pair, stretched the elastic, defined her shape.
She heard her name, afterwards, always
synonymous with the *Oh-no*-mistake,
like standing in front of every mirror in town
in ancient underwear, her feet
crammed into uncooperative heels,
her heart an obsessive suitcase packed tight
with important questions: Who will talk to me
about real things? What if my mother dies
too soon? When can I go home?
In her head, a grueling boxing match:

Suspended

a complex architecture of voices
yelled at the ring, where it looked like
there might be a death at the end,
and eventually, there was.

Hananah Zaheer

A Video Store Called Desire

My mother was a serious woman, suspicious of everything that did not go according to plan and, being a widow, frightened too. My father died in car accident a month after we left Pakistan and arrived in Kankakee, Illinois, leaving her alone to figure out a life different from what she had expected. Threatened by a culture that she was convinced would rob me of my innocence now that I had no male figure protecting me, she became my jailer.

She did this in the following way: Every morning she would call me the minute I left the room we shared at the Economy Inn where she was the front desk clerk. She called every five minutes after this, until I passed River Red Park, where she stayed on the phone for the entire minute-and-a-half it took to cross the green and I parked my '82 Chevy, bought for twelve hundred dollars from the inn manager, in the Kankakee Community college parking lot. She repeated this routine the second the clock hit two forty-five and punctuated my drive home with two-second repetitions of "OK?" meaning Are you OK? Are you driving carefully? Are any strangers following you? Did you talk to any guys?

I was never late, but she would test me occasionally anyway. She would skip her afternoon calls, and I would find her standing at the door of the inn. There was no way that she would have ever missed me from her seat at the front desk. I had to cross the parking lot and walk past the front office to reach the side stairs that led up to our room. Still, she would stand, lips pursed, a hand shading her eyes as if she was peering into a great distance, waiting for someone to return. She would look me up and down and, presumably satisfied, nod her head before heading back inside where she resumed her suspicious watch, in between reading passages from *Tess of the D'Urbervilles*, over guests that hovered by the coffee machine.

My mother loved words and teaching them and when her foreign qualifications failed to land her a job at local schools, I became her only student. She wrote ferociously, sending up to three letters a week to her family back in Pakistan. Often, she read me the contents of these, musings on what life might have been, had been, and what lessons she was drawing from her present circumstances. These included her plans too, for her and me—complex fantasies of life aimed mostly at success and a justification of the decision to migrate. Between her and the TV, which she turned on but rarely watched, our room was always filled with noise.

At work, however, she was quiet, often carrying out silent transactions with customers. She held herself in reserve, as if her words were only a privilege for those close to her. "Sure," she would say if anyone asked her to look up their reservation. "Thanks," when they took their keys and left.

I understood this. She was different people in different places. We were not unlike in that way, saving one side for each other, the other for the rest of the world, our real selves trapped somewhere in the middle.

I was not allowed to work. My mother believed that getting an education and then landing a professorship, like she had done in her previous life in Pakistan, was the only path out of the place fate had landed us in. This was also her scheme to keep me away from the outside world I knew. She oversaw this project with great dedication from her stool behind the front desk. I was expected to spend the afternoons with my books in the room behind the front office amidst paperwork and folded towels. Occasionally, if the afternoon was slow, she would ask me to take her place at the front while she threw stained bedsheets in the washer or sat on the plastic chair and rubbed her calves.

The way my mother worried about my character made me think I was in peril, that there was something wicked inside of me that might one day be released, like a genie from a bottle, and threaten the person that she was building with great care. The thought excited me. And in the few moments I had to myself at the front desk, I tested my powers. I practiced lifting my eyes slowly from the book in front of me when a guest approached the counter. I smiled only halfway, the way the women on the billboard on Route 52 did, mouths slightly open, eyes charged with something. Often my mother came back to the front and found some young inn guest, or the manager on duty, with a comb-over and a moustache, leaning on the counter asking me what it was I liked to do in my free time. This was cruel, I know, but I felt suffocated. I never went shopping with girlfriends. No one asked me to go to the movies or drive to Chicago for a concert because groups of young people always implied danger to my mother and she always said no. I was never even allowed to join any study groups because I couldn't leave the house once I returned unless it was in her company. I wondered if she would have been the same way had I been a boy.

Sometimes, in the afternoons, I didn't feel like studying and hung around the front, straightening the local attractions brochures that sat on a table near the entrance. Directly across from the front window of the inn office was a video store where Carla, my only friend, worked evenings. Junior, the night shift manager at the inn, also Carla's boyfriend, told me it used to be called Dee's Video Rental before Carla started working there. Now, there were several letters missing from the neon lit sign above the entrance, and the letters read, "DE 'S I RE."

My mother made the trip across the street to the video store on the occasional Friday afternoon to bring back movies, always two, and always something old that she considered appropriate and classic. She would go, seven dollars and the dog-eared video card in her hand, "stay" trailing behind her, implying that I was not allowed to take this as an opportunity to befriend anyone in her absence.

Once on a particularly busy Friday—there was an Indian wedding in town and the inn was crawling with guests who had driven in for the event—my mother was swamped with sorting out room keys and air conditioners that had stopped working and sent me across to rent the movies. *Gone with the Wind* and *Pride and Prejudice*. When I brought the movies up to the cash register, Carla was out, and an older man sat reading in a chair. He looked up at me through his glasses and smiled. I smiled back, a full one.

"Well, you must be Amal," he said and looked me up and down. "Give your mother lotta trouble, do you?"

I didn't know what to say. The man must have been more than sixty. Maybe even sixty-five. He had a hollow chest and fingers with skin that was cracked at the ends. His graying beard looked like it had grown because he had forgotten to shave one day, and then the day after that, and once it was on his face, had decided to just leave it there. It moved when he spoke, and he did so with great enthusiasm.

"It's a responsibility," he said. "Having a grown daughter. But I figure your mom is a smart woman."

I nodded my head. There was no arguing her intellect.

"She gave me this book to read." He held up a copy of *Great Expectations*.

I recognized the cracks in the spine, the tea stain on the front cover.

"I'm slow reading it, but that Estella ... lord."

I placed the movies on the counter and smiled again, not knowing what to say.

"Well, tell your mom Dee said hello." He rang up the movies and slipped them back across the counter.

"I will." I said and tried to smile again.

The idea that my mother had spoken about me to a stranger unnerved me. It made me feel like there was something about me, a secret that was sliding around in the world, something everyone knew but me, a big dark thing she might be afraid of. So much so that she, who liked her distance from the world, had felt the need to confess this to this man. Handful, he had said. I could imagine my mother saying that to him, tucking the wisps of her hair into the clip she wore, and something in me felt resistant. I did not like the idea of her sharing this intimacy with him.

The thought occurred to me that maybe, being her daughter, I was something like her. And if the reason she kept hiding me from everyone was so I wouldn't slip, like she had, with my words. I walked slowly toward the door, pretending to study the candy by the front.

I was almost there when Junior walked in, his eyes still heavy and swollen after a day's sleep.

"Carla here?" He asked Dee and from behind the counter, Dee shook his head without taking his eyes off the book.

"Can I use her account? We got a date tonight." Junior smirked at Dee, who gestured toward the store with his hand, meaning go ahead.

Junior gave me a quick wave and headed to the back wall where all the new releases were. I tucked the movies I was holding under my arm and pretended to look at the Westerns in the first row. I could see Junior's head, appearing and disappearing above the shelves as he read titles of movies, top to bottom. Slowly, I moved toward the middle of the store.

I met Junior as he was at the end of the last aisle, choosing between an action movie and a romance.

"Which one do you think?" He held both up to me.

I studied the covers for both. One had the close-up faces of two men facing each other, the ghost like image of a woman hovering between them. The title said *The Other Man*. The other one was *Hellboy II*, and a demonic-looking man stood against the backdrop of the horizon. I pointed to the first one.

"This, I think."

Junior groaned.

"Chick flick," he said. "Have you seen it?"

I shook my head, not wanting to admit that I would never be allowed.

"What are you watching?" He asked me, noticing the two cases I was clutching under my arm. I started to shake my head, but he reached out and, despite my protesting smack on his arm, slid them out.

"What the hell are these?" He laughed, looking at the titles.

I was torn between defending my mother's choices and wanting to join him in the disdain that he was offering.

"My mother likes them." I finally said.

"Ah." Junior leaned his head back like he understood and handed them back to me.

I thought I should leave. The visit across was already longer than I had intended, but Junior was studying me, his head cocked to a side.

"You know," he said finally, "these aren't the only movies Carla and I watch on date night."

I must have looked confused because he leaned in closer, like he was about to confess a secret, and said, "We watch some real action, too." And then he winked.

I had never noticed that his eyes were so black and from this close up. They looked like the kind of dark that can slide you inside it. They skipped around my face and left a trail of heat, resting, for a small moment, on my lips.

My heart beat faster. I was speechless and shy and, driven by some instinct I did not know I had, I bit my lip. At this Junior's eyes glinted, and he leaned back again, as if he had understood yet another thing.

"Wanna see?" he asked, although it sounded more like a statement than a question, and pointed behind him with his thumb. I didn't know what he meant, but he took me by the shoulders and walked me to the blue door at the end of the wall, across from the cash register where Dee had put the book down and now seemed to be staring out the window, head turned away. I had assumed this was just the back room, filled with paper and boxes of receipts, and maybe old tapes—a collection of things to sort, just like at the inn. But on closer look, I saw that the door said "18+ only."

Junior pressed against my back. "Let me show you."

But I was backing away and moving his hands off my shoulders.

"No thanks," I said, starting to move toward the front door.

"You are a good girl." The way he said it, it was both a question and a taunt.

"No," I said. "I don't feel like it. I have to get back."

I ran back across the road, not paying attention to the traffic, which was toward the heavier side at this time of day, which is to say a car went by every ten seconds or so. When I reached the entrance to the inn office, I turned to look back at the video store. Carla was just getting out of her car and waving excitedly at Junior who was standing just inside the door waving back. Dee was still behind the counter, and I could feel him looking at me. My breath was in disarray and, trying to maintain a calm for my mother who I knew was sure to ask questions, I turned and walked into the front office.

The manager on duty was at the desk, and I must have looked flushed because he said something about how I looked like I had been up to no good, something about the color of my skin.

"Where is my mom?" I asked him, my heart racing like I just run across a field.

He pointed to the back. I entered the small door at the side of the front desk and headed to the back room, but there he was standing in my way.

"Excuse me." I said, attempting the kind of firmness I had seen Carla use with the guys who, hoping for her attention, accosted her after class. My voice shook.

"Sure, darling." The manager looked me up and down and then walked to the computer, hands up in the air as if he was being held at gunpoint, but not before walking by me close enough that the front of his jeans brushed against my thigh. I walked into the back room and wished Carla was there.

☾

Carla knew her way around life. She lived in a two-bedroom close to Route 52 with her father and younger brother, and on nights when Junior was not working, stayed with him in his room at the inn. It was through her that I learned of all the perils out there in the world. She told me stories about her father and his girlfriends who came smelling of roses and alcohol and left in the morning, smeared and deflated. She slept with men and pulled me aside after calculus to give me details about what they did. Sometimes, she had issues with the men, too possessive, too violent, too distant, and she shared these with me too as we sat outside class, her smoking cigarettes, me high on her confidence. She snuck me copies of *Cosmopolitan* and *Glamour* and occasionally, when Junior wasn't looking, the occasional copy of his *Playboy*, which I hid behind my side of the headboard. I took these out only when I was alone and flipped through the pages, growing warm with envy at these women with absolute freedoms and shining skins.

Between her and my mother, I learned all there was to know about men and life, everything that was there to fear, and everything there was to celebrate. It was all theoretical knowledge, of course, and I had no real use for it. I did not have the boldness to move out from behind the front desk and run my hand up and down any man's arm, nor to display the goldenness of my skin to anyone. I went from home to school and back home.

One summer day I pulled into the parking lot at school in the morning, hung up the phone and an inexplicably sad feeling came over me as I watched groups of students making their way toward the buildings. Something about the ease with which they walked, arms swinging, saddened me. Carla, who was sitting on the curb smoking a cigarette, saw me and knocked at my car window, all energy and golden hair. She jumped into the car and made me drive her to the Taco Bell followed by the convenience mart and then to the River Red Park where we lay in the grass, the water flowing by us. She drank cheap wine and ate burritos and asked me about where I thought we would be in ten years. She told me about her dreams of being onstage in Chicago some day and, drunk on the sun, we both pretended that we would make it big.

"Don't forget me." I laughed and she laughed, too, her eyes sparkles.

"Never," she said. "Who could forget you?"

At nineteen, she was only a year older than I, but I was enamored with her life and her kindness in the way of a younger sister. She was confident and loud, and knew about men, which was like knowing everything. When I said I wished my father was still alive, she told me that I wasn't missing much. She said her father never even knew when she was around. He was depressed that his wife had left him, and drunk half the time, and so he may as well not have been there. That made me feel like we were the same, and I felt a lot better and a little indebted to her.

It was autumn now and the chill from the air seemed to have settled inside me as I sat in the back room and pretended to read. That day by the river had been hot, the grass pricking the backs of my legs, the air warm and the earth cool like it can only be in the summer. Carla, with her legs splayed out, her top lifted so the ring in her belly button glinted, wrapped her mouth around the end of the cigarette with a lazy ease. Had I known any better, I would have recognized it as being a sensual day. But I was just a girl on the outside of everything, held inside words and no action, with nowhere to go, not even sure how to make my place in the world, knowing nothing except the things she told me about: the taste of skin, the tremble of legs, the wetness and want, loneliness.

She told me, too, about Junior, and how he was different from the others she had been with. How he held her up against the wall and knelt in front of her and made her feel like the most important woman in the world.

"Do you love him?" I asked.

"Love him?" She laughed. "He makes me feel like magic," she said and closed her eyes, as if nothing more needed to be said.

I remembered seeing Junior at the inn before he and Carla became an item. He always entered the office just before seven, fresh from the shower, wet black hair combed back, yawning the remnants of sleep away from his dark eyes, ready to take over the night shift. Something in the way he walked reminded me of a jungle animal, perhaps a cheetah. It was the air of alertness about him, the way his body looked tense even when he settled himself on the stool behind the desk, hunching over and playing Tetris on his phone, as if he might spring into action any minute.

Sometimes he woke up earlier and walked across the road to see Carla. I envied him and how he managed to look so sure of himself as he stepped across the asphalt, dodging traffic, balancing caution with danger. I didn't know much about who I was or who I wanted to be, but I knew the knot I felt in my stomach when I watched him run across meant something.

When Carla introduced me to him, he shook my hand firmly and said how nice it was to meet me even though I had already seen him come in and out of his room at the inn. He asked me all the right questions and I could see why it was that Carla felt safe with him. He made me feel like I had all the answers, and laughed when I made a joke about both of us being nonpaying guests at the inn.

Junior was my neighbor, in the room right next to my mother and me. It was the exact replica of our room, the same brown-and-green-patterned bedcover, the same off-white curtains, the same maroon carpet. He had added to his room a radio and some colorful pillows, Carla's addition, I assumed, which I had seen whenever the cleaning ladies left the door ajar. We were hardly ever in our rooms at the same time. Junior spent the afternoons sleeping or with Carla while I was downstairs in the office. She often walked by, hair swinging, keys jangling in her hand, and waved at me through the glass of the front office before sprinting up the stairs. Even on the odd days when I was in my room in the afternoon, I could hear voices from across the wall, the slow steady squeak of the bed, or the bursts of sudden laughter.

That evening as I lay across my bed, flipping through the channels on the TV, I heard his door open and slam shut. Twice. My mother had not yet come upstairs and since this was an unusual time for him to be in his room, I turned off the TV and patted my hair into place before opening the door and sticking my head out.

He stood in the doorway, his hair askew, a cigarette dangling from his mouth. He was texting on his phone, and there was a frown of concentration on his forehead. When he saw me, he smiled, a quick hesitant pull of the lips, and went back to his phone.

"Hi." I said, not finding anything else to say.

With the sun glinting on my face, my eyes, which had been red and puffy earlier in the afternoon, must have looked awful because he didn't look up again but nodded instead.

"My mother is still downstairs." I said, stepping into the entrance so that my back was against the frame and I was holding the door open with my feet.

"I'll go down in a minute," he said, still not making eye contact.

Not finding anything else to say, I asked him where Carla was. At this, his face seemed to twitch.

"Her fucking dad," he mumbled.

"She left?" I asked.

"She left," he said and thrust his phone into his back pocket with some force. "I guess he needed her."

We both knew Carla's dad was trouble, and I didn't know what to say to this so, slowly, I slid out of the doorway until the door slid and clicked shut behind me. I leaned against it.

"My father is dead." I said. "Accident." This seemed like the right thing to say, something emotional, from the heart, to connect.

I wasn't sure if he heard me, but he shook his head and said, "Poor little girl. Poor, poor, little girl."

This encouraged me. I felt that he was being friendly and familiar, and the way he was looking out at the parking lot, head tilted to the side, made me feel like something was going to happen, although I did not know what and the thought excited me.

"So you watch a lot of movies?"

He shook his head. "Not really," he said. "It's Carla's thing. She's obsessed." Then, he squinted at me. "You? You like movies?"

I shrugged. I did not know what I liked and what I was allowed to like and the distance between the two confused me. I had been alone all afternoon and feeling an ache that had not disappeared since I had thrown myself on the bed a few hours earlier. At that moment I probably would have said I liked anything.

"You want to come in for a while?" he asked. "Till your mom comes back."

His offer felt like a small victory of some sort, and I nodded my head. He held the door open, and as I bent my head to slide under his outstretched arm into his room, I could smell him, the smell of earth and sweat and soap.

He followed me inside and closed the door. I had never been in a room alone with anyone but my mother and father and the realization that I was here—in a new place, with a man who knew how to make magic—was exhilarating. I felt my legs weaken and sat down at the foot of his bed, holding my hands under my legs to keep them from shaking. He lifted a beer out of the small fridge in the corner and pointed it at me. I nodded my head. It seemed like the right thing to do. He popped the top open, threw it at the trash can in the corner, missing it by a few inches, and handed me the bottle. The liquid tasted bland and bitter at the same time, and I took a few gulps, hoping that if I drank it faster, I would not have to taste it.

"Whoa." Junior said. "First time, right? Slow down."

I placed the bottle between my knees. It was cold and wet, and I rubbed my hands against my jeans. Across from me the TV sat on top of the dresser, the picture on it frozen. It looked something like an ear or a side of a face.

"Which one were you watching?" I asked him.

Junior, who had been leaning against the dresser, taking sips of his beer and watching me, smirked.

"Just a movie," he said. And the way he smiled at me made something thump inside of me.

"I want to see," I said.

Junior looked at me for a long time, and I met his look even though I could feel the blood burning in my cheeks. I expected this to make me look like Carla, bold and present. When he didn't move, I reached over and hit the play button and suddenly the screen was a jumble of arms and legs and skin and tongue and body parts that I had never before seen this up close. There was moaning, too—and *Oh yeah, oh yeah*—and even though I knew my eyes had opened wider and I was breathing shallow, I could not take my eyes away, even as Junior stood where he was, watching me.

I looked back at him. He stood against the wall, quiet. My skin burned and I felt a pull between us, as if in the air, inside me, there was suddenly something alive.

I put the beer down and stood up in front of Junior. I was not yet sure what it was that I expected to happen, but I knew that Carla had said he was magic. When he didn't move, I leaned in toward him, trying to find his mouth with mine. The touch, when it came, stung my lips, the feel traveling across my skin until I could feel my entire body buzzing. The idea that this is what my mother knew about and had been protecting me from set fire to my blood. My body moved in toward him in a way I had never considered, and I thought that I suddenly knew what to do, that he really did have magic. I felt both powerful and weak, and pressed against him, my fingers searching for his skin, breath in disarray, my focus on nothing but the desire for more.

When his hands touched my shoulders, I held my breath. Something was raging inside me now, and I knew he could recognize it. I smiled. But he did not go any further and held me that way for a while.

"Go home, Amal."

I opened my eyes. Neither of us said anything, but I could see that whatever had been flashing between us a few moments ago was gone.

He reached past me and turned the video off. I stood, not sure what to do, even though part of me saw that the streetlights outside had turned on and were shining brightly over the parking lot. I caught my reflection in the mirror above the dresser and was surprised to see that I looked no different. It was the same face, the same lips, the same hair that fell in disarray over my shoulders.

But that was not how I felt. Inside, I felt weak and aware at the same time, and like I had contracted a disease, and that it was now traveling through my veins, making my skin throb. The fever showed nowhere but in my eyes and looking back at them, I felt what my mother must have felt for me: afraid. I hurried out of the room and to my door, trying to steady myself before placing my hand on the knob. From inside, I could hear the sounds of the TV, which meant my mother was inside. I felt awful and certain that she would able to see the sickness in my eyes and tried to think of an excuse as I looked in through the window.

When my mother saw me, she stopped drying her hair with the towel and stared at me.

She was suspicious, as she always was, but as she stood staring at me, I knew that she was someone else, too, just like me, not just connected to me, but a woman with a life and conversations that I did not have access to.

"I went for a walk." I said and as she studied my face, it seemed that she was assessing me, too, recognizing something.

"You OK?" Meaning was I still who she expected me to be?

I nodded and walked over to her. She touched my hair, a gesture from my childhood, and ran a finger along my cheek. Then, putting her towel on the bed, she pulled me toward her and even though I knew she was smelling me, trying to discover what I hid, I held her and said nothing at all.

William Trowbridge

I'm Rubber, You're Glue …

In third grade, after an all-school convocation,
we saw the puddle in the contoured chair seat,
left by Dorothy Smith, whose name I've changed.

She'd been escorted out like someone
crippled, bereaved, or contagious. Maybe
she was ill, but I, who barely knew her,

turned her into those soppy pants, coining
"Damp Dorothy," which stuck and made her cry,
grade school miniature of "Wrong Way" Riegels,

whose Rose Bowl blunder lost the game
for Cal, or Ethelred "The Unready," doomed
to be the comic note in the Doomsday Book,

not to mention Slovenia's Vinko Bogataj,
Mr. "Agony-of-Defeat,"whose mega-ski-crash
opened *Wide World of Sports* each Sunday

for two decades. May Dorothy's trial have turned,
somehow by now, sweet as Vinko's, whose fall
bought a ticket to America for a week

of *Wide World*'s twenieth jubilee—Ali asking
for his autograph. I like to see it this way:
after high school, Dorothy, alone at a party,

on her third Black Russian, recounts
the seat-puddle mishap, and the little jerk
who nicknamed her, ending with a quiet laugh

that charms a charming guy so much
they end up married in a neighborhood where
she's treasured as just plain, well, Dorothy.

David Ebenbach

Nice All Day

I decided I was going to be nice
all day. I started with my neighbor—
Happy birthday! I said as she
came out of her apartment door.
It wasn't her birthday, but birthdays
are nice. She stood partway in and
partway out, holding her keys as I
went outside, and there was another
neighbor coming in, so I took his bags
in my hands and carried them across
the street that I was crossing, and
left them neat by his car.

I went to work, where I was nice
all day—I Xeroxed everything
I found on anyone's desk and
piled them up in neat, stapled piles;
I poured mugs of coffee until
every surface of the break room was
coffee. I have to say it felt great.
After I polished all the monitors and
sang jolly good fellow a few times, I
left to grab the bus, where I
gave everyone passenger safety tips.
You don't have a seat belt, but
you can still be ready. I stood
in the aisle and they watched me so
carefully. I could feel it: Around me

was a blue glow, a silence that
spread. It was like applause, but
silent.

Allegra Hyde

Chevalier

Edith Eleanor Watts, who everyone called Eddy, hit her head when she fell off the radio tower, after climbing eight rungs high to impress Lyle Baxter II.

The swelling started immediately.

So did Eddy's inquests.

"Was Lyle watching?" she asked, as we loaded her into the back seat of my Buick. "Did he look concerned?"

Trixie Everheart pressed an ice cream sandwich against Eddy's forehead, proclaiming Lyle's paleness post-fall to be a sign of affection.

"He always looks pale," I said, but no one took any notice. Everything was already decided: Lyle's complexion offered irrefutable evidence. He would ask her out. Tomorrow maybe—or the day after. Once he'd had time to regain composure.

A week passed, with no word from Lyle. Eddy's forehead, however, continued transforming—bulging—as if an egg were lodged in the center of her brow, and that egg were *hell-bent* on hatching. She kept her good looks, otherwise. Slim as stretched chewing gum, with brown hair blessed by a magazine sheen, and eyes like cracked geodes: full of crystals, depending on the light.

Her prettiness, though, made the swelling more conspicuous. An ugly person might have hid the disfigurement better.

Not that Eddy cared. She wore the swelling like a trophy. Told anyone who'd listen that she earned the lump by soaring through space for her One True Love.

I thought she'd earned it by being an idiot.

But as usual, I kept quiet.

"You should join a traveling circus," said Albert Hotchkins, who liked Eddy but pretended he didn't.

"Shut up, Albert," said Trixie, who pretended she did. "Eddy looks foxy hot."

It was Friday night in Chevalier, and like most of the town's youth population, we'd wound up at the bowling alley. Albert sipped his cream soda and offered it to Eddy. Eddy had her own, but she accepted his beverage anyway. Drained it in a single swig.

"You consider seeing a physician?" I asked, unable to ignore her distended brow. "It looks like it really hurts."

You would have thought I'd brought up tax brackets, or fungal growth rates, or the dissolution of the former Yugoslavia, the way Eddy rolled her eyes. "Are we going to start bowling soon or what?" she said to the others. "Lyle might show up any minute."

Eddy, Trixie, and Albert trooped off to rent bowling shoes, but I stayed sitting. I'd always been the nice one in the group—a title I held with some pride—but I'd been growing increasingly fed up with Eddy, same as I'd been getting sick of cream soda and listening to the Abba tracks my mother played every night during dinner. Of course, I could suffer the soda and even respect the way my mother had been deliberately driving my father insane the past five years, but I couldn't stand being treated like a doormat.

Especially by a friend. A close friend. A twelve-years-and-counting friend.

"Another strike!" exclaimed Eddy, and I saw Trixie give the signal for *boy-alert*: an alternating eyebrow lift. Lyle had arrived.

It wasn't Eddy's turn yet, but she plucked a bowling ball from Albert's hands and blitzed another ten pins.

Lyle squinted towards her, his hand on the lever of an arcade game.

Trixie's eyebrows began rapid-fire twitching.

And I stayed watching, feeling like a lost planet—like Pluto—orbiting the outskirts of a solar system that I maybe wanted part of. Maybe not.

It wasn't always like this. In fact, it wasn't even so long ago that Eddy cried to me in the submarine darkness of a routine sleepover. "Camilla?" she whispered, her voice fluttering like a trapped bird. "You awake? I really gotta tell you something."

I was awake. Bunked on the pullout couch in my family's den, I'd been listening to Trixie's chain saw snore and contemplating putting her bra in the freezer.

"It's a secret," Eddy added.

In those days, secrets came a dime a dozen—our incumbent crushes, the location of an older sister's nail polish. They were the currency of friendship, and Eddy liked to spend.

Still, a secret was a secret.

"I'm listening," I said.

Eddy's sleeping bag rustled in the pitch black. "I get this dream," she began. "I go totally invisible and everyone keeps walking by me, even when I yell and stuff."

She paused, as if struggling to describe something too horrible for words.

"I mean *everyone*," she repeated. "My mom, your mom, Trixie. Even Trixie's dog. Then I disappear."

The dream didn't seem like that big a deal. I'd had far worse involving my grandmother's collectible forks. But then Eddy's hand fumbled through quilts, clutching mine. She seemed genuinely spooked.

"That'll never happen," I assured her, in what I considered a grown-up voice: solemn and unflustered. "You'll never be invisible."

"You promise?"

I promised. In retrospect, I probably would have promised anything. While it seemed highly unlikely that Eddy would ever be ignored—by me, or anyone—I firmly believed that what one asked of friends wasn't supposed to make sense. Love wasn't.

"I promise," I told her, "forever and always."

Two weeks after the radio tower incident, Eddy's forehead had swollen to unprecedented proportions. So had her efforts to attract Lyle. We spent most nights, now, staking out his place of employment: Pisa Pizza. That, or calling his house.

I decided to write Eddy a letter detailing my concerns for her, for us. And I would have given it to her. Really. I brought the letter to school, was about to hand it over during third-period English. But then—right as our teacher, Mr. Stiegler, started jawing on the *Epic of Gilgamesh*—the lump on Eddie's brow made a hissing pop and split open.

"Oh my god," I whispered. "You OK?"

Eddy patted her forehead. "Honestly," she said, "it just feels like a giant zit."

Trixie laughed so hard she almost choked on the pencil she'd been chewing. Mr. Stiegler's bald head swiveled towards the back of the room, and I'm sure he wanted to say something smooth, like, "Just what's so funny about an unsuccessful quest for immortality?" But high school girls had a way of making him blush. Instead, he tugged at the collar of his own shirt, shushed, "Ladies, page twenty-three, please."

I noticed a bit of bone poking from Eddy's brow. A white nub, like an extra knuckle. "Maybe you should go to the nurse," I said.

Eddy ignored me, flipped through *Gilgamesh* without looking at the pages.

"Holy!" Trixie gripped her desk as if she'd just beheld the Second Coming. "Lyle just walked by the door. He's wearing argyle. That's an enterprising pattern."

Eddy nodded. "He's gonna ask me out today," she said. "I know it."

Lyle did not ask Eddy out. By sixth period he had not even said hello, despite multiple opportunities orchestrated in front of his locker. Eddy's forehead, however, had further evolved: the bony nub lengthened, stretched skyward as a narrow, pearly spiral, about six inches long and gleaming. A horn.

"It's like something you'd see on a mythical creature," said Trixie, as we crouched under the bleachers during gym class. "Like a unicorn."

I could tell Trixie was impressed, borderline jealous. She wasn't very good at hiding that sort of thing.

"Unicorns aren't real," said Albert.

No one ever invited Albert, but he had a way of showing up in conversations.

"They're about done with laps," I said. Peering through the opening of the bleachers, I could see the other kids bent double over knees, tongues lolling, eyes blank as chicken broth. I'd been watching them to avoid looking at Eddy, about whom I wasn't sure what to feel. She looked both ridiculous and magnificent.

Eddy, clearly, saw herself on the *magnificent* end of the spectrum. Strolling in among her winded peers, she said, "Anyone wanna race? I'm not even sweating."

I think she was expecting to cause quite a stir—and she certainly did collect a few curious stares, probably grounded in her ability to skip laps again—but then a red-faced kid projectile-vomited a neon green stream and passed out on a gymnastics mat.

"That's the coolest thing I've ever seen," exclaimed Lyle, who'd faked chest pains to sit out of class. He was not looking at Eddy.

The bell rang. Eddy toe-kicked a dodgeball across the room.

"Let's go, Camilla," said Trixie, tugging me out from under the bleachers. "Quit looking so smug."

So now Eddy had a genuine horn protruding from her forehead: hard as steel, beautiful as a narwhal nose. No one took much notice, naturally. Chevalier had its fair share of freaks and celebrities. Hell! We were the birthplace of the great running back Bobby Chanel and quilting champion Denise Dann. We had a guy with no arms who owned an antique store, and a couple of lesbians living on Abbott Street.

What was a girl with a horn to most people?

"You know, honey," said Eddy's mother, who was the only one to take any real interest, "horns aren't exactly the rage these days. Are you sure you want to keep it? I mean, do you even like it?"

"No," said Eddy. "Yes."

Trixie told Eddy that she'd heard Lyle thought it was fake. Eddy said she didn't really care what Lyle thought anymore. He was a bit of a bore, wasn't he? She wanted someone or something with a little more tooth.

"I've been thinking," she said one night, as we browsed the whoopie pies at Speedies' GasMart. "I might go somewhere."

Her words filled me with a fountain of hope. "What about Beauford?" I said, remembering our past trips to the neighboring town to see firework shows on weekends.

"Get real, Cam." Eddy inspected her reflection in a beverage cooler: the wet glint of lip gloss and an opalescent horn superimposed over Bud Lights for $6.89. "I mean *go somewhere* go somewhere. Like leave town for good."

I almost laughed. Then I realized she was serious. For all Eddy's caprice, hadn't she always at least been original? Everyone talked about leaving Chevalier. The idea was so formulaic it made me nauseous; people generally planned to go west, to California, where weed was speculated to be legal and workweeks four hours long. Or they talked about Europe, especially the guys who studied French and used *très magnifique* to describe their girlfriends. But hardly anyone actually left, or if they did it wasn't for long. What else was out there, really? Lonely nights? Lonelier days?

Chevalier could be boring, but that's why we had each other.

"I'm thinking maybe New York," continued Eddy, her thin fingers pinching a whoopie pie, as if testing the idea.

For such a seasoned performer she wasn't much of a liar—she'd obviously been considering this for a while—which felt like another slap in the face.

"We have these," said Albert, pointing to a display of road maps by the register.

Eddy selected a map, used it to fan herself. "Make me a purple slushy," she said.

The map was only good as far as Connecticut, but I decided she could figure that out herself if she was really so keen on the plan.

"Red is better," said Albert.

"Shut up, Albert," said Trixie. "No one cares what you think."

(

Trixie married Albert five years later. They had an "open concept" wedding—Trixie's idea, since she ended up studying interior design—and pretty much the whole town showed up. Even Denise Dann and Bobby Chanel's younger brother.

If I had to guess, Eddy was only invited to stroke Trixie's matrimonial ego. No one actually expected her to come. She damn well did, though: unfurling from a taxi ten minutes into the service. Black heels clacking over the minister's drone. Everyone seated on Albert's parents' front lawn ignored her—even Albert's mother, Mrs. Hotchkins, kept her eyes trained on Trixie's bouquet—but the effort was the stuff of heroics. It was one thing arriving late to important occasions, but quite another to take a cab. If you needed a ride in Chevalier, you called Patty "Jesus Saved Me From Cigarettes" Labash. Or, you called one of your friends.

But I suppose Eddy didn't have those anymore.

After the service, I hunkered down on the Hotchkins' screened porch. While I'd gained a bit of a reputation as a storyteller—

specializing in elaboration—that night, I wasn't feeling too talkative. Instead, I watched Eddy drift across the lawn like a loose newspaper page. No one said much to her, or if they did, it wasn't about her unusual choice in transportation, much less her five-year absence. Chevalierians are far too polite to bad-mouth someone to their face. Most folks went on ignoring her the same way she'd ignored us. We're a proud bunch; I'll give us that. Even when someone noticed her horn was missing, she was only asked if she'd met anyone famous in New York.

"I work in retail," she said, as if that meant something.

From the way Trixie carried on, one might have assumed she was too preoccupied by her nuptials to notice Eddy. But Trixie had seen her immediately. She was, like the rest of us, only doing her best to avoid the obvious: Eddy had been gone for years, she was a giantess in her heels, and Albert was clearly still in love with her. Even when Trixie eventually did swish over—cheeks flushed from champagne, and a bit of frosting smeared across her upper lip—she only said, "Lyle got pretty fat, didn't he?" and whisked away before Eddy could answer.

I kind of felt bad, in spite of myself.

Still, I remained in my screen porch hideout. History hung heavy in the air, brought on by dusk and the cinder-smoke of a char-grill, or perhaps by the rueful whine of an adolescent band, it clotted conversation, made even the mosquitoes drowsy with memory. A droopy-eyed woman mused on her first kiss: tongues gone xylophonic across teeth. A bearded man recalled working as a bag boy at the Phyllis N' Sons Grocery Store. I thought about the day Eddy left: how she'd caught a ride with some vacuum salesmen, the same day we were supposed to move in together. "Don't be mad, Cam," she'd called, leaning out the truck window, her horn glinting in the sun. "There's nothing here for me."

"I'm here," I'd answered, but only when she was out of earshot, my voice muffled by the exhaust fume wake.

I'm here. I said it to myself still, having made a point of staying in Chevalier, having made a life of it.

I'm here. Had it been worth it? Rather than answering my own question, I turned to the others on the screen porch, asked them what they made of Eddy's missing horn.

"Bet she sold it," said Albert, who couldn't find anyone else to hang out with, even at his own wedding. "Probably to a Chinese medicine shop or something." He peeled off a layer of sweaty tuxedo. "Rent's real high in New York. I've seen a movie about it."

From across the lawn, Trixie's laugh rang like jangling keys. Then someone suggested that maybe Eddy's horn had just fallen off. We don't consider ourselves intellectuals in Chevalier—in fact, we deny the title, given the chance—but we're not entirely unread. Even then, we knew that sort of thing happened.

"I still say it was fake," said Lyle, who hadn't gotten any cake and was cranky.

I got the real story, though. You might even call it the play-by-play. It was after the wedding, which stretched into the dingy part of the evening, long enough for the citronella candles to burn down and for Denise Dann to vomit in the birdbath and the town's teenagers to sneak off with the extra booze. There were loud good-byes from the newlyweds, whistles from a few guests, and the rattle of soup cans dragged behind Albert's parents' car. As far as I could tell, Eddy was gone, too.

I felt foolish. I might have at least said hello.

Then Mrs. Hotchkins hollered for help cleaning up, and everyone suddenly remembered a commitment to bedtimes. Guests stumbled into hydrangeas and foldout tables, looking for their shoes or an extra crab cake to take home. That's when I saw Eddy. She was on the move: striding across the lawn, high heels puncturing the grass. She was heading towards Mr. Stiegler, our old English teacher. She was smiling a big lipsticked smile—the first hint of happiness she'd shown all evening—and when she threw open her arms for a hug, I thought their reunion was rather sweet.

Then she held on too long.

I scanned the departing crowd for a reaction: for furrowed brows and tongues clucking. For Mrs. Hotchkin's shrill voice asking, "Who does that girl think she is?"

But no one said anything. It was as if I was the only one who noticed her.

Eddy unlaced herself from Mr. Stiegler and began twirling a strand of hair with one finger, the other hand on her hip. She giggled.

And still guests drifted away, oblivious, their shadows soaked up by the night. A tipsy Mrs. Hotchkins directed Trixie's brothers in the art of table-carrying.

Eddy stroked Mr. Stiegler's head, as Mr. Stiegler, bewildered, tried to explain something. She held a finger to her lips. She did not seem drunk, but rather steely and determined. She took his hands in hers.

"Eddy!"

Before I could stop myself, I was darting through the screen porch door and running towards Eddy, not sure what I was going to do, but certain that something needed doing.

"Oh, hello, Camilla," said Eddy, as if my panting appearance were the most natural thing in the world. "I was just chatting with—."

Mr. Stiegler, though, had already dodged away.

We ended up driving to the radio tower. Nothing in town was open that late, and it was too early to drive home, but for some reason I thought Eddy might want to see it. A fence had been installed in the past year, which we could have climbed if we'd wanted. Neither of us did. Instead, we sat on the hood of my car and looked towards downtown Chevalier: a low valley and a scrubby hayfield away.

Eddy didn't have much to say, so I did most of the talking. At first I tried to be terse and distant, but my words trickled into a torrent. I told her about my job at the primary school. About my parents' divorce. About the spring rainstorms and the flooding and how Pisa Pizza had closed from the damage. I told her how Albert courted Trixie: Once, he left a bouquet of chocolate roses in her car, but it was a hot day so they melted. I told her that while I still hadn't met the right man, I tried not to worry. There weren't too many options in Chevalier, were there? "Besides Lyle."

Eddy didn't laugh. "You're serious?" she said. "Pisa Pizza is gone?"

The focus of her attention irritated me. I considered mentioning Mr. Stiegler. *What? No other men in New York?* The question wriggled in my grasp, slick and ugly as a bullfrog.

"What? No other pizza in New York?" I said instead.

Behind us, the radio tower creaked, as if stretching awake in the night breeze. I remembered how years ago we'd carved our initials along the railing: *CAL+EEW.* Trixie hadn't carved hers because she'd been scared of the police. Albert had cut open his thumb.

"I suppose you want to hear about the city," said Eddy, yawning.

I didn't like the way she offered—as if I'd been begging—and yet there it was, that dark, sparkling thing: the answer to the question that had followed me those past five years. What *had* she left for? What had been so good that she hadn't come back?

"I guess so," I said.

Eddy drew in a breath, as if drawing in energy, sucking expectations out of the air. She'd always done this: made her audiences wait. It made me happy, despite myself: seeing the old Eddy emerge from this lipsticked woman in a glove-tight dress.

"First," she said, "was the Empire State building." She propped herself up on her elbows, cleared her throat, her voice slipping back into a familiar lilt: musical and reckless. "I caught a bus there and took an elevator straight to the top, a whole one hundred and two floors up in the sky."

Eddy kept going: getting louder, sitting taller. She said she'd gazed out from the observation deck, feeling all tingly and respectful—the way a person does sometimes at church—until she realized no one else was looking at the view. Everyone was looking at her. Not casually, either, they were staring: eyes wide, mouths open, coffee cups dropped on the floor. People looked at her, it turned out, wherever she went in the city. She stood out in a way she never had in Chevalier. People eyed her on the subway, peeped over the tops of their newspapers; they paused their Frisbee games when she walked through the park. Tourists took photos. She could barely stand to eat in restaurants.

"Halloween," she said, with a laugh that wobbled between amusement and ache, "was the only break I got."

Eddy told me about art museums full of bent neon lights and plates of rotting meat and couches with curse words carved into them. Even there, people stared. They held toothpicked cheese up to their faces and missed their mouths. In the streets, meanwhile, everyone moved in human rivers, gushed through skyscraper canyons so frantic with light that invisibility became impossible, aloneness out of the question. People got shot, people got hit by buses, people won prestigious awards, and yet everyone looked at her. They—.

"Stop," I said. I couldn't listen anymore.

She stopped, unperturbed, as if she'd been waiting for me to ask. Then we both looked towards Chevalier, as if the town might comment as well. Even from under the radio tower, we could see the matchstick glow of downtown street lamps, the neon wink of Speedies' GasMart, and the odd bedroom window lit up in the night.

A dog howled its lonely ideas.

"Not anymore, though," Eddy added quietly. She patted the place where her horn had been, almost sheepish.

It was a certain kind of night, the kind when young people skittered in and out of shadows, looking for something to do, trying to compensate for imagined cities: the unreachable wonders of other worlds. It was on this kind of night when a gang might gather to uproot the *Welcome to Chevalier* sign on Route 47. If everything went according to plan, they'd slide it into the town pool. I'd seen it happen before: the sign submerged, the town's motto, "Cela est suffisant," swimming like an alphabetic fish under water. People were proud of that sign, even if they didn't always know what it meant, even if they were the ones who splashed it into the deep end.

There remained so much more for us to talk about, but I noticed Eddy check her watch. It was a delicate silver number, the sort no one has a reason to wear in Chevalier: It would get busted doing dishes. I felt a hard knot of pride, remembered my sturdy practicality, my foothold in a town to which she'd never really be able to return.

"Sounds like you've got everything worked out," I said with a spasm of cheerfulness. "And anyway—," I eyed the dark space around her forehead, "—it didn't mean anything, did it?"

The question crawled around our shoulders, thick as sleepover blankets. Eddy glanced at me. There was scorn in her eyes: something, I realized, I'd never seen before. She looked at me as though I'd asked something she'd already answered. It made me want to apologize, that look: to tell her how much I'd missed her, that I'd only stayed in Chevalier to prove that I could. Then, recognizing the absurdity of such thoughts, I wanted to punch her. What a reckless girl. What a careless friend! I might have done either, but before I could, she brushed the hair away from her forehead and leaned across the hood of the car, so that for a moment I saw the place where her widow's peak pointed—a white circle, like a full moon or an inverse shadow— like a promise you can't remember, but can't forget.

Reviews

***Does Not Love* by James Tadd Adcox.** Chicago: Curbside Splendor, 2014. 200 pages. $14.95, paper.

James Tadd Adcox's debut novel, *Does Not Love*, falls under that category that might be labeled "Dark Comedies of Where We Are Now." Set in an "alternate-reality" Indianapolis, the novel discusses the powers-that-be that have a hand in the failings of interpersonal relationships.

Left in a miasma of emotional numbness after the latest in a number of miscarriages, Viola and Robert's marriage begins to break down. After a period of general dissatisfaction and disconnection, the couple's sex life begins to disintegrate: Robert, at one point, interrupts foreplay to plan the remodeling of the house. Later, the couple watches instructional videos on rough sex, which Viola has begun to fantasize about. Each of them begins to seek out meaning and authenticity in the larger world. Many hijinks ensue.

The shortish novel features a decent roster of players beyond Viola and Robert—Big Pharma, secret courts, a sadistic voyeur of an FBI agent, faceless rioters, and an underground community of test subjects all come into play at various junctures. One would be concerned that Adcox would lose or tangle a narrative thread here or there, but the thematic treatment is near masterful in its thoroughness.

Does Not Love owes quite a bit to Kafka towards the end, as the focus shifts from the marriage to the "secret" entities at work in the city's power structure. Here is where the best comedy of the novel resides: After the shooting of a pharmaceutical researcher, Robert is interrogated by police officers, who engage in a facsimile of good-cop-bad-cop that's simultaneously chuckle-worthy and deeply creepy. Forms of the words "menace" and "dread" are analyzed by characters to the point of farce.

The novel's only major demerit is Adcox's tendency to occasionally litter scenes with cutesy-clever lines, like here, after Viola locks herself in the bathroom away from Robert:

Robert considers the possibilities: He could break down the damn door. Breaking down the damn door could, to a certain manner of thinking, be seen as acting out of concern for his wife.

"I'm considering breaking down the door," Robert says. "I feel like that could be seen as acting out of concern for you. Would you see that as acting out of concern for you?"

Also, much of the dialogue in the novel consists of the conversational volleying of either purposefully bland mundanities or statements that read like topic sentences from a dissertation, which may make certain readers feel distant from the characters, though in my mind these awkward and pseudo-intellectual back-and-forths are of central importance to the thematic concerns of the work.

In the hands of a lesser writer, *Does Not Love* might crumble under the weight of its ambition, but James Tadd Adcox deftly sprinkles both comedy and great pathos into a novel that says some sad, funny, and ultimately important things about our culture, and that's the best definition of good satire that comes to my mind.

—*Matthew Stewart*, Moon City Review

((

The Belle Mar by Katie Bickham. Warrensburg, MO: Pleiades, 2015. 56 pages. $17.95, paper.

It makes perfect sense that judge Alicia Ostriker chose Katie Bickham's *The Belle Mar* as winner of the Pleiades Press Lena-Miles Wever Todd Poetry Prize. In both poets—Ostriker, with a dozen collections to her credit, and Bickham, with this, her first—the expression is frank. Both are straightforward social critics, and while the work is solidly poetry, it shies away from poeticism.

The Belle Mar takes as its project the job of telling the story of a Southern plantation house and the generations of people, both black and white, who have moved through it.

What the house and the people have seen through that history is nothing less than soul crushing. In Bickham's poems, each related through the consciousness of a different speaker, we see enslaved people beaten or shot to death, as well as terrible home deaths from illness and even the devastation of Hurricane Katrina. The house outlasts all of the tragedy, and it seems to have seen everything but joy in its long history.

What we have in *The Belle Mar* is not an elegy for times past. It is more like reportage upon our cruelty to one another—and especially to the people who began as slaves and, after generations, ended up as hired help at the home.

One of the most tragic poems in the collection is "Far Swamp, 1825." In it, a woman compares two deaths: that of her "milk sister," who was hung from her thumbs, flayed, and thrown from a slave ship into the sea, and that of her a fellow slave, who was beaten to death and buried in a bayou grave:

> At least this body—rotted from the day's heat
> while it waited to be boxed and buried—just got beat,
> fast and simple, no show to it. When they reach
> the grave, dug that morning by the body's husband,
> they look inside to see it half-full of gulf water.

The speaker ruminates on which is "the real evil"—a death that is swept away by ocean waves, "or graves in this thick water, / where nothing ever moves / or gets away."

The excerpt above is typical of Bickham's matter-of-fact narrative, which privileges truth-telling over ultra-poetic technique. Sometimes her poems shy so far away from figurative language and artful use of form that, on first reading, I had to ask myself if I was actually looking at poems. Here's an example from "Sugar House, 1992," in which old paintings on the wall of an outbuilding reveal some of the history of the plantation:

> It did remember. And if it could, what else
> had memories? Her pillow with the purple
> sham remembered her head heavy
> with sleep, folded down just right in welcome.
> She drew it, ridged with the pattern
> of floor.

These lines seemed very stilted to me on first read. Why break between "pillow" and "sham"? Or between "pattern" and "of floor"? But I came to see the choppy quality of the poem as reflective of the way history shows through the old building's walls in glimpses, the pictures only partial ones—while imagination is forced to fill in what seems unimaginable.

The Belle Mar faces our collective history unflinchingly, and in it, Bickham proves herself to be a bold new voice.

—*Karen Craigo*, Moon City Review

Buick City by Sarah Carson. Woodstock, NY: Mayapple, 2015. 80 pages. $14.95, paper.

In _Buick City_, Sarah Carson gives a close-up look at the backstreets and back doors of midwest life, the usually unexamined places where a dead end job at the twenty-four-hour grocery turns into a foundation for identity. For example, in the extended sequence, "Hall's Flat's," which uses the trope of a job application, skills such as "Experience working with minimal supervision / Ability to operate a manual/ powered pallet jack or Lift Product" are juxtaposed with things that are less able to fit in the blanks such as "In tenth grade I tried to join the wrestling team to be funny. / My favorite class was history. / I didn't go to prom." The result is a tracing of a future that is also the cold present of the upwardly mobile dream. In fact, that dream never happens in these poems, housed in stacks of pallets on loading docks and in trailers divided in half to get twice the rent. Sex comes cheap and warmth is a surprise, and when Carson writes, "It starts at six AM on a Sunday; there is a spider running along the Halloween display, and he won't kill it. He pulls down his zipper where the security cameras won't see him. I am surprised by his warmth." We are left unsure if the warmth is for the speaker or the spider, but we feel it and accept it.

Carson's sharp use of language and precise images compels the reader to pay attention to this place and the people who inhabit it. Strong prose poems begin and end the book, the first third a series of interlocking vignettes, the last third more centered on the speaker. Even though the lives shown may not have large dreams, they still have desires and opt for fulfillable dreams, as in the prose poem "Jimmy," where the titular character and his buddies "won't apologize for their waistlines. Nothing bad will ever come of this. Fifteen years later when Jimmy decides to move, the hot tub will add property value to his home." In this PBR-fueled utopia, all is well because the expectations are low.

Much is said these days about poetry collections and the need for a strong narrative thread that somehow binds the poems together and gives a sense that these poems together are much more than they could be apart. _Buick City_ has that necessary cohesion. The strong yet non-linear narrative carries the reader through each person and place until the completed book does what good poetry does, which is transforms

the reader into an inhabitant of that time and place, and in the end, expands their life experience to include another's.
—*Lanette Cadle, Moon City Press*

(

***Eight Mile High* by Jim Ray Daniels.** East Lansing, MI: Michigan State UP, 2014. 176 pages. $19.95, paper.

In his collection *Eight Mile High*, Jim Ray Daniels offers a haunting portrayal of Detroit through the lenses of his inimitable characters, all of whom are alive with grief, humor, and an eerie awareness of the world they live in. Throughout his stories, the character of Detroit itself evolves after each page, demanding to be acknowledged just as much as the human condition found in each of these characters; Detroit is Daniel's protagonist, one that begs to be understood not only for its rawness, but for its unnerving beauty. The setting, as the title suggests, gives foundation to everyone and everything else in the collection, whether it is a young man captivated by an entrancing mime or the meddling Mrs. Wakowski, who knew all the secrets in her pocket of the Polish burough.

These distinctive characters are painted with a precision of language, and—perhaps more importantly—with a precision of emotion. The pacing of *Eight Mile High* is seamless, and Daniels will have you laughing throughout an entire narrative, just to be hit in the gut with a raw sense of Detroit's ghosts in the concluding paragraphs. These ghosts are just as diverse as his characters, ranging from a Boy Scout dealing with inevitable existential questions to younger men facing the inevitable question of college, the army, or the Ford factory after graduation—and most of them went with the final option. "We stayed put, as our fathers and their fathers had done."

The structure of each story reflects its main character. At times, this creates a stylistic unreliable narrator telling a disjointed account, such as Terry, the nineteen-year-old in "Target Practice" who shot a man just before offering him one last warm PBR. With this in mind, Daniels uses several points of view to create the whole story for the audience. Terry himself divulges why Daniels did this: "I don't even know who should be telling this story to make it seem real with the emotional stuff. That's the thing with murder. How do you get people to calm down enough to pay attention and listen to something besides the blood dripping?"

Eight Mile High offers something beyond Daniels' innovative use of form or his grossly human characters; it gives the essence of a city that is unique to America but is oftentimes misunderstood. This collection begs readers to empathize with Detroit, to understand its imperfections, its violence, and also its vulnerabilities. Or, as Daniels puts it, a place where people had an "appreciation for the colorful anarchy of dandelions."

—*Bailey Gaylin Moore*, Moon City Review

☾

The Cartographer's Ink: Poems **by Okla Elliott.** New York: NYQ. 108 pages. $14.95, paper.

Okla Elliott's debut collection of poetry, *The Cartographer's Ink*, ambitiously explores historical and philosophical themes alongside memory, the importance of place and the imagination. The poems in *The Cartographer's Ink* are a mapping of the past, present, and future, and the speakers find meaning while dwelling in settings that range from Milwaukee to Africa to "The Stars of Orion." Elliott's verse is comprised of a seamless blend of narrative and lyricism that makes for a strikingly original voice, informed by literary predecessors as well as the culture surrounding the speakers in the collection.

The Cartographer's Ink features poems that use historical situations as backdrops and makes them relevant by juxtaposing them with a contemporary setting. The poem "Helpless" begins with the lines "Sejong the Great, fourth king of the Joseon Dynasty (15ᵗʰ / century), hired scholars to create the Hangul alphabet because / Chinese script, which the Korean Aristocracy used for writing, was too difficult for mass literacy." This is insight into a past culture. The poem goes on several lines later: "This is / what I want to tell my friend when she says she has miscarried, / but her body is still preparing for a birth, her stomach swelling." Elliott's use of historical situations to explain or give meaning to contemporary settings creates a binary between the past and the present, placing emphasis on the importance of past events while still maintaining the significance of personal experience in the present.

While poems such as "Helpless" use history to show the importance of the present, others like "Yard Work for My Dying Mother" use sharp images to demonstrate the immediacy of situations Elliott's speakers are dealing with. "Yard Work for My Dying Mother" opens with the lines "The mower drones, a hornet swarm / or lion humming the faithless tune / of battle hymns" which establishes a clear sense of a present place alongside the more violent images of battle hymns and the lion. The poem transcends the place by internalizing with the closing lines "The bodies will wash away / in sandy runnels, become scattered / chapter and verse on my mother's lawn, / where I await death's bulging arms," signifying both the poem's emphasis on the intensity of the present situation as well as the overarching theme of mortality.

The Cartographer's Ink is a striking debut collection of poetry that bridges gaps between history, imagination, and the present. Elliott's verse blends and binds narrative, lyricism, mysticism, and memory into a moving and cohesive whole while demonstrating arresting language manipulation. These poems are approachable and self-enlightening simultaneously, and they represent a brilliantly written debut poetry collection.

—*Terry Belew*, Moon City Review

☾

***In a Landscape: A Poem* by John Gallaher.** Rochester, NY: BOA Editions, 2014. 128 pages. $16, paper.

After reading John Gallaher's book-length poem *In a Landscape*, I had questions. The good kind of questions, I mean—the kind that is the poetic equivalent to a glass of sherry after dinner, and that pleasurable fire that starts to heat and weight your limbs.

And Gallaher is a very accessible poet, as it happens. He's in my state—there aren't a lot of us poets here—and I stood somewhere very near his office before, once, when I was at his university during a TESOL conference. I had been losing myself in the world of English instruction for speakers of other languages, a world I inhabit but often feel like a foreigner in, and so I tried to track down Gallaher's empty office on a weekend just to stand by his door and say, "Here. Poetry happens right here." It was enough to get me back to my conference and its free coffee table, and ultimately back into one of the conference rooms, where I learned some new ways to help students with English word stress. Standing where a poet walks centered me and reminded me of who I was and what I was about.

That seems entirely irrelevant, I know, but it's not. Gallaher's book is about all of this, and more. It strikes me as a book about the coordinates we rely on as we jerk from here to there in our lives. *In a Landscape*, briefly, is about the landscape of life and consciousness that we inhabit, and the little pins we stick into our grand topographic map.

One type of pin the book offers is death. People die matter-of factly all through the book—a toddler neighbor who drowns in a pool and is buried in a casket the size of a suitcase. A student who would marry her boyfriend in a year and lose him within four. The poet's cousin Lyle, whose airplane carved a groove into a Kansas field.

And there are other sorts of signposts. If death peppers the book, then surely ghosts salt it. Here, young John dresses up like Casper for Halloween. Here, he passes a funeral home at night, all the lights off but the front door open wide.

One of my favorite motifs is that of chairs, which show up again and again in the book, and always in a different way, like here in part III:

> You go to the room, and the place you like to sit
> is missing. This is an opportunity to trust, I suppose, or perhaps
> for blind panic, if one were to consider this a metaphor
> for something. But say it's not, say there are no such things
> as metaphors for a moment, and where does that get you?
> Presently, it gets me to a row of green and yellow plastic chairs,
> those 1950s-looking ones I imagine Kenton would like
> to collect.

Gallaher goes on to describe the scene as "lickable, how everything / looks like cheerful candy," but ruminates over what the row of joined-together chairs has to say about beginnings, or endings, "or if perhaps there might be a concept for no middle."

When is a chair more than a chair? When it's a coordinate, as the chairs that—well, they can't salt or pepper the book, can they? I said the dead people were pepper and the ghosts were salt. The chairs paprika the book, maybe—always a surprise when they show up, and in what they can mean: "Where You Sit Is Who You Are," part XVII tells us.

I don't know what else to tell you. It's a really good book, and it seems to be about ... everything. And the long, expansive, conversational lines, along with the LXXI Roman-numeraled poems (how many is that?), paint a landscape, a thorough one that is confusing and familiar—and tremendously personal, and, for all that, universal as well.

Just read the thing. If you'd like to talk about it, I'll meet you at Gallaher's office, which, by the way, is not at the university where my conference took place. I got my Missouri universities mixed up, and so went to the hallway where all of the creative writing announcements were and pictured this guy Gallaher, whose work I liked but whom I didn't really know, and in my imagination he was ghosting a hallway he's probably never inhabited in real life, his own university in another corner of the state. I think this anecdote is exactly the kind of thing the poet would appreciate, and maybe even write down, and assign it the number LXXII.

—*Karen Craigo,* Moon City Review

☾

***The Demon Who Peddled Longing* by Khanh Ha**. Los Angeles, California: Underground Voices, 2014. 296 pages. $13.99, paper.

Reading Khanh Ha's second novel, *The Demon Who Peddled Longing*, is like walking through a vivid painting of the Mekong Delta in southwestern Vietnam. Every page of the novel brims with the names of exotic flora, which provide an intricate and expansive depiction of the novel's setting. Ha's rich, descriptive language surrounds the reader like the dense, lush jungles through which his protagonist, Nam, travels on his path to avenge the rape and murder of his cousin, with whom he had once been in love. Khanh uses Nam's journey to parallel what he sees as an inherent duality in man: a primitive nature by which one survives and through which one suffers.

Ha uses the vibrant, inexorable qualities of the Vietnamese jungle to parallel the violent nature of Nam and his desire for revenge. Yet the jungle also serves as a metaphor for the ways in which people are constantly returning to the most primitive of traits to resolve the problems derived from the intricacies of modern life. This circularity manifests itself not only in Nam's character, but in his journey as well, which, along with the themes of reincarnation found in the novel, suggests the constant rebirthing of the individual as they move from one stage of life to the next. Nam becomes the very individual he is seeking to destroy and discovers in himself the same qualities he finds abhorrent in the men he is hunting.

What sets the novel apart from others is Ha's ability to maintain an economical style of writing while incorporating innumerable layers of detail and description. His use of colloquial names for plant life (a field guide to botany might prove to be a worthy supplemental read to this novel), the depth of his characters, and the inherent tension within their struggles make Ha's work one of those novels where something new is discovered on every read. Once Nam falls in love with the beautiful wife of the wealthy landowner for whom he works, the story becomes one of passion, rage, and forgiveness, allowing Ha to explore two polar sides of humanity while maintaining an effective and cohesive narrative.

Yet while there is the exploration of the convergence of man and nature in the novel, Ha also portrays another side: the dramatic rejection of man by nature. Ha's employment of this perpetual cycle of assimilation and repudiation emphasizes the finality of an individual act and the permanent burden an action can have on a life while at the same time emphasizing a natural, sometimes forgiving, process on a larger scale. To put it simply, Ha's characters experience both the repercussions of their dramatic and questionable actions while also coming to the realization that their pasts are over and cannot be fixed in the present.

The theme of the reciprocity of benevolence between the characters endows the novel with a humanitarian perspective. Ha's adherence to a gritty and believable story world, paradoxically, emphasizes and reinforces this theme while at the same time providing a dramatic juxtaposition of the opposing tendencies within Nam to both save lives and take them. It is this unique quality of Ha's writing that makes the novel not only one that is difficult to put down, but also one that forces readers to examine their own internal confluence of thought through the presentation of Nam's struggles in an exotic and enigmatic landscape.

—*Ryan Hubble*, Moon City Review

☾

Brain Fever: Poems **by Kimiko Hahn.** New York: W.W. Norton, 2014.
144 pages. $26.95, cloth.

Brain Fever examines the collage of a human like a fever dream
remembered the only way it can be: subjectively. Neuroscience and
philosophy are both used thematically, as if the speaker, suffering from
brain fever (a dated term used for people who most likely suffered
from encephalitis or meningitis) grasped at the concrete to soften the
emotional shock of exploring one's own history.

Kimiko Hahn's ninth full-length collection is not only influenced
by neuroscience and philosophy, but by the Japanese language and its
dependence upon word association and homonyms. These three aspects
echo through all eight sections of the book, its speaker having suffered
a crisis, though that crisis simply could be life. Her children are grown.
She has lived through the infidelities of her husband, forcing her to
scrutinize her identity as wife, mother, and individual. Is she split in
two? Into countless fragments? Is a life split not by who we love but by
time and perspective?

The collection begins with the poem "[Kimiko's Clipping
Morgue: BRAIN file]." There are files on memory, dreams,
poetry, and miscellaneous, the final item being "BRAIN split (see
CONSCIOUSNESS, see WIFE)." This establishes the collection's
crux—the self as an entity forced into a single body, prey to one's own
thoughts and others' expectations. How can a person remain sane?

The book's first section, "consciousness," contains several quotes by
Benedict Cary, a science reporter for *The New York Times*. Here, the
brain is awakening to reality, most likely still riding the emotional
shock waves of trauma. We first glimpse that maybe the husband is less
than faithful. We see the speaker's tendency to do things she dislikes
simply because of expectation. In the poem, "The Dream of a Little
Occupied Japan Doll," our speaker begins by describing her favorite
porcelain doll from all those she has collected:

> I keep on my desk the first one
>
> though she—or he—is not doing a darn thing.
> Here in sleep, rivalry is reserved.
>
> And as dreams "tune the mind for conscious awareness"
> perhaps this favoritism suggests

I've quit hoarding and now collect myself."

The rest of the poems repeat this feeling that the speaker is on the precipice of seeing herself, and society, without the comfort of delusion. In "The Secret Lives of Planets," Hahn has arranged lines from Dennis Overby's scientific article, "Now in Sight: Far-Off Planets," to create a poem that compares parents to failed stars:

> The problem seeing other planets is picking them from the glare
>   of parent stars—
> or failed stars—
> giant planets in the other reaches, [leave] plenty of room
> for smaller ones to lurk undetected in the warmer inner regions—
> whether parents are really failed stars—
> telescopic, mirrored and warped—

The highly-lyrical nature of *Brain Fever* complements its themes of philosophy, identity, and love, and the poems' brevity, precise imagery, and echoing of that imagery will make readers return to the collection, finding new connections each time.

—*Sara Burge*, Moon City Review

☾

Paper Doll Fetus **by Cynthia Marie Hoffman.** New York: Persea Books, 2014. 80 pages. $15.95, paper.

Cynthia Marie Hoffman's second full volume of poetry and runner-up of the Lexi Rudnitsky First Book Prize in poetry, *Paper Doll Fetus*, may bely one's expectations of how a poem tells its story. For instance, "A Stone in the Field Falls for the Goat's Placenta" relates a rock's unrequited love for a glistening pile of goat placenta, and in doing so it sends the reader tracking between title and content to confirm nothing has been misread. This poem hardly stands alone as equally arresting dramatic monologues pervade Hoffman's work (notably "The Liver Speaks to the Ectopic Embryo" and "The Lamb's Wool Strap Speaks from the Gurney, 1915") but even her more straightforward narratives, such as "The Cesarean," ring with her particular and peculiar voice. Hoffman gleans such perspectives from medical texts of the late 1400s to the mid-1600s. With this research, coupled with her own contemporary hindsight, she presents an evocative portrait of the ongoing struggle between science and superstition as well as tension between mind and body. This book, composed of many strange and striking persona poems and third-person narratives, often leaves the reader agog at her inventiveness.

The mystery and allure of her disturbingly whimsical narratives hinge on the cohesiveness of her imagery. Descriptions of the female body, particularly of reproduction and its potential abnormalities, permeate these poems, and this lends a sense of continuity that, as the reader progresses through the collection, intensifies in effect. This quality is perhaps most evident in poems such as "One Child" and "Testimony of the Imperfect Lamb," as both concern narratives of infants born with deformities that result in their deaths. As demonstrated by these poems, Hoffman illustrates what gives this collection such command: her ability to create characters that, despite her proclivity towards the strange, the reader never feels divorced from. We empathize with the grotesque, as in "The Calciferous Substances Speak to the Sleeping Fetus," in which the growth comforts the baby as it dies. Stated so bluntly, the thought might make one cringe; however, Hoffman's ability to weave her narratives, odd though they may be, with the familiar renders their often-alien voices incongruously human and, like us, unable to close their eyes to hope.

Hoffman's bizarre narratives are complemented by the clarity afforded by her relatively conservative structure. Her accessible verse and tendency to use a long, descriptive line function as a grounding principle to the lyrical and often associative leaps she makes within her poems. This collection—comfortably varied in structure—is blank verse at its best. Her content, which could be construed as experimental, is balanced by its conservative form. These poems, then, are not resigned to those familiar with the genre but extend to anyone with daring taste who does not shy away from forays into those shadowy parts of the mind that are as dark and clandestine as a womb.

—*Allys Page*, Moon City Review

☾

Border States by Jane Hoogestraat. Kansas City, MO: BkMK, 2014. 65 pages. $13.95, paper.

In *Border States*, Jane Hoogestraat conveys the many textures of the American landscape, winding across destinations to demonstrate that any place can be home if the feeling is right. She is clearly a careful listener, adept at recognizing the particulars of the natural world. Graceful yet precise, Hoogestraat knows that the best way to paint a vivid scene is through the rhythmic music of everyday experience. The poet urges readers to stop and take notice of all that is living, in order to more fully position one's self inside of this complex and beautiful ecosystem. Equally comfortable across all four seasons, Hoogestraat uses natural wonders as a canvas: "Planting the fall bulbs yesterday," she writes in "To See Beyond Our Bourn," "I thought as I often do / of what it means to settle here, to plan ahead for spring." In this carefully considered collection, the poet provides a heartfelt roadmap of profound vistas. For example, in the final poem of the collection, "Near Red Lodge, Montana," the poet examines a place situated "far from human fear or desire." Here again, nature takes center stage, as "the water rinses a little soot from the edges of a still-charred rock." Hoogestraat's keen insight and observational talents provide the engine that drives this collection forward.

With a sharp eye for the world and a robust vocabulary for the many treasures of terra firma, this is a book chock full of poems that sing while exploring locations near and far. The poet has provided us with a roadmap full of wondrous surprises, joys rooted in the depths of the earth itself. Like the work of Ted Kooser or Mary Oliver, these poems point out the extraordinary qualities of the everyday, while also celebrating the genuine workings of a new day: "This morning," the poet writes, "the darkest green, the coldest spring fell away before a sunlit clearing." These poems have a firm compass within them, one that is humbly set to track the passage from dusk till dawn. An ambitious book with a striking scope, these are poems to which the reader will return again and again, seeking out just the right moment, honing the moment to stop and invite a deep breath.

These poems have a distinctly restorative quality about them; they feel like a pleasant tonic in a world that is usually too busy—perhaps too connected to the technologies and platforms that are commonplace in networked existence. In such an environment, *Border States* is a vital book, especially for the way that it encourages the reader to take notice of her or his surroundings. This is a book that will appeal to anyone who enjoys a thought-provoking read, from undergraduate students of poetry to close observers of the planet. Given the complexities of the new millennium and the enduring qualities of the land itself, we are fortunate to have Jane Hoogestraat as our guide. For their truly admirable focus, these poems do well to invite us to reconsider the world and our place within it.

—*Peter Joseph Gloviczki, Coker College*

☾

***Unaccompanied Minors: Stories* by Alden Jones.** Milwaukee: New American Press, 2014. 165 pages. $14.95, paper.

Unaccompanied Minors follows Jones' debut book, *The Blind Masseuse: A Traveler's Memoir from Costa Rica to Cambodia.* The stories in *Unaccompanied Minors* take the reader on a journey from a North Carolinian homeless shelter, to the bland suburbs of the U.S., a small Costa Rican town—starkly contrasted by a feces-laden San Jose brothel—and back stateside for a Floridian wilderness retreat. While Jones' characters are very much a part of their settings, a sense of universality builds throughout the sequence of stories.

If you are looking for whimsical tales of youthful misadventures or, perhaps, tales of profound charity or gratitude, *Unaccompanied Minors* is not for you. There are no villains in Jones' stories, but no heroes, either. She turns a sympathetic eye toward the less-than-ethical thoughts and desires we all pretend not to have. With themes of sexuality, survival, and loneliness, each protagonist struggles to find a sense of responsibility. In "Thirty Seconds," a teen babysitter tries to rationalize her lack of guilt in the drowning of her young charge. "Sin Alley" finds a Costa Rican man choosing between the male prostitute with whom he is enamored and his own troubled niece. An irresponsible lesbian in "Flee" learns to put the needs of another over her own libido.

Of seven gracefully arranged stories, the first four serve as a sort of warm-up. These characters are a bit immature, but fairly blameless. The babysitter isn't really at fault for the child's drowning. The young girl in "Freaks" is honestly trying to connect through her own physical disfigurement and her friend's anorexia. "Something Will Grow" and "Shelter" feature slightly older narrators, but at most, they reflect on youthful hardships and remain largely innocent. The final three stories, "Heathens," "Sin Alley," and "Flee," feature young adults who have fallen prey to their own demons. On first read, these stories may seem to reveal the seedy underbelly of humanity. There are, however, no easy choices in these stories. These protagonists are not white knights or messianic allegories. They are each struggling to decide who to care about, and what, and how much in a world largely indifferent to their own needs.

Jones' characters have an almost palpable need to become lost and find themselves at home in a strange place. *Unaccompanied Minors* is not about learning to make the "right" choices, but about learning to make your own choices. The collection concludes with the words, "It was time to grow up." By this point, the reader is sure of only one thing: No one grows up the same way.

—*Kelly Baker,* Moon City Review

☾

***The Dead Wrestler Elegies* by W. Todd Kaneko.** Chicago: Curbside Splendor, 2014. 120 pages. $14.95, paper.

Kaneko's mantra in *The Dead Wrestler Elegies* is an old *Superman* tagline: *You will believe a man can fly*. This is appropriate for the subject, because for many people pro wrestlers like Andre the Giant were real-life superheroes. Yet all that lay ahead for these men and women was a cocktail of death and disappointment.

"You Are Looking At Dr. Death" meditates on how the body can waste away. Steve Williams, who died from throat cancer, shriveled away to nothing towards the end, a mountain of a man in his heyday:

> You are not the sound a body makes
> as it collapses to the floor. You are not
> those sounds a mouth makes after our bodies
> fall apart. You are not a body.

Let it be said that there's no shortage of material when it comes to writing a book about pro wrestlers, an embarrassment of riches that can be funny, disgusting, and cripplingly sad.

With two of the most infamous deaths (Owen Hart falling to his death from the ceiling of the Kiel Center and the double murder and suicide involving Chris Benoit), Kaneko explores the dangers of an existence that most enjoy exposing as "fake." Chris Benoit's name is mentioned in the epigraph but not the poem itself, an echo of reality considering that the WWE has actively erased any mention or glimpse of the once-loved Canadian Crippler from its broadcasts. Kaneko captures the disbelief and disquieting effect that the murders had on the wrestling fan base and the outside world:

> Somewhere there is a place for all of us
> to figure out what evil things we are
> capable of believing. We want to understand
> the distance between love and fury, the damage
> a brain can do to a body.

Other poems highlight the unique existence of men who couldn't exist today, like Bruiser Brody. The embodiment of a savage madman, Brody incited riots wherever he was found stomping. Proving that no man is invincible, this legendary tough guy was stabbed to death while touring in Puerto Rico.

> This life is not a thing to be finished,
> not this busted smile, not this forehead,
> scar over scar, not this body left bleeding
> in a grimy shower stall.

Kaneko's book is about pro wrestling on the surface, but underneath it's about the relationship between fathers and sons. Often we create bonds with our parents through different forms of media. Sometimes the only way to remember them is by association:

> In the tavern where my father fell, I find
> no bloodstain shaped like my father's body,
> no dent where his head clashed
> with the floor: The bartender says they talked
> about all the men they once watched
> wrestle on television

If pro wrestling has taught us anything, it's that the world moves on without us. Sometimes there's a trail of bodies we can trace back to imagine why.

—*Anthony Isaac Bradley*, Moon City Review

☾

***The Spirit Bird: Stories* by Kent Nelson.** Pittsburgh: U of Pittsburgh P, 2014. 336 pages. $24.95, cloth.

Kent Nelson's first collection of short stories, *The Spirit Bird*, follows his first two novels as the 2014 winner of University of Pittsburgh Press's Drue Heinz Literature Prize. The collection is an exploration of loneliness, wild landscapes, and human-avian connection. From Gambell, Alaska, to Panama City, Seattle to New Mexico, Nelson writes with enough detail to allow the reader to settle into each setting without being overwhelmed with image. The varieties of landscapes, as wild and untamed as the characters they contain, act as destinations of the reader's migration from story to story.

In "The Beautiful Light" both reader and protagonist are presented with the idea that "birds measure the health of the planet." Without over-demonstrating his knowledge as a seasoned birder himself, Nelson represents various species of birds throughout the collection either by utilizing "birder" characters or with the details of the physical setting. The title story combines both as it follows the protagonist's journey up an off-limits mountain in search of the Eurasian Dotterel and into a frozen burial ground. The constant presence of birds (named or unnamed) throughout the collection works to remind the reader of the characters' health and connections to the Earth.

The stories are connected through each protagonist's struggle with their own brands of loneliness: physical isolation like in "Alba" and "Joan of Dreams," seclusion from family ("Seeing Desirable Things") and community ("Race"), or, in the case of Danny Pendergast, mental isolation. This unifying emotion fuels the consistent motion of the characters in and out of relationships and provides an accessible emotional platform when beginning a new story.

Haunting and ethereal, each story of *The Spirit Bird* has its own unique atmosphere and landscape, but when collected together, the stories lend themselves to conglomerate into a world more aware of its ability to isolate, but also to bring together.

—*Sierra Sitzes*, Moon City Review

☾

All the Wasted Beauty of the World: Poems by **Richard Newman.** San Jose, CA: Able Muse, 2014. 102 pages, $18.95, paper

Richard Newman's third collection of poetry, *All the Wasted Beauty of the World,* explores and uplifts the melancholy and mundane aspects of everyday Midwestern life into an eclectic mix of poetic forms, including sonnets, villanelles, and the ode. That said, the collection is not limited in form or in content to just strict poetic forms and Midwestern life, but instead the speakers seek to find meaning in a rather turbulent world that ranges from St. Louis to Latin America during the times of Conquistadors. The multitude of speakers and subjects alongside Newman's ability to brilliantly manipulate traditional poetic forms makes for a haunting and rhythmic collection of new poems.

All the Wasted Beauty of the World introduces a series of odes on subjects that are here depicted in a negative light, subjects such as Mulberry trees, brown-banded cockroaches, and Asian Carp. With these poems, Newman takes undesirables and seeks to compare them with elements of humanity, with lines like:

> Mutt plant—genitals dangling purple, black,
> red, pink and white. You sticky the very ground
> from which you sprang. Slut fruit. Jackberry,
> prized only by the innocent,
> your leaves like mittens in the lost and found

Another example:

> Mama Cockroach, you mate but once in life
> then spawn 600 children in a year,
> tote perfect tic-tac capsules full of eggs
> before you seal them to our kitchen cabinets,
> a molting nest of legs, spent shells, and spit.

Newman's juxtaposition of vivid object description and personification seek to strike at the hearts and minds of readers, bringing to question the importance of seemingly ordinary surroundings and the speakers' places in the world.

Newman seems to stray away from personal narratives in this collection, instead seeking to explore the world around his speakers, with poems like "Four Kids Pissing Off the Overpass After a Cardinals Game" and "The Ugliest Woman Sitting at the Bar." As opposed to using a first-person speaker to describe the world, Newman unifies the speaker with the reader with lines such as "Our lives span diaper to diaper, / and in between we piss on anyone / we can, in this case anyone with tickets." In doing this, he seeks to maintain existential solidarity among experiencers with a collective and resounding "we" that encapsulates the reader and speaker as one looking through the same lens at the world around.

The poems in *All the Wasted Beauty of the World* look for meaning among the everyday occurrences through the music of poetic form and the exposure of the correlation between objects and situations that are taken for granted or overlooked during the daily grind, as well as a collective speaker sharing these trials in conjunction with the reader.

—*Terry Belew*, Moon City Review

☾

The Turtles of Oman: A Novel **by Naomi Shihab Nye.** New York: Greenwillow Books/HarperCollins, 2014. 304 pages. $16.99, cloth.

"Aref knew that the Green Turtle would return to the exact same beach for egg-laying for *decades*. Turtles had invisible maps inside their shells." Aref loves his life in Oman, and he doesn't want to move to Michigan for three years no matter how many times his mother tells him it will be an adventure. He will miss the turtles laying their eggs, his cat Mish-Mish, his room, his friends, and his school, but he'll miss his grandfather, Sidi most of all. Nothing truly important fits inside a suitcase.

The Turtles of Oman by Naomi Shihab Nye is a thoughtful children's book intended for 8-12 year olds about Aref's weeklong journey with Sidi to say good-bye and imprint an invisible map of Oman into Aref's memories. Like the turtle, Sidi promises that Aref will return to the home of his heart. Aref and Sidi's relationship is the heart of this children's story. Sidi shows Aref a world of beauty and wonder, a world where people once placed candles on turtles' backs to light their gardens at night, a place where everyone is his friend, a place where Aref is loved absolutely. Every moment Sidi spends with Aref, he encourages him to capture the essence of the day: breathe in the smell of the desert, soak up the night sky so a star map will always be there, feel the wind off the ocean. Sidi's joyful and reverent worldview helps Aref work through the fear of moving and saying good-bye. Oman will be waiting, and it will remain part of Aref even if he is 7,283 miles away.

Nye effectively uses lists to build Aref's character and create a visual break for her readers. The lists capture Aref's sweet curiosity and optimism. With a handwritten look and large letters in slightly crooked lines, the visual disruption of large blocks of text with Aref's personal notes is appealing and helps speed up the pacing of the story. *The Turtles of Oman* is a character-driven novel with a slower, more reflective narrative. Nye writes with simple but elegant prose, painting a vivid landscape and poignant emotions, but for more reluctant readers or readers who don't visualize the written word as well, the lists of facts provide concrete information as a boy would see it.

Nye is a voice of hope, optimism, and acceptance. She was awarded the Jane Addams Children's Book Awards in 1995 and 1998, which is given to children's books that "effectively promote the cause of peace, social justice, world community, and the equality of the sexes and all races as well as meeting conventional standards for excellence," and she was named laureate of the NSK Neustadt Prize for Children's Literature in 2013. *The Turtles of Oman* continues to show Naomi Shihab Nye's warmth, insight, and humanitarian spirit through Sidi's joyful and reverent worldview and Aref's excitement and energy.

—*Jennifer Barnhart, Missouri State University*

☾

Baby's on Fire by Liz Prato. Winston-Salem, NC: Press 53, 2015. 144 pages. $14.95, paper.

Baby's on Fire, Liz Prato's short story collection, is at once familiar and new. The characters are people you've met before, maybe your Colorado cousin, or your drifter brother, or even yourself. Prato captures the voice of her characters precisely, letting the reader into their minds and lives, while invoking a sense of nostalgia in her reader, for these are stories they most likely have lived before.

"Baby's on Fire" sets the tone for most of the stories. This is the story of a young woman who has graduated from college and lost everything, even the house. A reader should not expect a happy ending, as the selection ends with "The smell of burning waffle batter hung like storm clouds in the air," promising a still-unruly life for our hero, while giving the reader some beautiful imagery to ponder. Another story, "A Space You Can Fall Into," features a protagonist who fancies herself a city-slicker stuck in small-town Nebraska. The kids she falls in with are not so wholesome as she might imagine and she is left burning.

While the stories capture the voice of their characters very well, it is the voice that makes some of them feel repetitive. The protagonist of the second story can easily be mistaken for that of the first, albeit in a different situation. However, Prato's stories are still delightful, and well worth a read.

—*Ana Berkovich*, Moon City Review

❨

Put This On, Please: New & Selected Poems by **William Trowbridge.**
Pasadena, CA: Red Hen Press, 2013. 208 pages. $19.95, paper.

In *Put This On, Please: New & Selected Poems*, there's a refreshing simplicity in the language William Trowbridge uses to reel the reader into his poetic landscape, a light-heartedness that captivates and stokes that inner playfulness through his masterful use of popular culture while lending the true meat of his poems that deeper impact, making us pause and reflect at what the core of his works are trying to bring to the surface.

One evident example is in the poem "Screaming B-Movie Victims," examining the common tropes of the campy horror film: "A few stumble and sprawl / or stand there staring up in terror, / shot from the creature's viewpoint / as they're about to be pancaked / or devoured." That image finds itself intertwined with the atrocities of Auschwitz or the invasion of Iwo Jima, permitting the reader to weigh the absurd with the absurd, or what terrible things are presently being engraved into our history.

Through this collection of poetry, the reader embarks on a journey of meshing with the "whole," often from the viewpoint of a misfit. Kong's attempts to fit into society: "If it had worked out, I'd be on a train to Green Bay, / not crawling up this building with the Air Corps / on my ass," or the Fool's failure at mass sympathy in the poem, "Pity the Fool." Through the quirkiness with which the misfit persona goes about it, we're given a look at an underlying desire to be part of the social order and, by the same token, a desire to embrace simple human nature.

His liberal use of pop culture icons such as King Kong, Abbott and Costello, and Wile E. Coyote does not diminish the strength of his poems, but rather gives them a context with which to pull the deep emotional core from their fruity exterior: "Lou whines, retriggering the blows, / again and again as Lou keeps / stumbling on the tripwire of this schtick / that won't stay dead."

This collection reveals its abundance of complexity through blatant simplicity and the relatable cultural references, giving ample room to ask the question of whether we're seeing things through the right lens or not.

—*Daniel Wright, Missouri State University*

((

By Light We Knew Our Names by **Anne Valente**. Ann Arbor, MI: Dzanc, 2014. 200 pages. $14.95, paper.

A whimsical jaunt, a coming of age, a self-identification through smooth and surprising prose, Anne Valente's *By Light We Knew Our Names* is a short story collection worth spending the weekend on.

Each of the stories takes on a unique detail by which every other detail in the story functions: a giant pile of tea, transfiguring mothers, ghost grandparents, and a very compassionate baby. The metaphors that each of these details provoke form the perfect balance when placed within the effortless prose.

The collection opens with "Latchkey," the imaginative story of a young girl learning that she has a gift much like those in her circle of friends, but unique from theirs. She must find her place among them as she matures and discovers herself. Though parts of the story are left ambiguous, it isn't disappointing. It is filled with details of magical realism and elements that leave the reader guessing and surmising the meaning of things right along with the protagonist.

Another standout story is "To a Place Where We Take Flight," where two young boys practice playing music in order to play for the oncology ward at the hospital where one of their mothers resides. Though more realistic than magical, the experience for the boy becomes greater than an amateur show, greater than a moment to make a parent proud. It becomes an understanding of life and death, and of where the grief and the happiness are found among it all.

The most dramatic and heart-wrenching story of the bunch goes to the title story," By Light We Knew Our Names." The plural narration tells of the lives of abused women, a chain reaction of emotions. The first two sentences, poetic in nature, set the tone for the entire story: "Through summer, we waited. We waited through June, through July, when the sun ripped a white fissure from tree line to sky, a sky that burned all day and night, turning away from us for only moments, four hours, five, settled into its own sleep."

Just when the stories seem as if they could go on for too long, they open the reader up to new perspectives and conclude with magnified certainty. *By Light We Knew Our Names* is a well thought-out and inspiring read that would enhance any reader's bookshelf.

—*Elizabeth Alphonse,* Moon City Review

☾

The Wynona Stone Poems by **Caki Wilkinson.** New York: Persea Books, 2014. 80 pages. $15.95, paper.

In Caki Wilkinson's *The Wynona Stone Poems,* Wynona is a basket case.

She "is having trouble broaching. / She likes to float. A quick sip now and then, / the one indulgence she can't not allow, / appeases." While Wynona herself both observes and is observed, Wilkinson presents her character through a variety of introductory expositions. "Wynona ruins people, mixing parts / of bodies parted with parts / in progress." "Wynona almost never thinks of sex." "Wynona pleases well." She's "a character / about to break: she's ... well just standing there." Wilkinson's and even Wynona's language speaks with an almost delightfully demented rhyme pattern that both emphasizes Wynona's innocent perspective and breaks Wilkinson into her own poetic verse through some free and indirect discourse.

Though the reader flows whimsically through the almost-fairytale Grimm poems, it is through the sound of a warped music box. The reader experiences the immediacies of Wynona's artificial everyday. Her world is built on its own folk culture, reminiscent through other characters who ping against Wynona's psyche and the interlaced voice of the omniscient narrator and the character. It is a world seeking structure and built with the frame of the many formal poems throughout the collection that both emphasize and detract from Wynona's submerged mental space and her seeming need to breach.

The separation of Wynona from the narrator, the distinction of world and setting, beg the question of a societal purpose for the collection. Does it serve as a mirror of a specific culture or only the psyche of an individual character, her projections, obsessions, and various other intransitives? The collection's final poem, "Arts and Crafts," observes the creation's comment on creation. Wynona criticizes memory, artistic sensibility, and classification, and even her own generation of external material, experiencing a secondary birth in her own way. "Wynona needs / material / with edge, surer / shapes that hold / a crease or secret." It is this sub-consciousness of a creation within its own confines, absent of any metaphysical properties, and the quality of lyrical language that make this collection singularly unique and eerily provocative.

—*Taylor Supplee*, Moon City Review

Contributors' Notes

Michael Albright has published poems in various journals, including *Tar River Poetry, A NARROW FELLOW, Pembroke Magazine,* and *Cider Press Review.*

Elizabeth Alphonse is a student at Missouri State University, majoring in creative writing.

John Andrews' poetry has appeared in the collection *The Queer South: LGBTQ Writers on the American South* (Sibling Rivalry, 2014), as well as in *Columbia Poetry Review* and *Short, Fast, and Deadly,* among other journals. He is currently a PhD student at Oklahoma State University.

Kelly Baker is working toward her MA in English at Missouri State University. She is a contributing author to *Edgar Allan Poe: A Guide for Readers Young and Old* (Moon City, 2013) and an assistant editor of *Moon City Review.*

Tyler Barnes is an undergraduate at Missouri State University, studying creative writing.

Jennifer Barnhart is a student at Missouri State University, majoring in professional writing with a creative writing minor. Her work has been published in *Drunk Monkeys.*

Kate Belew is a student of poetry at Kalamazoo College. She interns with Sundress Publications and the reading series at the Kalamazoo Book Arts Center. She has received the Nature in Words Fellowship and has been published in journals such as *Minetta Review* and *Collision Literary Magazine.*

Terry Belew is a graduate teaching assistant at Missouri State University, where he serves as an assistant poetry editor for *Moon City Review.* His work has appeared in *Tar River Poetry*, *The Fourth River*, *Word Riot*, and *Beecher's*, among other journals.

Roy Bentley's poems have appeared in *The Southern Review*, *Shenandoah*, *Pleiades*, *Prairie Schooner*, and elsewhere. His fourth full-length poetry collection, *Starlight Taxi*, was released by Lynx House Press in 2013. He teaches at Georgian Court University.

Ana Berkovich is a student at Missouri State University, where she studies technical and creative writing. She serves as an assistant editor of *Moon City Review* and an associate editor of *Logos: A Journal of Undergraduate Research*.

Jennifer Jackson Berry is the author of the chapbooks *When I Was a Girl* (Sundress Publications, 2014) and *Nothing But Candy* (Liquid Paper, 2003). Her poems have appeared in *Harpur Palate*, *Booth*, and *Whiskey Island Magazine*, among other journals. She lives in Pittsburgh.

Ace Boggess is the author of two books of poetry: *The Prisoners* (Brick Road Poetry, 2014) and *The Beautiful Girl Whose Wish Was Not Fulfilled* (Highwire, 2003). His writing has appeared in *Harvard Review*, *River Styx*, *Rattle*, *Mid-American Review*, and many other journals. He lives in Charleston, West Virginia.

Kevin Boyle's book, *A Home for Wayward Girls*, was published by New Issues Poetry & Prose in 2005. His poems have appeared in *North American Review*, *Pleiades*, and *Virginia Quarterly Review*. He teaches at Elon University in North Carolina.

Jo Brachman has previously placed work in *Birmingham Poetry Review*, *Poetry East*, and other journals, as well as in *The Southern Poetry Anthology* by Texas Review Press. She has work forthcoming in *Bellingham Review*.

Anthony Isaac Bradley's stories and poems have appeared or are forthcoming in *Slipstream*, *The MacGuffin*, *Atticus Review*, and other journals. He was nominated for a *storySouth* Million Writers Award.

Sara Burge's collection of poems, *Apocalypse Ranch*, won the De Novo Prize and was published by C&R Press in 2010. Her poems have appeared in *Virginia Quarterly Review*, *River Styx*, *Cimarron Review*, *The Los Angeles Review*, and elsewhere.

Lanette Cadle is an associate professor of English at Missouri State University. She has previously published poetry in *Connecticut Review, NEAT, Menacing Hedge, TAB: The Journal of Poetry and Poetics,* and *Weave Magazine.* She is a past recipient of the Merton Prize for Poetry of the Sacred.

Matt Cashion's second novel, *Our 13ᵗʰ Divorce: A Love Story,* is forthcoming in 2016 from Livingston Press. Other work has appeared in *Willow Springs, Grist, The Sun, Passages North,* and elsewhere. His website is www.mattcashion.com.

Grant Clauser is the author of two poetry books: *Necessary Myths* (Broadkill River, 2013) and *The Trouble With Rivers* (FootHills, 2012). His poems have appeared in *The American Poetry Review, Cheat River Review, Mason's Road,* and other journals. He also writes about electronics and teaches poetry at Musehouse Writing Center.

Brian Clifton's work can be found in *PANK Magazine, Juked, burntdistrict, The Laurel Review,* and *The Boiler.*

Amanda Conner is a graduate student at Missouri State University, studying fiction. She serves as an assistant editor of *Moon City Review.*

Karen Craigo is a poet and essayist living in Springfield, Missouri. She maintains the blog, *Better View of the Moon.*

Kelly Davio is the poetry editor of *Tahoma Literary Review* and the author of *Burn This House* (Red Hen, 2013). She is a reviewer for *Women's Review of Books,* and her work appears in *Best New Poets, Verse Daily, The Rumpus,* and other journals. She blogs at www.kellydavio.com.

David Ebenbach's first full-length collection of poetry, *We Were the People Who Moved,* won the Patricia Bibby First Book Award and will be published by Tebot Bach in 2015. He is also the author of a poetry chapbook, two collections of short stories, and *The Artist's Torah* (Cascade, 2012), a nonfiction guide to the creative process.

Hannah Farley is a creative writing major at Missouri State University. She hails from Smithton, Illinois.

Matthew Ferrence lives and writes at the confluence of Appalachia and the Rust Belt. His essays have appeared in journals that include *Blue Mesa Review, Colorado Review, Creative Nonfiction*, and *The Gettysburg Review*. He is the author of a book of cultural criticism, *All-American Redneck* (U of Tennessee, 2014), and teaches creative writing at Allegheny College.

Jessica Forcier's fiction has been previously published or is forthcoming in *New Delta Review, Coal City Review*, and *Paper Nautilus*. She has also been a finalist in fiction contests for *Indiana Review* and *Hunger Mountain*, and she received an honorable mention in AWP's Intro Journals Project. She received her MFA from Southern Connecticut State University.

Katherine Frain's work has been published or is forthcoming in *The Journal, The Adroit Journal*, and *Rufous City Review*. She is the poetry editor of *The Blueshift Journal*.

Melissa Frederick is a writer and blogger from suburban Philadelphia. Her poetry and prose have appeared in numerous publications, including *Crab Orchard Review, DIAGRAM, Mid-American Review*, and *Helen: A Literary Magazine*, and is forthcoming in *Hippocampus Magazine*. Her poetry chapbook, *She*, was published by Finishing Line Press in 2008.

Jeannine Hall Gailey recently served as the second Poet Laureate of Redmond, Washington. Her fourth book, *The Robot Scientist's Daughter*, was published by Mayapple Press in 2015. Her website is www.webbish6.com.

Peter Joseph Gloviczki is an assistant professor of communications at Coker College. His first full-length collection of poetry is *Kicking Gravity* (Salmon Poetry, 2013).

Mitchell Krockmalnik Grabois has had over six hundred poems and works of fiction appear in literary magazines in the U.S. and abroad. His novel, *Two-Headed Dog* (Xavier Vargas E-ditions, 2012), is based on his work as a clinical psychologist in a state hospital. He lives in Denver.

Alex Vartan Gubbins was a finalist for *The Iowa Review*'s 2014 Jeff Sharlet Memorial Award for Veterans and for *North American Review*'s 2015 James Hearst Poetry Prize. He is also the recipient of the 2014 Witter Bynner Grant for translation.

Britt Haraway's work can be found in *Natural Bridge*, *New Madrid*, *BorderSenses*, and *South Dakota Review*. He teaches creative writing at the University of Texas-Pan American and edits fiction for *riverSedge*.

Wei He is a bilingual fiction writer and playwright from Inner Mongolia, China, and is currently an MFA candidate in the dramatic writing program at the Carnegie Mellon University School of Drama. She holds an Her fiction and poetry have been published internationally in the United States, China, and Taiwan.

Patricia Heim is a retired psychotherapist who divides her time between Main Line, Philadelphia, and the Eastern Shore of Maryland, where she lives with her husband, Jay. Her essays have appeared in *r.kv.r.y. quarterly literary journal*, *APIARY Magazine*, *Epiphany*, and *The Dos Passos Review*, among other journals.

Julie Henson is an MFA candidate at Purdue University, where she serves as poetry editor and Looseleaf Director Writing Workshop director for *Sycamore Review*. Her work has appeared or is forthcoming in *The Pinch, dislocate, and Yemassee*. She was a semifinalist for *Boston Review*'s "Discovery" poetry contest.

Gabriel Houck, originally from New Orleans, studies in the creative writing PhD program at the University of Nebraska-Lincoln. He has MFAs in writing from the California Institute of the Arts and the University of Iowa, and his work has appeared in *Western Humanities Review, American Literary Review, PANK,* and *Mid-American Review,* through which he won the 2014 Sherwood Anderson Fiction Award.

Ryan Hubble is currently working on his MA in creative writing and will be starting on an MA in rhetoric and composition in the fall of 2015.

Jane Huffman is a Michigan-based poet and playwright. Her work has been featured in *Arroyo Literary Review, RHINO,* and other journals. She is currently studying at Kalamazoo College.

Allegra Hyde's writing has appeared or is forthcoming in *The Missouri Review, New England Review, Denver Quarterly,* and *Southwest Review,* among other journals. She serves as prose editor for *Hayden's Ferry Review*. Her website is www.allegrahyde.com.

Donald Illich has published work in *LIT, The Iowa Review, Nimrod, Passages North,* and other journals. He lives in Rockville, Maryland.

Toshiya Kamei holds an MFA in literary translation from the University of Arkansas. His translations include Liliana Blum's *The Curse of Eve and Other Stories* (Host Publications, 2008), Naoko Awa's *The Fox's Window and Other Stories* (UNO, 2010), Espido Freire's *Irlanda* (Fairy Tale Review, 2011), and Selfa Chew's *Silent Herons* (Berkeley, 2012).

Leonard Kress has had fiction and poetry in *The Iowa Review, The Massachusetts Review, The American Poetry Review,* and other journals. His recent poetry collections are *The Orpheus Complex* (Main Street Rag, 2009), *Living in the Candy Store* (Finishing Line, 2011), and *Braids & Other Sestinas* (Seven Kitchens, 2011). He teaches at Owens Community College in Ohio.

Jill Kronstadt's fiction has appeared or is forthcoming in *Tin House* Flash Fridays, *Sou'wester, New South, Scribner's Best of the Fiction Workshops,* and other journals. In addition, she is currently an assistant editor for *Narrative* and a staff writer for *Bloom.*

Ken Letko's poems have appeared in five chapbooks as well as a number of anthologies and magazines, including *Alehouse, Bloodroot Literary Magazine, The Dos Passos Review,* and *Natural Bridge.* He currently edits *The Kerf* and teaches at College of the Redwoods-Del Norte in Crescent City, California.

Alexis Levitin's translations have appeared in well over two hundred literary magazines, including *Partisan Review, The American Poetry Review, Grand Street,* and *Kenyon Review.* He has published thirty-five books of translation This fall, two new books will be appearing: Salgado Maranhão's *Tiger Fur* (White Pine) and Sophia de Mello Breyner Andresen's *Exemplary Tales* (Tagus).

Salgado Maranhão is about to publish his tenth poetry collection, *Opera of Nos,* in Brazil. In 2012 he was honored as best poet of the year by the Brazilian Writers' Congress. In 2014, his book, *Mapping the Tribe,* was named best book of poetry of the year by the Brazilian PEN Club. His second book in the U.S., *Tiger Fur,* will come out in September from White Pine Press.

Cate McGowan is the author of the short story collection *True Places Never Are*, winner of the 2014 Moon City Short Fiction Award and published by Moon City Press in 2015. Her stories appear in publications such as *Flash Fiction International, Glimmer Train, The Louisville Review*, and the English fashion magazine, *TANK*.

Ana Merino, originally from Madrid, is an associate professor of Spanish at the University of Iowa, where she directs the MFA program in Spanish creative writing. She is the author of seven collections of poetry, including *Preparativos para un viaje* (Reino de Cordelia, 2013), winner of the 1994 Premio Adonáis de Poesía, *Juegos de niños* (Visor Libros, 2003), winner of the 2003 Premio Fray Luis de León, and most recently *Curación* (Visor Libros, 2010).

Bailey Gaylin Moore is a graduate student at Missouri State University, where she teaches English and serves as an assistant editor of *Moon City Review*.

Joddy Murray's work has appeared or is forthcoming in over seventy journals, including *The Lindenwood Review, The McNeese Review, Minetta Review*, and *The Southampton Review*. He currently teaches writing and rhetoric in Fort Worth, Texas.

Jason Olsen teaches writing and literature at Utah State University Eastern. His work has appeared in *Rattle, North American Review*, and *Hanging Loose*, among other journals.

Allys Page is a graduate student at Missouri State University, where she teaches creative writing and is an assistant editor for *Moon City Review*.

Jeff Pearson is finishing his final year in the University of Idaho's MFA program. His work has appeared in *SHAMPOO, Heavy Feather Review, Otis Nebula*, and *saltfront*.

Charlotte Pence recently published her first full-length poetry collection, *Many Small Fires* (Black Lawrence, 2015). A professor of English and creative writing at Eastern Illinois University, she is the editor of *The Poetics of American Song Lyrics* (University Press of Mississippi, 2011).

Tatiana Forero Puerta is originally from Colombia. She holds a BA in philosophy from Stanford University and an MA in philosophy and creative writing from New York University. She is currently a philosophy and yoga instructor, living, teaching, and writing in Manhattan.

Mary Quade is the author of *Guide to Native Beasts* (Cleveland State University Poetry Center, 2003). A graduate of the University of Chicago and the University of Iowa Writers' Workshop, she is the recipient of an Oregon Literary Fellowship and three Ohio Arts Council Individual Excellence Awards. She is an associate professor of English at Hiram College in Ohio.

Michael Robins is the author of three collections of poetry, most recently *In Memory of Brilliance and Value* (Saturnalia, 2015). He teaches literature and creative writing at Columbia College Chicago. His website is www.michaelrobins.org.

Paul Arrand Rodgers currently lives in Athens, Georgia. His work has appeared or is forthcoming in *Hobart*, *Atlas Review*, *CutBank*, and elsewhere. He writes online at the website, *Fear of a Ghost Planet*.

Sierra Sitzes is a graduate student at Missouri State University and an assistant editor for *Moon City Review*.

Curtis Smith has published close to one hundred stories and essays. His most recent books are *Beasts and Men* (stories, Press 53, 2013) and *Communion* (essays, Dock Street, 2015). His next book will be *Lovepain*, a novel from Aqueous Books, due out in 2017.

Marjorie Stelmach's most recent book of poems is *Without Angels* (Mayapple Press, 2014). Earlier volumes include *A History of Disappearance* (University of Tampa Press, 2006) and *Bent upon Light* (University of Tampa Press, 2009). Individual poems have recently appeared in *Arts & Letters*, *Cincinnati Review*, *The Iowa Review*, and *Prairie Schooner*.

Matthew Stewart is working on an MA in literature at Missouri State University, where he is an assistant editor for *Moon City Review*. In his free time, he writes essays and stories about the Ozarks and occasionally other places.

Pablo Piñero Stillmann's first novel will be published in the summer of 2015 by Tierra Adentro. His work has appeared in *Ninth Letter, Cream City Review, Electric Literature's Recommended Reading, The Normal School,* and other journals.

Shane Stricker completed his MFA at West Virginia University in 2013. His work appears or is forthcoming in *Midwestern Gothic, Whitefish Review, Lake Effect,* and *Crossborder.* His story collection, *One Eye Closed Tight Against the Coming Jesus,* was named a finalist in Leapfrog Press' 2014 fiction contest.

Taylor Supplee attends Missouri State University, where he studies poetry and serves as an assistant editor for *Moon City Review.* His poetry has appeared in *Rattle, Revolver, SLAB,* and other journals.

Rob Talbert's poems have appeared or are forthcoming in *Alaska Quarterly Review, The American Poetry Review, Ninth Letter, Passages North,* and other journals. He received his MFA from Virginia Tech and is currently working on a PhD in creative writing at Florida State University. His first book of poems, *Jagged Tune* (2015), is available from MadHat Press.

Eugenie Theall completed her MFA in poetry from Sarah Lawrence College and currently teaches creative writing and English. Her poetry has been published in *Carquinez Poetry Review, Hawaii Pacific Review, The Hampden-Sydney Poetry Review,* and *Silk Road,* among other journals. Her work also won first place in the Elizabeth McCormack/Inkwell contest.

Jen Town's poetry has appeared in *Mid-American Review, Cimarron Review, Iron Horse Literary Review, EPOCH,* and other journals. Her manuscript, *My Happy Apocalypse,* was a semi-finalist for the 2012 Perugia Press Prize and a 2014 finalist for the Moon City Poetry Award. She lives in Columbus, Ohio.

William Trowbridge's latest poetry collection is *Put This On, Please: New & Selected Poems,* from Red Hen Press (2013). He lives in the Kansas City area and teaches in the University of Nebraska low-residency MFA in writing program.

Shelly Weathers holds an MFA from Goddard College. Her work has appeared in *Redivider, Reed Magazine, Clockhouse, Sou'wester*, and elsewhere. She received the 2013 Beacon Street Prize for Fiction, as well as the 2014 John Steinbeck Award for Fiction.

Charles Harper Webb's latest book, *What Things Are Made Of*, was published by the University of Pittsburgh Press in 2013. He teaches in the MFA in Creative Writing Program at California State University, Long Beach.

Steve Willis is a professor of art education at Missouri State University. His artwork addresses sacred spaces and personal experiences within Native American and non-Native spiritual ceremonies. To see more of his images, visit www.stevewillis.org.

Daniel Wright currently attends Missouri State University as an undergraduate.

Kirby Wright is the author of the companion novels, *Punahou Blues* (Lemon Shark Press, 2005) and *Moloka'i Nui Ahina* (Lemon Shark, 2007), both set in Hawaii. *The Girl With the Green Violin*, his fourth poetry collection, is forthcoming from Etched Press in 2016.

Changming Yuan, the author of *Chansons of a Chinaman* (Leaf Garden, 2009) and *Landscaping* (Flutter, 2013), grew up in rural China, holds a PhD in English, and tutors in Vancouver, where he co-edits *Poetry Pacific*. Yuan's poetry appears in literary publications across thirty countries, including *Best Canadian Poetry* (Tightrope, 2009; 2012; 2014), *Best New Poems Online*, and *The Threepenny Review*.

Hananah Zaheer lives, writes, and teaches in Dubai. Her recent work has appeared or is forthcoming in *Gargoyle, Willow Review, Concho River Review*, and *Word Riot*, among other journals.

GINGKO TREE REVIEW

The Body Issue

Now considering stories, poems, essays, plays,
and more on the theme of the Body.

Send to gingkotree@drury.edu.

For more information, visit us at www.gingkotree.org.

Gingko Tree Review
Drury University
English Department
900 North Benton Avenue
Springfield MO 65802

Mid-American Review is pleased to announce the

2015 Fineline Competition

for prose poems, short shorts,
and anything in between

$1000 First Prize • Deadline: June 1, 2015

2015 Final Judge: **Michael Czyzniejewski**, author of *Chicago Stories* (Curbside Splendor, 2012) and *I Will Love You For the Rest of My Life* (Curbside Splendor, 2015)

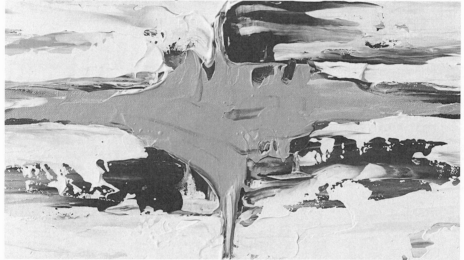

500-word limit for each poem or short. $10 entry fee (payable online or by check/money order) for each set of three works. Contest is for previously unpublished work only—if the work has appeared in print or online, in any form or part, or under any title, or has been contracted for such, it is ineligible and will be disqualified. Entry fees are non-refundable. All participants will receive *Mid-American Review* v. XXXVI, no. 1, where the winner will be published. Submissions will not be returned. Manuscripts need not be left anonymous. Contest is open to all writers, except those associated with the judge or *Mid-American Review*, past or present. Judge's decision is final.

The 2015
Moon City
Poetry Award

• The Moon City Poetry Award is for an original collection of poetry written in English by a single or collaborative author; no anthologies will be considered.

• Individual pieces in the collection may be published in periodicals or chapbooks, but not yet collected and published in full-length manuscript form.

• Open to all writers not associated with Moon City Press or its judges, past or present. Students, alumni, and employees of Missouri State University are ineligible.

• Manuscripts should be at least 48 pages long.

• Manuscripts should be submitted via Submittable, https://mooncitypress.submittable.com

• A $25 entry fee is due via Submittable at the time of submission; entry fees are nonrefundable.

• Simultaneous submissions are permitted, though manuscripts should be withdrawn immediately if accepted elsewhere.

• Deadline: May 1, 2015. Winners will be notified in late 2015 and the winner will be published in the fall of 2016.

• First prize: $1000, publication by Moon City Press (including international distribution through the University of Chicago Press), and a standard royalty contract. Ten additional finalists will be named and considered for publication.

• For questions, please visit http://mooncitypress.com/ or contact Moon City Poetry Editor Sara Burge at saraburge@missouristate.edu.